The Winding Stick

Elise Valmorbida

*For dear Roger
with love and thanks
and X xx
Elise*

TWO RAVENS
PRESS

Published by Two Ravens Press Ltd.
Green Willow Croft
Rhiroy
Lochbroom
Ullapool
Ross-shire IV23 2SF

www.tworavenspress.com

The right of Elise Valmorbida to be identified as author of this
work has been asserted by her in accordance with the Copyright,
Designs and Patent Act, 1988. © Elise Valmorbida, 2009.

ISBN: 978-1-906120-35-1

British Library Cataloguing in Publication Data: a CIP record
for this book can be obtained from the British Library.

Designed and typeset in Sabon by Two Ravens Press.
Cover design by word-design.co.uk and Two Ravens Press.
Hopper Petrol Station photograph © Alberto Urbinati.

Printed on Forest Stewardship Council-accredited paper
by CPI (Antony Rowe), Chippenham.

FSC
Mixed Sources
Product group from well-managed
forests and other controlled sources

Cert no. SGS-COC-2953
www.fsc.org
© 1996 Forest Stewardship Council

About the Author

Italian-Australian émigré Elise Valmorbida runs a communications agency and teaches creative writing at Central St Martin's in London. Honoured as a Trailblazer by the Edinburgh International Film Festival (2007), she is the producer of award-winning indie feature film SAXON, released in 2009. Her published works include *Matilde Waltzing, The Book of Happy Endings,* and *The TV President.*

For more information about the author, see
www.tworavenspress.com
and
www.word-design.co.uk/fiction

For Francesca

With thanks to:

Tara Wynne

Raj Kajendra, Rajeswary Balasubramaniam,
Shasha Canagasuriam, Raj Rajarajan, Bala Canagasabey

Naga at Archway Temple, Dr Raj at East Ham Temple,
Glen at Islington Fire Brigade, Giri at Shell

Greg Loftin, Elizabeth Fairbairn, Charles Boyle

The ZenAzzurri writers: Simon Campbell, Susan Clegg,
Anita Dawood-Nasar, Kate Grunstein, Richard Hughes,
Margaret Laing, Roger Levy, David Lucas, Steve Mullins,
Annemarie Neary, Sam Patterson, Joanna Pocock,
Mike Roberts

1: Lust

For her it wasn't love. Not at all. I know that.

She was the girl who lived in the corner shop and had a craving for men. There's a word for that. Whenever there were deliveries, she'd pull down the blinds and close the shop for hours. You don't have to be told what they were doing inside.

It was a shallow house with a double front. Not a proper building going all the way back like the rest of the street, but a thin one just deep enough to have a shop below and two rooms above. When you turned the corner, walking past, it was gone in no time. The neighbours said you had to shuffle sideways like a crab indoors, and sleep in a straight line stiff as a rod.

The assurance society said she could live there until the day she died. She paid all her bills on time – which was more than some people could say. She had the knack of money. You could tell just by looking at her stockings.

Her name was Claire. Some ginger man delivering snacks and biscuits once a month told her *Claire* meant nice things in French. (He'd been fighting across The Channel.) So she twirled her hair and counted up the boxes, and before you could say *Cock Robin* she was locking the door and pulling down her blinds.

Next time and then every time, she took him to the pub three doors up for a pint of bitter beforehand. And all the locals holding onto their drinks just minded their own business, kept themselves to themselves, marked the keen look of luck on his face.

Claire wasn't as pretty as he said her name was. She had dull skin and canary legs, for a start. But she didn't keep her knees together and her eyes were hungry as a cat in spring. She had a laugh like a falling bell. As for him, the snack and biscuit man, he never stopped his fidgeting in the pub. He hardly said a word, just gulped his drink. (He bought whatever she drank.) His ginger eyes were all over the place. He was meant to be working, had his address list to get through, kept checking his watch – but

1

he couldn't help himself, just thinking about it. His meat. Her sweets. His hands. Her secrets. With bitter on his lips, he was on his feet as soon as she was. Out the door. Up the street. Behind the blinds. No-one knew if he was married.

But it wasn't just him. She had an ache, an ache that wouldn't go away. There was the rude-faced man with the milk who delivered most days. His mouth was pinched like an anus (anyone would say it) and he walked with a stoop. It wasn't about handsome looks. Then there was the tobacco man who sometimes brought lucky charms for her bracelet. He didn't bother taking off his wedding ring. And another married one with not a hair on his head and a maroon van full of sundries. If you picked the wrong time of day, never mind if it was flint you needed, or the papers, or whatever. She'd be in there, legs wide apart as a baby bird's beak and just as eager. On the stairs out the back or up in her bedroom. On the shop floor. Even against the rattling door. (Never mind the buses in High Street – this was Chapel Street, known for its quietness.)

It wasn't love. Not at all. Not the sort of thing you could take to a clergyman and ask for a blessing. More like a curse. Like gambling, or being a drunk, when there's only the meanest bit of pleasure left in the thing itself but you'd spend your whole life just thinking about it, conniving plans with yourself or anyone else just to get satisfaction.

The doctor had an idea of Claire's reputation and told her she'd gone and caught some creeping venereal disease. There were symptoms he could see with the naked eye. Looking inside her with his light on, he said it would be a lifelong affliction, but it was best to nip it in the bud. She tried to see the things he saw in a mirror. She tried again back home at the shop. There was nothing special to see, but she had to take his word for it.

Claire went to the VD hospital, clutching her special blue vanity case and fearing the worst treatment. They told her someone had made a mistake and how lucky she was – this time – but it was probably a sign to change her ways in any case. She was lying on a high table. Legs open. Eyes closed. There was no disease after all, they said. Just a kind of unsightliness, a slip in her physical making which had the look of early infection. She had to hear them say it twice before she would open her eyes again. Written all over their faces she was sure she could read the message: *Don't be fornicating all over the shop.*

After the VD hospital, Claire got home and did the first thing she could to celebrate. You don't have to be told what. Weeks of abstinence and fear of being damaged in the body and feeling locked up inside can drive a woman up the wall. She felt it between her legs like a hunger she had to be rid of.

There was a jobbing builder working on the terrace in Baron Street that was wrecked in the air raids. He went into the corner shop in the shallow house to buy a paper and before you could say *Jack Rabbit* she was satisfying her craving with him behind closed doors, never mind the doctors' warnings. He called her names, shouting loud enough for all the world to hear, his voice getting louder, and meaner, as they carried on.

Unless you poked your head inside, then and there, with the shaking doors and the worked-up builder letting himself go, you wouldn't know the dull colour of her face and the single look in her eyes. The way she cleaned up afterwards like spilt milk or a job done. He paid for his paper and she gave him his change. After that he bought his things at another shop unless he felt like a quick one. And she used the sharpest vinegar to head off any consequences. Took the bottle straight off the *Condiments & Miscellaneous* shelf.

No need to say she didn't know which one was the father of her child. If you were looking for fidgety or rude-faced or balding or loud, you'd get the lot with any baby. Never mind the delivery men. Never mind the passing builders.

After the lying-in hospital, Claire went back home with her special blue vanity case and rearranged the goods and put the old merchandise towards the front and fixed a leaking bag of sugar and mopped the cement floor. She took her baby to a clergyman and asked for a blessing, but all she got was a lesson. Written across his holy face she was sure she could read the message:

3

Don't be fornicating all over the shop. She dangled her lucky charm bracelet over the cot in peace-time and all the child could do for years and years was cry at the blurry sight of the Four-Leafed Clover, the Lucky Clog and the Three Gold Monkeys who Heard and Saw and Spoke No Evil.

Claire carried on managing the shop and keeping up the business like there was no tomorrow, paying all her dues and sloughing off her yearning as and when, legs loose as a pair of old scissors. Opening hours or after dark, you could hear the sound of the shop door locking and unlocking. A delivery man groaning and cursing. Another one thrusting and thumping her. Another one gripping her head in a wax-paper bag because she asked for it. Mostly they ignored the baby or had it shut out of sight upstairs, but the sundries man had a soft spot for children – there were nine, with his wife, in a picture in his pocket – and one of the men liked to play games. The glass panes rattled with their blinds.

There was no sign of a father moving into the narrow space, and no chance of a proper routine. Feeding happened when it did. Sleep fell when it did. Nappies whenever. Growing up, teething, soothing ... whenever. Daylight or half-light or night life, one dropped and tumbled into the other.

Hardly surprising that such a baby could grow to have the gift of insight, could learn how to expect things and see through things before knowing how to walk. It began with needing, simple pictures like food. Milk. A maroon van. And then it went deeper. Resentment. A mother's coldness.

The child was due to have trouble with its eyes, the sort of trouble that wouldn't go away, but the mother didn't know that yet. The mother was due to die from too much of one thing, not enough of the other. More and more sex, less and less air. Although she didn't know that yet. And when her infant opened its sexless mouth to scream at the idea of losing her, bawled out its orphan grief long before the event, the mother could never know that it wasn't just another bout of hunger or growing pains sent to try her patience and bring out the blame. She picked the

4

child up sometimes but she always put it down.

Nightmare you are, with all that crap in your eyes. You cost me an arm and a leg, but you'll always be rubbish. Shut up. Shut your bloody face.

The shop was locked, of course, when she died. The blinds were pulled down. But you don't have to be told that. You know exactly what she was up to inside the wax-paper, inside the cramped space.

Everyone heard the sounds of the child left to cry and cry over her dead body.

The man slipped away just like the fathers, all of them, quick to close their zips until another time. Some people were convinced it was the tobacco man, because of the lucky charm lying loose on the counter: a Golden Rabbit's Foot. Some of the neighbours said it was the shouting man who'd learned new ways to hurt her. But others insisted it was a passer-by, a stranger idly walking, delivering nothing, paying for nothing, taking nothing away.

Nightmare you are. You'll always be ugly. You cost me an arm and a leg, you suck me dry, but you'll never amount to anything. Ugly, ugly, deformed bastard.

I don't know how many times she said these things to me.

2: Avarice

I see reflections, lights, tricks. Wherever I look, my face is in the way. It's out there, shot through with traffic, or waiting on the forecourt between jams and jellies, but it's always too big. Like a head out to haunt some crook in an old film. I squint. *You'll always be ugly. Shut your bloody face.*

From the inside looking out, you get the picture. The shop fridges blend with pumps dispensing carton milk. Motorbikes ride through rows of juice in boxes. And brown teddy bears, lined up for sale on the top shelf, sit bigger than humans on car roofs.

On my first night, way back when, I thought all the customers were a bit short. A dwarf, followed by a squat man, followed by a child-driver reaching up to pay for petrol and tobacco. Then I remembered my built-up floor. I laughed to myself that night, alone in my glass box. From the outside looking in, you might have felt sorry for this man with bad eyes, perched on a stool, giggling like a girl in a lit-up photo booth. But, chances are, you wouldn't have noticed.

I am raised up so I can look down. Between my cameras and my eyes, I see everything. Seven cameras. Two eyes. One camera is trained on me, although my manager knows I won't steal. I've got the knack of money (it runs in the blood) but Siv knows I wouldn't steal. He even lets me sit in his office. He leaves the door unlocked. Sometimes I need to go in there, away from the glare of the shop and the forecourt. If Siv has been working late, he leaves behind his smell of musk in amongst the smell of papers. I suck it up with my nose. Musk, more musk. Siv's dark sweat and paper mixed with musk.

I wipe the discharge from my eye with my finger. *Nightmare you are, with all that crap in your eyes.* I look at my reflected face and I hear the song of the expectant pump as my first customer shoves the premium nozzle into his tank.

Ti. Ti. Ti. Ti.

Pump Number Two.

To authorise, I wipe the icon on the computer screen with my finger. Pump Number Two gets a green light.

I watch him through my window. I watch him on camera as he fills his car with my petrol. His hair like pelt has ridges where the fat skin rolls at the back of his neck.

My computer sings to me. The flow has finished.

My customer comes to me, puts the ball of his face up against my slot and speaks. 'Pump Number Two – and *The Truth*.'

There's a picture of a dead teenager on the front page. She is smiling. All day and all night. Piles of her. I slip her through.

He pays. He won't look me in the eye. Our fingers touch with the slink of coins. He goes. I can't see the place he goes to, or the things he's done – I don't always know.

Not everyone is porous.

Out there, beyond the forecourt, is the huge stream of lights – too many – cars, constant, lorries rumbling, people processing, driven, road without end. In here there's just me and the hum, the air conditioning and the breath of fridges.

At my feet there's a big grey padded bar. If I kick it, the emergency wall will shoot up, metal and wood six inches thick. Faster than blinking. A shield that makes everything invisible. On the inside it says: *KEEP CALM*. And there are two red buttons to jab for the police.

The time is 23:15 on the camera.

Pump Number One is singing. It's the furthest pump, at the edge of the road. A small businessman in a pinstriped suit. I authorise. He fills up his motorbike and my computer closes the deal with a *Ti*. He comes to my window, tripping at the step.

'Number One' is all he says. He's hiding inside his crash helmet, but his eyes are red grapes swimming in the drink and I know where he's been before he tugs at his suit pockets, feeling for change, and pulls out the red polka-dot tights. Her feathered G-string flies out like magic. When he opens his wallet I see his kids inside, stuck behind plastic. (I think of the sundries man who nozzled my mother, the man with nine children kept in the dark inside his pocket.)

My computer sings again. Pump Number Six. A green or black van with the bonnet up, pissing water like an old horse. I authorise the pierced white couple. They're sick of each other.

Pump Number Three. A silver saloon. I authorise the black man in a tracksuit. For him, white people are a kind of cancer.

Pump Number Two. I authorise Adam. He's filling his old Escort. He's nearly blind with age. He should be asleep, he shouldn't be driving, but he's been poking about in a woman's drawers. I don't want to know his name. I turn away, try to think of other things: the thief who drives off without paying, the two-eyed emergency button, the smear on the glass across my view.

But the petrol is pouring like a story. The smell of it seeps through the slot at my window, rubs itself all over my skin, prickles my eyeballs, makes them weep. His petrol is free-running, clear. Adam still has a craze for saving. He married the wrong woman and he lived through the war.

~

Beatrice and Adam lived through the war. Not any war. *The* war. When they moved into their rooms in Baron Street, newly wed, the war hadn't started yet. There were no letters in Beatrice's drawers. And in any case, Adam knew not to go poking about in a woman's things.

It was a small flat, just enough space. They did it up with help from no-one. Third floor, powder blue walls, cosy, not an inch to spare for lodgers. The local streets had names like Duchess, Pleasant and Lordship, but the area wasn't what it is now. And you'd never know from the outside looking in that Beatrice was an orphan at eight years old. Or that it was left to her grand-mother to do all the bringing up.

Dragging up, Beatrice would say.

They lived on handouts from neighbours. The odd stroke of luck. A young woman downstairs offered to pay the rent in exchange for a bit of housework, which was fine until the day she jumped off Beachy Head.

8

In the war Beatrice sewed great-coats and khakis at the factory. She came home one day and the top of the terrace the length of Baron Street was all blown away and sifting into the sky. Powder blue walls turned into dust. The government gave her and Adam a pittance to start all over again. A salvages man (in a poorly finished uniform) picked his way through the rubble and told Beatrice what would do after bombing and what wouldn't, making valuations on the spot. All the while, the broken walls just powdering into the sky.

Adam had a craze for saving. If it was up to him, the gas fire wouldn't go on, not for himself. Nor hot water. Nothing for himself. It was a craze he had, nothing to do with being selfless. And if he couldn't save it, he'd count it. Adam loved keeping a tally, had the number of everything, things that didn't matter. He was a decent man (anybody would say it) and he had the measure of things, but he didn't like being made a fool. No man worth the socks on his feet would.

They were courting when the grandmother died.

The rent was too much.

Beatrice suffered from the anxieties.

There was nothing for it.

They got married.

For her it wasn't love. Not at all.

But it was enough for Adam, and they both needed a roof over their heads.

Not like the girl who ran the corner shop across the road and had a craving for sex. She always had a roof over her head and a gift with money.

With two little boys after the war, Beatrice had to work from home. The rooms in High Street were nowhere near as nice as the powder blue walls. Nothing so fresh or romantic. There was a Jewish lady who brought her hand sewing work. Lining and finishing for a furrier. After machine work, the garments were all messy. Beatrice did the padding, the hooks and eyelets, and all the linings. Her work was beautiful. The furrier let her know she was a class apart. He gave her the deluxe jobs and paid her

9

handsomely – which kept her going through all the anxieties. His name was Cosier. Funny.

Adam's craze for saving became a kind of vocation. At the end of a working day in the London Underground, his pockets were full of fares in the hand. He kept them all. No, not all – Adam was no fool. No need to say that keeping *all* the ticket-money would arouse the suspicion of your superiors. Walk into the flat in High Street and there'd be all his half-crowns and two-bob bits in piles lined up on the mantelpiece.

Adam never learned a love of spending, but Beatrice did.

There was enough money to buy new carpet. All over. Green as the sea at Broadstairs. Thick, swirling, deep enough to drown in. There was enough money to keep their boys in new boots. Enough money to buy a luxurious fur stole with the help of Mr Cosier. Mink. The whole anatomy: claws and snout.

The two young boys never knew the meaning of poor. Or unlucky. They played on green carpet, thick as you like, cushioned from the word go, because Beatrice and Adam never stopped working and saving in all the years till they went on the pension. Money in shiny piles on the mantelpiece. Fancy lace and fur in the drawer. Most people would say they were good sons, and that Beatrice brought them up, not dragged them up – she who grew up with the shame of cardboard in her boots.

A pity Adam never got the chance to sweep her off her feet before the wedding, but truth be told he never once raised a hand to her in all his life and he never got drunk or mad (apart from the savings) nor any other of the vices. Funny.

Beatrice would say it wasn't romance between the two of them, not at all. Never was. Times were what they were, and in one moment there it was: the rest of their life. The rest of her life. But Adam would say different.

That's why, after twenty-one years on the pension, with a dwindling stash of old fares like tips in the new money lined up on the mantelpiece, clacking hips and not one tooth left to count or call his own, that's why he was the way he was when he found the letters she had saved under her smalls. Fifty-three of them. He

10

counted. Her drawers were always her own business and nobody else's. A private place to keep her lady's things, her hosiery, little bags of lavender. Being close enough to ninety, Adam should have known not to go poking about in a woman's things. After all that time. And he knew Beatrice suffered from the anxieties. But he didn't know about Mr Cosier. Years and years of him – who could count how many years? Sewing those furs, hundreds of furs for him, delivering herself to him, spending herself, throwing herself away on him, letters tied in ribbon, yellowed letters from after the war full of passion enough to make a man blush. Enough to throw an old man off his feet, make him lose his balance. A kind of sea-sickness. Talk about the girl who ran the corner shop and pulled the blinds down.

Adam was a decent man, but he was no fool. Until he raised his hand to his wife and smothered her with a pillow, her old woman's breath easy as a blind kitten's.

~

Adam demands a receipt, claws at his change and counts it with a passion. Twice.

'You can't be careless with the shrapnel,' he says, and looks me in the eye for cheating – instead he sees the swollen skin, the seeping.

'How much was that a gallon?'

Actually he doesn't want me to tell him. He snorts as if he's answering himself, clips his fumbling wallet shut and turns to strut. Stops. Changes his mind. Turns back and points up, his stringy arm straight as a military salute.

'I'll have one of those.' He indicates the top shelf. 'How much?'

The big brown teddy bears are discounted to clear, but it's the end magazine he wants. It's called *Kitten*. She purrs without sound all over the front cover, her eyes meet his from above and she has been waiting, panting, begging all her life for him. She wants to spend herself on him. She wants him to paw her, stroke her, lick her clean off the paper. He is lost in her gape but

11

he counts out the price he knows exactly. The coins stick to his fingers like honey.

I'm getting hard, I can't help it.

Her huge bare nipples scrape against the window as I pass her through. Her lips rub against the rubber edge on the glass. His crooked fingers jab at her eyes. If I'm not mistaken, there's a wet dot on his trousers.

'A receipt,' he says, rapping her head impatiently. Big clean fingernails. Gnarled knuckles.

And she purrs.

~

In Siv's office there's a picture on the desk: some idol with too many arms, dancing almost naked inside a circle, a circle sprouting tongues of licking fire. (*NO NAKED FLAMES* the signs say on the walls, the forecourt, all over the shop.) The idol has curvy hips, shiny lipstick, eye make-up. I can't tell if it's supposed to be male or female.

There's a third eye in the middle of its forehead, but it doesn't take much to see it as the private parts – the gape – of a woman. A snake is winding through the limbs, squeezing against the skin.

I sit on Siv's swivel chair.

I turn my back to the security camera.

I'm thinking about Beatrice.

Finishing off the hooks and eyelets.

Private parts.

The kitten.

Fur coats.

And Cosier.

And Adam.

My dad.

A blank.

And carpet.

Thick carpet.

Fur coats.

And musk.

And sweat.

The gape.

The snake.

The gape.

The snake.

The gape.

It's over.

Over.

I lean back in Siv's swivel chair, pump number one in my hand, Adam's story all over me like milk. The door out to the shop lets off a little sigh from its hinges. The computer is singing. *Don't be fornicating all over the shop*. Someone is waiting at the window. The pierced man. The computer is singing.

I notice Siv has left me notes as usual, stuck on the desk. He never leaves me in the dark.

Foods delivery due tonight. See order book.

Close Pumps 1 & 2 after 3am.

He always leaves me notes. I sniff them for his musk, the oil from his skin. I feel drained. The computer is singing. The pierced man is waiting. Seven hours till my shift is over.

Another note. It's hardly a duty. *In places without tanks gods are not present*. Siv's handwriting is all over the place.

3: Sloth

Every season feels the same in here. Out there it blows from winter to summer, from dark to bright, but the station is always the same. When a tube dies I make a note to Siv. He is the one who calls in the electrician to fix it.

Every night I empty the waste bins into the big dumpers around the side. Every night I take the leftover news out the back. Yesterday's dead teenager is gone. She was more popular than the road rage victim who hit the ground in a bundle early this morning. There are still at least a hundred of him, pressed in layers, holding his law degree, dressed in a graduate gown and sash. He'll be returned after midnight – but not to his father, a tiny weeping Greek in the corner.

Every month the security videos are recycled. Day and night are cancelled. Unless there's been a crime, actions are undone. Seven memories are made to forget.

When it's quiet I slip into Siv's office and watch myself on playback. My eyes look better on TV. You can't see the seeping. I watch myself sell anything to anyone. Under-age drivers with bloodshot eyes. Girls who ask for tampons, laughing or hiding in the glare. Black men doing night shifts. Insomniacs. The prostitutes and dealers who meet their customers at the forecourt edges. Tired couples. Gangs sorted by colour. I get sick with other people's conditions. I cry or faint or get hard. I hate the leaking smell of petrol but it's better at night, and it's better on video. The stories get in amongst me. Sometimes, when I think about it, I wonder if it's not a kind of thieving.

I watch black-and-white re-runs of the big lorries delivering food and sundries. The tankers backing in with fuel. Even on fast-forward they're slow. On rewind they head out, front first.

I look for my father in the face of every delivery man, but they're nearly all too young to know the girl in the corner shop who had a craving for them. In any case, I don't have anything to go by. No photograph to match. No comparisons to make, except with my own reflection.

So I look for my face in the faces of older taxi drivers, worn-out post-office workers, stooping pimps. I look for my face in the face of every man I see.

I see Siv on the screen sometimes, coming out of the office and checking forms with someone on day-shift. He moves like he's on wheels. On video his dark face splits when he smiles. Maybe he has a word with Giri, maybe with slick-haired Naga. These days all the cashiers are from Sri Lanka except for the African called Ken. And me. I am white. Whiter than spilt milk. Whiter than the chalk cliffs where people jump at Beachy Head.

People in the day are different. I see mothers with children in uniform. A skulking schoolboy who takes his shortcut through the station every day at 08:15 and 16:00 on the camera, give or take a few minutes. Huge stains on the forecourt, lit up by sunlight. Walkers with dogs. A mouthing alcoholic who appears whenever he feels like it. And sometimes birds – just a smudge. Their songs have turned to silence. I see the mechanics. That small book-keeping woman who does the phones and accounts for Siv.

She's alone, bent over the ledger. Tears are falling in great drops from her eyes. She wipes them off and smears her ink across the page, but she keeps adding up. Her fingers play the calculator. I can almost hear music. She answers the phone with a grin because she knows you can hear a smile even if you can't see wet eyes. She books in a service, a clutch replacement, a new exhaust. She makes tea for the mechanics and the big chipped mugs tremble on her tin tray as she pushes the security door open with her back, edging out in reverse. She mothers them. She tells them something in a spill and waves it off with her laughing hand. She washes their mugs afterwards, and scans the notice above the sink. *Keep your mess to yourself, you lazy – yes you!* She made the sign herself, with red felt-tip on cardboard. She's the only one who reads it. Her careful letters have been blotted with upward-flying splashes.

~

It's midnight in my box. No customers outside. I fill in the shift control sheet.

Name: Terry.

My eyes sting.

Sign-on time: 23:00. Sign-off time: 07:00.

Safe drops.

Day deposits.

Night deposits.

I go to the sink behind the partition and splash my eyeballs. Still no customers. *Keep your mess to yourself, you lazy – yes you!* I push the security door open with my back, just like that woman does. The lock clicks shut behind me.

I walk through the aisles of the empty shop. The light hurts.

Two security bolts, and I'm out.

The roar of traffic from High Street is like a big sea with rocks, a place to drown. At Pump Number Six I pull on some diesel gloves and start to empty the forecourt bins. Every now and then I look up at a lens, saying things to myself, my twin tomorrow. I pose for the video, stand up straight, hold in my stomach, tell myself to read my lips. I am the main actor.

I play all the parts.

I play my self.

Boy.

Girl.

Old.

Young.

Then.

Now.

I try to walk like Siv. I try to feel it from the inside. But Siv's not easy. I wish he was.

I move like the woman who does the books. Little steps, almost hopping. Fur coats wouldn't make her happy. Fur coats don't make me happy. Men don't take away her ache. She doesn't even want her husband back. She lives for the twins she gave

16

birth to, who broke her heavy sac and slid, sprawling, out of her gape. Legs wide apart as a baby bird's beak.

Never let anyone tell you it's hard having one, she says to the mechanics.

I look down. The tarmac is stained all over with her leaks and oozings.

I look up at the camera.

I join her on video.

We're together inside *Terry's TV.*

~

Never let anyone tell you it's hard having one, their mother would say, when she had the chance to say it. She winced to think of triplets.

It was hard work enough to get them into the world, one twin after another, two for the price of three. Hard work enough to keep them in nappies and food and sleep and entertainments. She got the divorce through when her boys were just fourteen – they said it was a bolt out of the blue but they carried on as usual – and she never looked back, or forward either. Just kept them in food and entertainments while they fell away from school and told each other secrets like twins do.

She had the flat above the betting shop in High Street. On the left as you looked at it from the street, there was the aluminium and glass door full of painted dogs tearing round the bend and snarling after their own muzzles. On the right as you looked at it, there was the wooden door with the buzzer and the filth climbing up like a black tide from all the rain and buses. The postman never got the doors mixed up and no-one else did either.

You'd be hard-pressed to hear Ray and Desmond telling each other their twin stories. The buses filled the rumbling flat with rattles loud enough to stop you thinking, but the boys had their own words for things which stopped even their mother from understanding. Sometimes their voice became a kind of sigh or another kind of whimpering. They leaned together close enough and barely moved their lips. It was like a private language.

17

Every night there was the blue light of their television glaring up, then down, as you'd expect in any home, then flickering like a war inside the room. And sometimes there *was* one. Voices went up, things fell, their words were mangled. No telling what they were fighting about. But mostly they were soft and nestling, let the TV make a scene, spit it out.

And in the day, if you could see it, the TV light still played up and down and flickered on their eyeballs (all four) side by side and still as stones. Ray and Desmond, Desmond and Ray, all the hours from morning to morning, from the slinking out of bed and slinking back in. Identical mirror twins.

From the outside looking in, you could say it was just laziness they didn't get a job, or go to the shops, or learn to drive, or buy the papers, while at the garage their mother earned their keep. (Out of sight, she did the books and phones.) Or make the dinner once in a while or even have a flutter just downstairs.

You could say their mother was like some kind of small bird with two great cuckoos in her nest, taking up all the space, eating the bacon as fast as she could bring it home and wearing her out.

But the fact is, the twins got large for a while, grew to being grown-up men, and then slowly, slowly they started to dwindle, while the mother just kept on with the job at the garage and all the work she had to do in between. (No need to say how much shopping. Or washing and ironing. And cooking and cleaning. And cutting their hair and clipping their nails. And doing the bills. And getting the videos, and taking them back.) But there was nothing she could do about the dwindling.

Desmond and Ray, Ray and Desmond, after a while took up the space of one person. Desmond's left hand on the remote control, Ray's right hand on the weekly guide. Ray's good left eye, Desmond's good right eye, focused together. (They never once saw an eye doctor, except on *Hospital Lives*.) And if you didn't know better, you'd say that Desmond's heart was on the left side, where it should be, and Ray's was on the right, where it shouldn't.

18

And there was the mother like a frail bird, heaving hot up the stairs with all the shopping and them not lifting a finger until she'd turned the shopping into dinner. Desmond with the fork in the left hand, Ray with the knife. Dinner on their lap, the blue light flickering on their shiny eyeballs, Ray and Desmond slowly chewing, grinding the food between their sixty-four teeth. (They never once went to a dentist, except in video.) But they went to the toilet when they had to, and that alone was inconvenience. They dragged their feet and wore the carpet thin with their unwilling, left foot after right, right after left. No need to be a gambler to guess what those twins did day after day for twenty years, just judging by the worn-out carpet.

And there was the mother, heaving hot down the stairs with all the rubbish and them not lifting a finger while she stacked it up outside in the pavement space between her blackened door and the betting door painted with racing dogs inside the glass, forever baring their tearing teeth, the noise of her lost in the roar of buses, never mind the television.

Good chance if I was locked out by accident my boys wouldn't even let me in, she said at the garage to the men. She was writing out their invoices and clipping them to car keys, or she was doing their tea and biscuits. And they laughed in their blue overalls and blew smoke and didn't know she meant it, that her boys with their clean fingers and secret meanings would not even miss her food. Just the videos.

The Blue Lagoon. The Mouse That Roared. Cape Fear. Brigadoon.

The rubbish grew bigger and bigger with left-overs, all the things her boys didn't eat. And their mother tried not to mind, or take it too much to heart, thinking this was just another of their secret-meaning phases. (She was the last person to make a scene – anyone at the garage would say so.)

This Is Your Life. Candid Camera.

So she prepared their dinners day after day, creeping in like a shy bird so as not to make a noise above the television, leaving their tray of food and creeping out again, knowing that they

19

would hardly touch it. The more she cooked, the less they ate. Maybe, she thought, they were doing an experiment.

Cosmos. The Body in Question. The Fly.

But, sometimes, on the outside pavement in the space between two doors she stood and sobbed, tired with wondering at their foreign garble or their lazy leanings. Her clutching the keys till her hands were red and white and shaking.

Day after day, Desmond and Ray shrank like documentary war-orphans before swelling out like Biafrans off the news right there on the sofa in the living room.

When the twins heard their mother shouting from beyond the doorstep, her voice was like a distant seagull drowned in traffic. She was locked out with the rubbish. They were watching *Baywatch*. It was after-hours and the betting shop was closed. They turned the volume up – but Ray was touched to save her. He couldn't walk any more, so he crawled and dragged his blown-up belly past the path in the carpet all the way to the top of the stairs.

Ray looked down. He was out of breath and wondering. His mother was doing the buzzer and shouting into the letterbox, her fingers pressing through the flap in the door, her lips in the space calling his name.

Which is why Ray fell down the stairs and broke his leg.

At the doctor's Ray garbled and cried out all his first-time fear and great lack of willing, blinking as if he couldn't see, searching for his brother Desmond. And the doctors fixed his leg in plaster but there was nothing they could do about the liquids on the lungs or the swelling on account of starving, which was what got him a week later.

Accidental death was the official verdict. There was no way in the world his mother would accept the self-neglect bit. She was never one to make a scene, but (she told the men at work) those reports really took the biscuit.

And Desmond, with his heart hurting in the left side of his chest, feeling only partial comfort from the endless light shining into his eyes, never stopped the watching – except to coax his mother into taking him all the way to the cemetery where his Ray lay alone now, keeping himself to himself, stuck forever in the outside world.

~

I'm staring into the bin at Pump Number Two. I've taken the lid off. I can't move.

When the cuckoo fledgling opens up wide, it makes a huge pink crying picture, like all the pinkness of a clutch of tiny warblers put together. It knows how to cry like baby warblers – not with the voice of just one, mind you, but a proper nestful. A host of throats. The foster mother can never seem to find enough food. It's worse than a leaking bucket.

I'm crying into the bin at Pump Number Two. I've taken the lid off. I've taken the contents out. I burrowed out from the gape of the girl who ran the corner shop and had a craving for sex, legs pink apart as a baby bird's beak. More trouble than a hole in a bucket. I'm cursed. I see too much. I'm crying into an empty waste bin. I can't move. I can't do a thing. I've been here for years. So many years. You could say it was just laziness that I don't get a better job, or learn to drive, or do things in the daytime like other people. But you'd be wrong.

I wipe my eye with diesel gloves wet from the leak at the bottom of the bags. I should never touch my eyes. Sometimes I wish I was blind. The traffic on High Street is angry, drowning out the mothers who don't scream, so loud I can't even hear myself cry. White and red lights are streaming. Lava eyes. Too many. I know the filthy black tide is rising slowly up our doors. I check the camera. I know my face is a blubbering mess. One day soon I will watch myself crying into the bins on TV and it will bring tears to my eyes.

I drag my bags of rubbish to the dumpers by the pavement. The contents stink: fast food containers, sick and savoury, in heaps of paper wipes reeking of fuel.

You'll always be rubbish. You'll never amount to anything.

This is security's last frontier. I pose for the camera – holding

21

the bags with my arms outstretched like a statue – before heaving the lot up, over and in. I kick the cage of gas cylinders. The frame rattles and the locks hold fast. Everything is the way it should be. The camera is my witness.

~

06:30

Beyond the station, weak light creeps slowly in amongst the traffic. My shift is nearly over. I look rougher than usual, bad in the eyes, but today there's no-one to see me like this, not even Kandy.

4: Gluttony

The lottery till is separate from the cash till. On my side, where customers can't read it, the lottery company sticker keeps asking me: *Have you asked for that extra sale?*

Questions are things that fly out, like darts.

Have you asked for that extra sale? This question is more like the painted dogs tearing round the bend on the betting shop door. Always darting – but caught dead in its tracks and stuck forever. Whenever I look, the question is still trying to fly. I don't ask anyone for that extra sale. I can't even say the questions I want to ask.

Maureen was my foster mother for a while, the first one I can remember. She had two legitimate children, and me. She had thin lips and thick hair, a heart so big she gave me my own room to sleep in. She got paid by the government for my clothes, toys, food. We said grace every night before dinner. She taught me the Seven Sins and the Seven Virtues. Maureen tried hard to treat me just like her own, but no-one ever made any pretences. Everyone knew that my mother was dead because of men. And that no-one had any idea who my father was.

Maureen had a job at the supermarket. Things ticked over nicely for a while. The problem was her husband, Mr Foster. Of course, that wasn't his real name. It was a misunderstanding, but the name stuck with me. It was because of Mr Foster that I ran away. He could never look me in the face because of my eyes. I was thinking of Mr Foster whenever I had accidents. The way I saw it, every criminal in the newspaper headlines was him. Every slippery fornicating abdicating father. In the end, Maureen had to take me back to the social services. There were plenty more where she came from. And no end of Mr Fosters.

Fingering the screen, I authorise a pizza delivery boy. He fills his motor scooter. His pizza is getting cold. He has a black eye and L-plates. He pays.

01:02 on the monitor.

23

There's a straggle of clubbers on foot. They're in the mood to make a stir. They're pointing at me and laughing amongst themselves: *he's got tits! Tits!* They shield their mouths and shriek through their fingers, their lips in the space calling me names. *She-male.* They're under the influence. They're right. *She-male.* With my poker face on, I take their money. I give them change. But inside I can see it from their point of view. At the window-slot, their hilarious hands are shaking. Hysterical. On the outside I sag – I am the sad thing in the display case. I have tits. I'm wearing a girl's lucky charm bracelet. (Your average parasite – your leech, your worm, your barnacle, your lonely limpet – goes from he to she without even noticing.)

A prostitute cuts across the forecourt corner. Shoes for falling over. She's depressed, but she earns more than she ever did in the office, and tonight her boyfriend cooked her dinner.

A patrol car pulls up. I authorise. Police need petrol more than most. All those blue light missions can leave them caught short. False alarms. Accidents. Call-outs to where the twin lies broken on the stairs, where the son lies poisoned on the floor, or the family lies burned in their beds ... It's just like TV.

Tonight everyone pays. The stash accumulates in fits and starts. I drop my fifth night deposit into the safety chute and write the figure on the shift control sheet. I make a note of the time: 03:33. I close Pumps One and Two, the ones nearest the main road. Their lights go off.

The prickling smell of petrol seeps into my booth through the slot. I read today's *Truth* and the sickly whiff of newspaper ink curls up with the breath of shop fridges. Black print clings to the pores of my skin and darkens my hands – but Siv's are darker. Terrorists attack a bus full of people. Bullying in schools has got worse. A brother strangles his sister and she stares, forever young, from underneath her veil. Negligence in hospitals is fatal. I feel all choked up and it's as if my heart is irregular and I press my hot eyes with the cool of my fingertips. There is no relief from the news. There is nothing I can do.

In Siv's office, I find the usual notes. His handwriting is worse than a doctor's. He has worked out the due deliveries and the changeover shifts. My name is written in boxes across all the nights.

He's made a list of chores for himself, scribbled on a scrap of paper.

1 *Creation*

2 *Preservation*

3 *Destruction*

4 *Veiling*

5 *Grace*

I'm half tempted to look inside Siv's diary, but that would be like thieving, and Siv knows I wouldn't steal. My mother called me *parasite,* but it was my fathers who deserve the credit.

I try to imitate Siv's handwriting, think as he might – but it doesn't work. I don't know much about Siv. Not everyone is porous. And in real life I hardly ever see him. He does days. I do nights. Bharathi was the garage manager before him, and Bharathi said to me: *Terry, you're a piece of furniture.* I know that in Tamil he was thinking a compliment. It was Bob before Bharathi who gave me the job – he knew I had the knack of nights – I haven't moved in years. You could say it was just laziness. But you'd be wrong. I would say that the more you see, the less you can do.

I catch sight of myself in the idle monitor. I've got black eyes from the news. Tonight my head is full of taunts. In the curved glass I wonder at my half-hearted breasts, just proud enough to push my shirt out. I put yesterday's security video on to play and *Terry's TV* comes to life.

When the usual schoolboy cuts across the corner of my forecourt at 16:01, I press the button and make him pause. He's stuck. He's frightened. Blurred. He'll never amount to anything. Instead of growing up and out, he's somehow growing inwards.

~

Walking home from school, Mark Register stopped to sniff irises and fondle the blossom in public while other boys wrote stuff

25

on walls the length of High Street.

ROBS a twat

You'd say a rose smells sweet and hawthorn smells like meat on the turn. That petrol prickles. That an iris leaning through the railings smells of something see-through and there's nothing like a graveyard for the shiver of cypress in your nose.

MR Stinks

On a Monday, scattered rubbish took the edge off things. Butts and bones and old teabags all over the pavement smelling of neglect.

Your mother sucks more cocks than I've had hot dinners

Mark had spots on his face that hurt when he moved or pressed, and all anyone could say was *it was hormones and don't touch your face with your hands*. He was only fifteen and nothing like the songs, not one of them, but he was greedy for the things he found in magazines.

Mark lived in the middle of the terrace in Studd Street, the big house with the double front and the perfect paint. From the outside looking in, you could see books up the walls, floor to ceiling, enough to show that his mother had a job in writing and his father was a kind of politician.

Mark did his homework by himself every night, but he never got any thanks for it and the girls didn't ring him up either, like they did the other boys, and he knew it wasn't on account of his marks (which were good), and it wasn't on account of his mother and father having reputations to look after (which were good), so he wondered if it wasn't because of the skin on his face that hurt the flesh when he leaned over and the pressure went building into his pores. Or on account of his smell.

MR Stinks

Initially, the words in black paint looked like they meant to say *Mister Stinks* – like Mister Moneybags or Mister Spock – but there was a day when Mark Register walking home from school read it differently in the tiniest sideways glance. There was squinting sunlight passing straight through petals, net curtains, car windows. The fat smell of flesh going off in open bags and bins.

The whiffs of cheese and cat spray. No-one else on the street.

In his sore face, Mark felt a flush of heat. It melted up into his hair and burned the back of his neck.

MR Stinks

He checked his armpits just to be certain: a quick tilt of the head, not enough to hurt. At the gape of his school shirt he sniffed.

The Japanese say that Westerners have the odour of putrefaction because they can smell the sour milk in our blood, Mark's mother once said over dinner. She was telling the story about how, years before he was born, his father went on a student trip to Russia – which was all restricted, meat and vodka, pickled onions, communist cigarettes. He'd come back reeking from the inside, pungent to the bone.

It wasn't him, she said. *He was someone else altogether.* An unwashed tramp she could barely kiss at the airport. She'd had to hold her breath, and even wondered if she loved him. *But (and this was the point) he was oblivious to his own odour. For him it was business as usual. He had no idea at all! It was days before he was himself again.*

MR Stinks

Mark didn't know the hand that wrote it and he couldn't remember when he first saw it. The dot on the *i* was like a halo. The letters were shiny, looked wet in the sun, as though they would never dry. Mark barely shut the front door of his big house in Studd Street and his uniform was on the hall floor. No-one was home. Standing there in just his underwear, he pawed sticky at his pits but all he could make out was the morning's deodorant, a scent like talcum powder leaving a white film. A slight bitter sting of sweat. He peeled off his socks. One at a time, he twisted his feet up to his face, losing balance. Pressed as close as he could to his crotch, little pains bursting out all over his bent face. All he could smell was the faint scent of himself.

But (and this was the point) he was oblivious.

Which was how it all started. In the bathroom cabinet, there was the spray his mother used. *Violet Mist.* Hollows, crooks, bends. Not the scent of real violets pure enough to wipe out your woes, but satisfactory. And then his father's spray. *Active Sport*. Hardly any left in the can. Mark studied his body in the mirror for more than an hour. He tested all his muscles, to see how they looked, as if they could be some kind of compensation. He posed, practising photo smiles, making his eyes go out of focus and pretending his skin was clear in the blur. He stared at the mirror for long enough to try and catch himself looking like a stranger, a face for the first time, the way a girl might see it. He learned his back off by heart like a map of China, every lump and spot. The stretch marks around his waist (from when he had a growth spurt) looked like a foreign river. He checked his armpits and sniffed at his groin. *Violet Mist* and *Active Sport*. Nothing else. The cans were light, nearly empty. He had to have more.

The parents said they could taste deodorant in his sixteenth birthday cake.

By then, he sprayed it on at least three times a day, from top to toe. Every crease and join. Every bit of skin and hair you could think of. The tuck of his ears, the soles of his feet. On his back it stung. His cupboard was full of aerosols (the best ones that dried without turning to nuisance powder). *Pure Vanilla. Indulgence Natural. Blue Heaven.* He went through them like an old soak going through his gin. And he kept spares in a secret place under the bed. He couldn't get enough of it. It was more than a habit or a taste. You could say it was an appetite. Worse than a hole in a bucket.

But it wasn't just on the outside. Mark learned to guzzle mouth-wash – so thirsty for it he couldn't help but swallow, regardless of what the label said. He loved to feel it wet his gullet and reach his gut, drenching him from the inside. Sweet to the bone. It made him feel like someone else altogether.

Still the girls didn't ring at night, or give him the twice-over at school in daylight. Mark wondered if they noticed his haircut, if they talked about him, if they cared at all. But there were never any signs. Maybe like him they felt alone, keeping their secrets to themselves, putting on a brave face and holding on till the day when they would open out like a flower – is how he looked at it. And in between his thankless homework Mark studied the magazines full of beautiful skin and scent and perfect sex. He couldn't get enough of it. Pages and pages of close-ups. Pores. Spotless backs and bottoms. Faces like fresh petals. Lips parted. Glossy smiles with flirting breath. He hankered for the touch of real waxed thighs and marshmallow chests. Got drunk on his rosy notions.

Mark's heart attacked in the middle of the spring term. His windows were closed. No-one was home. It was his morning spray, the first of the day, the last straw if you like. Propane. Butane. Breathed into the blood. Day after day. Just waiting to go off.

When his parents got home, Mark was on the floor, his face a kind of lilac colour. They could taste deodorant in their mouths, even when the coroner talked about accidental inhalation. They thought of his sixteenth birthday cake and his mother howled like a storm.

They buried their son just past a clump of violets grown big as a hat between graves. Through the evergreens they saw a little woman pushing a wheelchair with a fat man slurping at his nose, so blocked up with missing his other half that he never smelt a thing. But the air was full of cypresses, violets (real ones) and the smell of new dirt damp in the sun.

~

Pause – I press the button and bring Mark Register to life again. In black and white, he finishes his shortcut across the garage forecourt. His head is full of taunts. My head is full of taunts. Instead of growing up and out, he's growing inwards like a toenail or a hair.

29

5: Rage

There's a stink to the news that fills my nose and creeps further in. It feels like a sickness inside me. Today's *Truth* disgusts me, but I can't resist it. I get poorly with other people's conditions. The newspaper headlines sound the same as graffiti, the same as the shouts and sniggers scrawled on High Street walls. Crimes and insults. There's nothing I can do about it. I keep myself to myself. I'm not one for meddling. And if I don't improve myself, or stick my neck out, idleness is not the reason. The more you see, the less you can act.

My first foster mother said that sloth was one of the Seven Deadly Sins, but animals without souls commit the sin all the way through Nature from barnacles upwards. Waiting was never a shame for tape worms. Guinea worms, hornworms, hookworms, roundworms, lungworms, flatworms – ask any worm that waits: the meek inherit the earth.

I watch. I wait. I count up the change in the till. It's neat. It always adds up. I love the sound of it, most of all the clatter of coins. I've got the knack of money. I'm as good as any of the others. I could be a banker. Bharathi, the manager before Siv, told me that his kind have it in their blood. He said I was as good with money as any Sri Lankan.

Tamils, he said, *know how to make ends meet.* They make good accountants. Administrators. Mathematicians.

Everywhere in London, Bharathi said, *Sri Lankans are cashing up in all-night garages and grocery shops.*

No-one else wants this kind of job any more. Except me. I do nights. I stand out. I want this job. It's mine. It's me. I'm as white as Mother's Pride. I've been here for years and I never want to leave. I've never missed a shift. Siv has never had to stand in for me. Nor any other manager before him. I've locked myself in. Screw. Hook. Sucker. I call it survival of the stillest.

Siv comes from a faraway island. On the wall of his office, in amongst the timesheets and the legal notices, his map is a tear-drop in the ocean. Brimming. *Giant's Tank. Elephant Pass.* Waiting to fall. *Brief Garden. Adam's Peak. Kandy.* The easy names sound like big things, sweet and wet things. But I couldn't say half the names if you paid me. Restless words like Paraiyanalankulam or Ratmalagahawewa. There are dots of jabbed biro around a town called Batticaloa. I have memorised the name, even if I don't know how to say it. I think this is where Siv comes from. He's not see-through in the way that some people are.

Siv is dark: browner than a penny, darker than diesel. He moves like he's on wheels. He acts like a man who has the answer, or a plan, for everything, and it looks to me as if he has lived everything before.

On playback I've seen him comfort the mourning book-keeper with his hand touching lightly on her arm and she flinched. I saw him talk to her with all the tenderness of a father, his eyes like olives, wet and black. I saw his dark hand touch her white arm and she flinched. I played it over and over again, so long in the gap between customers that afterwards I've watched myself watching the video. And I flinch.

~

One of my foster mothers had thin carpet worn through from grazing, and shiny lino in the kitchen. Her husband Mr Foster left lumps of mud from his boots on every floor and wouldn't pick it up. He smelled of kerosene sometimes, but that was just the way ale turned deep inside him. He was a builder. She stirred dinner at the white stove. She sewed buttons, or darned gloves and jumper elbows. In the corners of her curtains there were discs which felt like real money. Through folded hems I rubbed the coins, believing in some kind of mystery luck. I would need money – secret money – if I was ever going to run away. I would have to pay people to feed me, to hide me, to give me a ride in their car to some place miles away from Mr Foster.

When no-one was looking, I tried to tease the hidden coins out, but layers of cloth were forever in the way.

One day at last I did it.

31

My foster mother flinched sometimes when Mr Foster gripped her, kissing her with kerosene and tugging at her top. I was thinking about her flinching when I pressed my spoils into Mr Foster's shepherd's pie. He stuffed his mouth and cracked his tooth on a grey lead weight. He yelped and then he hit me. The wetness from my eyes on his hand made him flinch.

~

At night, you get the stray insomniacs who believe everyone else in the world is sleeping. If they venture from bed, they don't notice all the other unsleeping eyes: the dilated pupils, a pizza delivery boy's black socket, an alcoholic's cherry-eye, the certain gape of prostitutes. Not to mention the indifferent looks of lorry drivers and delivery men.

I wonder how eyes become windows to a body's soul – and I don't mean the surface flecks or spots and stains. I mean the look inside that comes outside, the secrets of a life's story told without a word and spilled without a trace – you'd be hard-pressed to explain the physics of it to a blind man.

A tipsy couple on foot straggles up to my window. She buys a packet of condoms, even though he hates the idea and refuses to pay for them. The computer sings. A postman in uniform peers at a security camera to get my attention. I stare right back at him on the live screen till it switches over to another view, the edge of the forecourt at High Street. The time is 03:05. The postman at Pump Number Six slaps it like a slow horse. I authorise him. He begins to fill his little car. Tomorrow he's on strike. They want to turn his sorting office into luxury apartments – no-one ever imagined the heights that things would soar to.

At the edges of the forecourt, beyond the glare of my glass, through the jams and jellies lined up in reflection, a heavy figure passes. I saw her yesterday around dawn, and last week just after midnight. Once, a long time ago, she came up to my window and bought some sore throat pastilles. She had lost her voice.

On playback I've seen her again and again. Shuffling across the grease-stained corner, clutching at her cardigans, clammy from her sleepless bed, treading by night on oil and water. She panics. She roams. The most important step in a parasite's life is that final journey: leaving the host. But she always returns to her mother's blonde voice. It fills every last corner. The daughter's nightmares are nothing – there is worse to come. It's just a matter of time. I've read the truth. I've seen it all.

I check the live action monitor. The camera shows only a familiar patch of dark grease in the cement and I scour the scene for some new sign – but you'd be wrong if you found any rhyme or reason in spots and stains.

She's already at my window and tapping the glass.

'A packet of aspirin, please,' she says.

I'm filled with her horror. I want to cry out and tell her what I see, her past, her future, but I feel paralysed, caught, like a question on a sticker.

'The more you know, the less you bet,' I say. It comes out in a stammer.

'I beg your pardon?' Her top lip pulls up on invisible hooks. Her father was some kind of gambler. He's gone for good.

'It's much worse than a headache,' I say. 'It won't just go away like that. Try not to fall. Don't slip up. Make sure the drawers – the doors are closed …' I search for the words. 'Before the horse bolts. I mean, before –'

'Excuse me. I just want some aspirin.' She's deciding not to come back here again unless she's desperate. She thinks I'm lucky to have a job, in my state. Her mother is blonder than Jean Harlow, and it drives the daughter mad.

~

Elizabeth Sturgess. A blonde name. Lucky for blondes: when they go white they keep looking blonde. She was a handsome woman before the stroke. (Anybody would say so.) It took away bits of her. Facial movements, sipping, get-up-and-go. She lost sight in her left eye. She lost movement in her leg. But she never lost the art of cursing, and she never lost her teeth.

Elizabeth Sturgess. At the launderette. On the phone. The way

33

she said her name made it sound like she had a million pounds in the bank for each and every tooth she owned.

Twenty-eight, she said, tapping the front ones with nail-tips. Mouth open like a horse sucking a strong mint. *Twenty-eight, and the bastard dentist wanted to rip them out when I was expecting.*

Mary the daughter had brown hair, thin and wispy. Too much scalp on show. Overcast by her mother in the street, on the estate. Fifth floor, you'd see The Blonde Head bobbing along the balcony wall, but The Brown just disappeared into the bricks like a shadow. Shorter too. Mary had a job in the council doing permits and paper documents.

Typical job for The Brown, Elizabeth Sturgess said at the shops, the doctor's, generally to all and sundry. She was forever out and about, exercising her right to roam. You couldn't pin a good woman down. Born between the wars you were guaranteed to have a lust for your own ways. She called it independence. Played in bomb-sites all the hours. Went to live with all sorts of people in all kinds of places. Never mind the swinging sixties. Never mind your council daughter conceived in proper wedlock, in the dreary days before the boom.

The times were brown, and my daughter is of the times. Elizabeth Sturgess would shake her head in the hairdresser's chair. Check her roots in the mirror.

No perks either. The tendons in her neck like ropes.

As if Mary should have done more with herself, been more successful, got herself a job in the aristocracy.

From time to time, the council threatened Elizabeth Sturgess with paper documents. Parking fines for some car she didn't own. Taxes a woman her age didn't have to pay. Penalties and charges. Worse still, they made outrageous demands upon the long departed Mister. Mother would press on daughter, demanding she pull some council string or other. But there were never any strings.

I'm in permits, not in finance. Quiet Mary fairly screamed. Brittle as a biscuit.

The Brown was forty-nine when her mother had the stroke. Her father had run off without his personal things when she was

34

only twelve. He wasn't around for a single birthday every year after that. But in her middle age she still had a whiff of him in her mind's nose, his hairdo oiled well past the fashion (leaving stains) and she had a nightmare of his underpants.

G.B. Sturgess. Mary could see the name in fuzzed blue thread across a white tag. The dye had run in the wash. The letters wavered. But it wasn't the tag that troubled her.

G.B. Sturgess. Her mother said the initials stood for *Gambling Bastard,* even if a croupier couldn't. The day he left, he wiped the palms of his hands in the air just to show that they were empty. A single stroke. Like he was quitting a table for the next shift. Anyone else would have waved, or slammed the door. Something normal.

Elizabeth Sturgess kept only his name. Took all his leavings to The Salvation Army. His black suit with the sewn-up pockets. His shaver. His underpants. Taunted for weeks by his pointed shoes arranged pigeon-toed in the main shop window. She stopped dead in her tracks the day they disappeared from the display. Then her hair made a blaze of blonde in the glass reflection.

Mr Gambling Bastard-Sturgess, Esq. She stood at the window and swore loud enough for all the world to hear. *Double barrel. Unlucky for some. Good riddance, Mr Chips.*

When he left (before the shoes) Mary was in the hating phase. Breasts like little strawberries and single brown hairs in her armpits. He passed wind at the dinner table on days off. He teased her for her clumsy slips and accidents. He slept long but lightly, twitching in all directions. If he had stayed, not left, perhaps he could have tamed her, charmed (and not disgusted) her with fingers dexterous from the punters' chips. Forever stacking the cork coasters because they were there. Coins, cards, keys in a bunch. Slicing, shuffling, twisting. Sleight of hand.

Slight of mind, his wife would say. (And, truth be told, he was a little simple – she wasn't the first to say it.) If he had stayed on, he had no hope of taming *her.* Not blonde Elizabeth Sturgess with the handsome face before the stroke.

Getting up to the fifth floor was no mean feat for someone

who'd lost their get-up-and-go. There was a blind tiled corner in the foyer, and three steps to the lift with a make-do ramp. Elizabeth Sturgess learned to make do, but mostly with the help of Mary. Which caused no end of cursing. Both mother and daughter making a scene. You could hear them down the corridors. Fighting on the edges, through the walls, on the landings.

Mary didn't sleep at night. She was always listening out for her mother's voice. She woke up twitching. In her mind's eye she'd be feeding a hungry mouth that kept on moving like a game. It made her clammy. Or there were animals under the bed sometimes, big and restless. She could hear them panting, ready to bite if her feet touched the floor. (Which meant not going to the toilet even when she needed to.) And some nights she was at the office getting sacked, over and over again. Which made her cry without a noise.

I can't be doing this all the time. The daughter grumbled at the lift in daylight, tired of moving her mother's weight. Out of breath. Wishing she was deaf.

You think I like this bastard condition? The Blonde Head jawing. Half the face muscles looking smudged and still. But all her handsome beauty pacing about the other half. *Why don't you get that bastard council of yours to help us?*

I'm in permits, not in social services. Mary in public places, holding the scream in clenched teeth, a vice.

And what about getting us a posh new garden flat? Het up. Not listening. Never listening. Although both the ears worked as well as before.

I'm in permits, not in housing.

You couldn't move The Brown once she'd made her mind up. She was in permits. She was full of stubborn council talk. She was a rude little sign on a bullet-proof window. Department closed. Ungiving as the day she was born, after two days in labour and the damage to prove it. Enough to drive a sane woman mad. Twenty-eight teeth but only half a daughter. (What could you expect with only half a father, a simple cheat who couldn't even slam the door like someone normal?) Refusing to help her own mother as usual. Plain as a bucket – anyone would say it – and a talent for mistakes. Lucky to get a job anywhere, never mind the bastard council, with those eyes like a car-shy pony and that sulking lip. That head of thin brown go-nowhere hair. Lucky to have a friend, with the drab old-woman clothes she wore.

Six months after the stroke, Mary took herself to the housing department, where she had a friend, and to social services, where she had another one. From the outside, you could see they were friends, just by the look of them. You could tell by the way they moved, their shoes, their hair. They had a meeting.

Mary got a handful of white paper documents. It was official. Her mother needed special care and there were homes you could go to, with all manner of services on tap, entertainments laid on like hot and cold running water, bars in the toilet, young nurses who never grumbled or sulked, no make-do ramps on the stairs, and endless company your own age to die for, all dreamed up specially for old women who ailed and cursed.

Mary brought the two friends home. She put their coats over the settee stains. (Somehow the old hair oil stood out in public – darker, shinier – took her back like a trick to the hating phase when she was bumping into things with her young woman's hips.) There were slick-marks on every soft chair. A familiar smell in the living room.

With people from the council all of a sudden in her place, The Blonde Head knew full well to go through the motions – as best she could.

I'm in housing, said the brown friend in the comfort of the kitchen.

And I'm in social services. The other one too cheerful.

Elizabeth Sturgess stood at the sink, bit her lip (the half she could) and kept mum. Nodded her head and made herself a cup of tea, just to show what kind of metal she was made of, stroke or no stroke, her good arm working. Listened with both her ears and slurped her tea, just a little spilling down the side. Wiped her chin too often, just in case. Combed her hair with the right fingers, deft. Knew she was wearing the wrong trousers, caught unawares in her worst slacks.

Twenty-eight, she said, tapping her front teeth with nail-tips. Mouth half-open. Only half the set showing in a gape.

She raised her voice. *And they're seventy-something years young if they're a day. And you know the bastards wanted to rip them out when I was expecting. That's the truth. Put that in your pipe and smoke it.*

The Brown Friends gave each other the special look. Sipped their tea as one. (Not a drop spilt.) Rested their cosy elbows on the table, straightened their cuffs. Smiled.

We understand, the eyes said. Saying nothing. *We know.*

But Elizabeth Sturgess knew better. She farewelled the ladies from the council. Kept her position standing firm by the sink.

Left alone with Mary.

The Brown was looking somehow lighter, fairer, the pinch smoothed from her lip. She was armed with paper documents. And bastard witnesses in the guise of friends.

Well then, Mary said. Expecting things.

Elizabeth Sturgess was feeling cornered, but the last thing she expected was the short hard feeling of the kitchen knife in her good fist stabbing at the ungiving gut of Mary Sturgess, slipping like a silver fish out of her hand and onto the floor. (Not a drop of blood spilt.)

The last thing on her mind was the way that the daughter could topple and fall on the open drawer and scupper her spine, her brown eyes full of a pony horror, stiff as a stick from the neck down and losing control of all the bodily functions forever except the thinking part of the brain.

Nor did the mother set her mind to imagining the daughter being moved out of the flat on a stretcher, or the unlucky nurse who turned the hospital machine off by accident some time afterwards, when the daughter needed it just to carry on breathing.

You'd be wrong to suppose that The Blonde Head thought any of these bastard things, whatever she said before and after the stroke.

Sleight of hand. Slight of mind. Over and over, that's all she was thinking, Elizabeth Sturgess. Her handsome beauty free to roam about half her face.

6: Pride

There are three realities: god, souls and bondage. Siv has doodled this on the first page of his work diary. It feels as if I'm stealing his private thoughts, but he knows I wouldn't actually take anything from him. He can trust me. Other managers keep their cashiers locked out of the office.

The Sacred Entrance serves as the passage to go in and come out of the Temple. This is the most important part of the Temple and we should offer our prayers here.

This is printed on a torn-out page that smells of incense. There's half a picture on the back. Why has he kept it? He's scrawled a message in biro across the space. Numbers. Names. His writing is worse than a dying man's, it's so hard to read. As I say, he's not porous. He doesn't let things come out like others do.

03:24 on the monitor and the office camera is watching me now. I sit quietly on the stool and do what I'm best at: nothing. Pale as a limpet in the gloom.

It's not a personal diary. Most of the spaces are empty. *Tiger. Tank. New recruit. Fundraising. Promo.* I close the cover. I can't make head or tail of half of it.

Siv's idol picture is judging me, its third eye narrowed.

The camera inside the shop takes its turn to wake up and stare. The teddy bears huddle together, oblivious. The Hollywood video-boxes flare, and the *Kitten* magazines hide behind each other. Canisters of car oil line up, gather dust. Unbought copies of the *Truth* wait in piles. Three boys on foot press their faces to my window.

They want cigarettes. According to the law they're far too young – they shouldn't even be out on the streets at this hour – but if I don't sell them what they want, someone else will. Besides, I can feel their craving. It's like a hunger, and hunger was never a sin for tape worms or any other living creature.

The boys want to shout, forever, without going hoarse, the

length of High Street. They've got huge black felt-tip pens in their pockets. They've got words ready in their minds.

I have none, no words in my mind except theirs. *Terry the tosser. Your mother sucks more cocks than I've had hot dinners.* It's as if they're shouting at me, through me – but it's my customers who have porous skin.

They pay. They go.

~

At 06:45 on the TV screen Giri turns up for the changeover in the dirty light of morning. He has a mop of thick black hair. His eyes are bright. He's left a pretty wife and four children at home in bed, slowly waking up for school. Giri wears a crucifix at his neck. His wife was Hindu before they married. A tiny gold and silver god with an elephant's head stands on her dressing table, next to a statue of Jesus whose naked heart sits proud on the surface of his robes.

Giri sets about checking the changeover float. I open the shop doors. The coldness from outside pours in. Two blocks away, fire-truck sirens are whooping. Giri stops counting for a moment to authorise a yawning Turk who stops for petrol on his way to the house he's painting. A van pulls up and drops off a pile of the *Truth*. Public transport is in chaos because of bomb scares. A little girl has been tortured to death. Through the shop, I return to my glass box.

Giri is still counting.

A legal secretary lifts the nozzle at Pump Number Two. She had sex with her boss last night. I authorise. A woman from Bethlehem pulls up in a khaki-coloured four-wheel drive. In the back seat, her daughter dozes against her violin case. The computer sings. I authorise. A bank manager pulls up to Pump Number Five. He has a private passion for little boys. It's unrequited. I authorise.

Everything is in order. Giri has checked the float. It all adds up. I sign the book. He signs the book. It's 07:00. Time to leave.

~

Some days in London are still-born. I cut down Sillwood Street, away from the roar of cars. The street lamps are on even now, leaking yellow light in pools. After the terrace of old houses come the modern flats. I slip into the third slit between the buildings and climb up Kandy's stairs. Outside her door is the familiar ceramic plaque: the little painted fox she had done for her, specially, by mail order. So homely. Tiny brush-strokes: licks of a moth's tongue. Real-looking fur and shadows. Sparks in the eyes. The animal turns to look at me. Through me. My little fox. Number seven. Unlucky for some. I press my finger lightly on the bell.

The Sacred Entrance serves as the passage to go in and come out of the Temple. This is the most important part of the Temple and we should offer our prayers here.

Kandy lets me in. The kettle is on and the windows are steamed up as usual. She has sprayed perfume in the air – musk, my favourite – but it doesn't mask the smell of fresh and stale smoke. Cigarettes and joints. The TV is on. It's 24-hour cable news, but she's turned the sound off because she knows I like the flickering pictures. Kandy's been up all night, like me.

'How was work?' she asks.

'The usual, you know.'

In my head I sort the people into categories. I've absorbed their stories. I tell them to Kandy – she's studying psychology – but I only tell her about this week's dead and dying.

'How's your night been?' I'm standing in the middle of her carpet.

'I haven't stopped.' She sighs.

The kettle sings and Kandy carefully prepares my tea: three sugars, lots of milk, the mug she had made specially for when I visit. (It says *Terry's Mug* in a pattern all over.) Watching her is soothing. With her good hand she passes the mug to me.

'Sweets for the sweet,' she says, half smiling.

There's no expression on the right side of her face, so it always

41

comes across as a sneer. But it's not like Elizabeth Sturgess – Kandy had polio when she was little. When she smokes she holds the cigarette with her weak right hand, gripping it hard at the wrist with her left. When she drinks, likewise. She prides herself on giving head without having to use her throat. Her senseless cheek does just as well and no-one has ever noticed the difference – except me, of course. With Kandy I feel tender, close. She's always there for me, more faithful than a fiancée waiting after a war.

I'm sitting on the sofa-bed, drinking tea. I'm watching the silent news. *There are three realities: god, souls and bondage* – whatever Siv says in his diary, men's dreams are always bondage. When I put down my very own *Terry's Mug* on the bedside table, Kandy comes to me. My heart is singing. She sits at the edge of the bed, unclasps the calliper from her leg and slips off her robe. My heart is singing. She undresses me like a baby. My heart is singing. She climbs on top of me. My heart is singing. She lets me in.

The Sacred Entrance serves as the passage to the Temple.

I pray out loud into Kandy's ear and Siv authorises.

~

When it's over, I tell her this week's story.

We're lying on the bed, side by side.

Kandy's not porous and she listens like a professional.

The TV news is on, but the sound is switched off. I know more than any newsreader.

Kandy smokes.

I close my eyes. I've seen it all.

~

A live cigarette butt rolled, rolled. This way and that in gusts of wind. Standing in the middle of the pavement, Safina stared at it. She thought about picking it up. She smelled the smoke and hankered after it in her nose. And the way this butt rolled, and rolled, seemed to tempt her with her own weakness. She was a sinner. She always did things wrong. She knew that.

The day of the butt with its red-hot end was Safina's last one. It was written in her fate, is how she would have said it. And even though she didn't stoop to pick it up, the first picture that came into her head as she gave up her breath once and for all was the burning cigarette butt earlier in the day, rolling this way, then that. She was wearing her favourite plum lipstick. Umar's favourite too. She didn't even think about the baby inside her. Or her first child, still an infant, and looking like his absent father.

The first one's always like the father, Safina's mother would say. She had her theories. It was Mother Nature's way of keeping a man from doubting or straying – only in this case, she had to admit, the baby's face had not done the trick. Safina's brother Abul was the spit of his own dead father gone forever to rest in paradise, which proved the point about likeness for anyone who cared to notice. Problem being, Safina's one on the way was the first one for a second father.

Young Umar was the last word in romance. He smelled nice when he sweated, he hung on Safina's every word, made no complaint when her baby cried from the pram, distracting them in intimate moments. Umar had a reliable job but he was – and anyone would say it who'd call a spade a spade – *inferior.* He was a fitter and turner, marked by grease, and he suffered from diabetes. No match for the daughter of a pharmacist and his widow. But you'd be wrong if you thought that was the only problem. Umar should never have taken up with a married girl, no two ways about it, even if she was deserted by her real husband gone to spend her dowry and live in amongst country peasants till God knows when.

Safina was angling secretly for divorce, but she wasn't going to get one, and she knew it. Something else was written in her fate. There were moral rules to take account of, and there was no-one like Safina's mother for making them stick: she'd learned a kind of vigilance, the sort that didn't stop at home. She was strong and built like a ship, and she'd come to London on one. Marched right up the stairs of their flat in Duchess Street, and painted the walls before the week was out. Picked out all the floral plaster trims and scoured the stinking kitchen. Got herself regular piece-work, sewing toys and putting the stuffing in.

Maybe it was because of the mother's vigilance that Safina turned out to be such a sinner – there's always some child who's contrary, who'll go the other way from family expectations. The mother had her consolations, but it broke her heart when local children tore at her daughter's headscarf and called out names, or flicked her with balls of gum from the back of the bus. She stuffed Safina's blotted cloths into the freezer, in amongst the ice cube trays and frozen peas. She couldn't think of another way round it.

Then, when Safina turned fifteen, she was formally engaged – but not to the one she loved already. Her brother knew nothing about the grease-stained mechanic at the local garage, or the go-between at school. One thing he did know was that the world is rife with tricks and tests.

In honour of a deal made before she knew how to walk or talk, Safina's groom was sent for specially from overseas. He was drawn by the strength of her dowry. And her photo helped. He was an administrator. The lands he managed spread so far and wide it took more than a day by horse to cross them. Safina might have looked like a sinner in the picture, with her dark lipstick, her close-set eyes full of a darting pride, her hair too tight across her head. But there were shadows under her eyes that made her sad as a kitten and just as wanting. There was no way of knowing her heart was secretly accounted for, even if her body wasn't.

We can be proud of our family, Abul said in a speech at his sister's wedding. He was working at the superstore, training to be a manager. Safina was seventeen and ripe for children. *Two respected families coming together.* He wasn't to know that the young groom was already making plans for another life back home, to disappear forever to his country province.

The family has great honour, their mother would say, by way of self-defence, before, during and after. It wasn't exactly like it sounds. The way she saw it, no-one here would understand it.

Pride is another word, but what did that mean to a judge whose Christian children would rip at modest veils?

Abul was deputy manager at the superstore when Safina's second known shame started. He was so busy with one thing or another that it was an age before he noticed her go off her food like she did first time around. Coffee. Onions. And mushrooms. Just some things.

But even then, she lived like a nun on a separate floor, so you never could be sure. And it's not the sort of thing you'd want to believe when you had to set an example and hold your head up high in public. *We are proud of our family* – Abul said that in court, as if it would change things. But his mother was already fainting at the verdict, then the sentence, her being one to stick to morals all her life, give or take the odd exception. Collapse she did, with a groan, all over the pew, made a great bruise and lump on her ageing forehead. They had to stir her up with smelling salts.

But it was her that made the shroud to wrap her daughter in. Her that kicked Safina in the belly to make her bleed it out, the great insult. Her that stuffed Safina's mouth with headache pills to dislodge the family demon. Her that made Safina clean out the travelling trunk, the one she'd brought from home on the ship, to clear a space in readiness. And (because it was far too late for doctors) it was her that held Safina by the feet to keep her still. Crying hot tears of shame all the while.

And it was Abul that taught Safina a lesson – he nearly died of shock to hear she'd made sly vows to marry the father of her unborn guilt, the fitter and turner Umar marked by grease and weak with diabetes. It was him that stretched the flex across Safina's throat, crying tears of pouring sorrow minute after minute until she died, her body going slack as the beast who gives up the ghost on TV documentaries, knowing that it's written in its fate. The brother kissed the sister, saying sorry to the dead thing inside her. Then he kissed the living baby orphaned in the cot. The mother held the daughter's feet down all the while, just in case.

Abul drove the double-dead body of his shroud-wrapped sister

45

pressed into the travelling trunk up and down big ring-roads near the superstores, and onto crowded motorways, and small winding country roads, until he finally found a tip to dig it in. His mind went back to the kitchen freezer, the folds of dark cloth stuffed in amongst the ice-cream tubs, the look of his upset mother breaking frozen gum off scarves. His sister lashing out: accusing him of doing, and wearing, whatever he wanted.

She was unlucky. She chose her fate. That's what Abul said in court by way of self-defence, although he did admit to panic. His mother had asked him to think of his father. He could barely remember him, but that wasn't the point. It was easier than taking the part of the groom.

Honour. That's what the mother said to the English barristers, praying quietly to God in public. It was simpler back home: you wouldn't have gone around hiding clues as if there'd been some pointless crime. You'd make a show of it in your window. Everyone would know that the son was defending his father's name. He had always been his mother's pride and joy.

When Safina saw the live cigarette butt rolling this way, that way, with each gust of wind, she rubbed her sore belly kicked by her angry mother strong as a ship. To cheer herself, she imagined her handsome Umar shaving, kissing, smoking, smelling sweet, despite the grease on his muscles. His black fingernails. His close-up smile in bed. Safina, who never smoked, stopped in the middle of the street and stared and wondered how it would be to pick up the butt and suck on it. She wondered what kind of person with germs had smoked it. She suddenly noticed all manner of filth and nonsense. *Your mother sucks more cocks than I've had hot dinners* scrawled by an idiot on the wall. Droppings left by an owner's dog in front of a neighbour's gate. A pizza offer flapping against the railing. *Buy one. Get one free!* A fortune-teller's flier with no end of spelling mistakes promising ninety-eight per cent accuracy. And all those blackened balls of spat-out gum, pressed flat to the ground by generation after generation of stamping feet.

Safina stood there, frozen still, feeling her illegitimate baby kick from the inside. *Dying to get out to all the filth and nonsense,* was how she saw it. She rummaged in her bag until she found her favourite lipstick, the plum one Umar liked most. She pulled back her headscarf. She held her mirror to catch the best light and did her mouth. Right there in public, in the middle of the pavement. *For Umar,* she thought. *My own true love.*

At home behind closed doors her first child waited. Her brother and her mother waited. With a spade, a length of flex, an empty travelling trunk and a hand-made shroud.

~

'Is that the end?' Kandy asks.

'Yes.' I don't open my eyes. Not yet.

'Someone always dies at the end.'

'Yes.'

'And they're kind of local.'

'Yes.'

'Which garage was it?' Kandy asks. 'The same place you work?'

I shake my head.

'We're all capable of anything that shows up in court,' Kandy says. 'Every one of us. There's nothing we can't do.' (She always says that.)

'Yes.'

'She could have run away, pet, but she didn't. She was part of the deal.'

We both lie there for a while without saying another word.

Kandy's not porous. She knows not to say too much.

Kandy is not her real name but it's the name that sticks, the same as Mr Foster.

'I hate all those pizza fliers and junk mail, don't you?' she says at last.

I nod. At home I keep them all in piles, years and years of them. I don't throw anything away.

I open my eyes and check the clock. It's time, nearly to the minute. Time to get up.

47

When I'm dressed and ready to go, I pay.

Kandy props herself up against both pillows. She holds a cigarette to her lips with her right hand, lights it and grips hard at the wrist with her left. 'See you next week,' she says, neat as a therapist.

'Thank you, my own true love,' I say. 'Don't move on account of me – I'll let myself out,' I say, and I go.

~

I'm walking home. The traffic is thickening. Someone has dropped a live cigarette butt onto the pavement. The birds are carrying on in the trees. Stock brokers and gamblers are dreaming of today's bets. I want to wake them up, shouting till I'm hoarse: the more you know, the less you'd bet. At this hour the men who make all the money know precisely which suit to wear. Lawyers prepare themselves to pass without too much trouble from one host to the next. The mourning mother of twins is waking up to her alarm clock. The mechanics are on their way to the garage. The half-smoked cigarette on the pavement behind me rolls this way, then that.

Who enjoys it more: the ladies or the gents? Safina or Umar? The sister or the brother? Judging by the risks she takes to get it – the dangers she brings upon herself for the sake of satisfaction – the answer's got to be the lady. Look at the trouble Beatrice went to way back when, despite Adam, despite everything, despite what people were saying about the girl in the corner shop, my aching mother. *Don't be fornicating all over the shop* – but she did. She went ahead and fornicated all over the shop. And it wasn't for love.

I'm frozen, standing in the middle of the pavement, looking at the messages all around me, the dirty flap of newspaper wrapped around a bollard, the special offer in the gutter, the childish writing on the wall: *LUV U 4 EVVA*. I zip up my jacket to hide my breasts.

I think of all the devices dreamed up to take away dead Safina's pleasures, to tuck her out of sight and keep her down just like a genie in a bottle. But she still pops out. The ladies enjoy it more – you'd be hard-pressed to tell me otherwise – because there's deep-down pain in it for the gents every time. The drinker always blames the drink for his madness. He hides his bottle under the bed. He goes to great lengths to bury his weakness. It's got something to do with pride, but I haven't put my finger on it. The more you see, the more you see, and there's the end of it. I've got the gift of insight, but it doesn't mean I have the answers. That much I do know.

~

Home is called the Nightingale Estate, but the only singers here with tongues for real music are the blackbirds. They're so plain they're beautiful. The morning light is grimy. Street lamps are still on. Bedrooms here and there are lit-up boxes. People are on the move. Engines are revving. I keep my eye to the ground. My feet pass other feet. I am drained, at the end of my shift, my vision sapped. Security floodlights glare down from on high. I make my way, in hurrying steps that take forever, one after another, inching along my road, my concrete path, my tiled lobby with the blind turning, my steps, my scraping metal lift with corners damp and stinking. I ride up high on the usual smells of public piss and last week's disinfectant. In wipes of red light, the numbers come alive, from ground to one to two to three … all the way up to fifteen. Thirteen and fourteen are always missing, like floors that don't exist. I want to get inside my flat, my home which is where my heart is, where the door clamps shut and no-one comes knocking, where the carpet is worn bald with paths between the papers, where everything is kept and nothing is lost. The keys are ready in my hand, moist sweat in the teeth of them. I unlock my door. Three locks, one above the other. Inside, I close myself in. I settle down, burrow into my bed, grip at the edges of my quilt, blend in with the wallpaper. There are goings-on like a storm of filth and nonsense all around, but my windows are shut tight and the blinds are drawn. I close my eyes, ready to sleep – properly, soundly, without dreams. You could call it survival of the stillest.

7: Envy

I turn up for work at 22:50 on the monitor and do the change-over with Naga. I'm counting the float, note by note, coin by coin, while Naga deals with customers. I'm old enough to be his father. He's only twenty. He's already emptied the forecourt bins and taken a big delivery of sundries.

Naga is lighter than your average Tamil. He could be something else if you didn't know different. Before the likes of Naga, and Giri, and Bharathi, and Siv, things used to have another complexion. Of course, there's the African called Ken. And there's me. I'm paler than chicken.

The float adds up all right and it's time for Naga to go. He signs the book. When he gets back to his bedsit he'll stay up till all hours doing homework. He's studying economics.

'Siv has left your pay. It's on the desk,' he says.

In the office I pick up the envelope scrawled in Siv's illegible hand. *Terry – Wk 7.* I tear it open and the cash is there, my week's earnings in tidy notes held together by a rubber band. A few loose coins. A payslip. I hide the lot in my inside pocket. Naga is waiting. I come out into the brightness of the glass box. There are no customers. The computer is silent, but I'm not.

'Why do Tamils work in petrol stations?' I can't usually say the questions I want to ask. Questions are things that fly out, neat as darts. Until this moment my question has been like the painted dogs tearing round the bend on the betting shop door. Darting – but caught, paralysed inside me.

Naga looks surprised. He's putting on his outdoor jacket.

'For the money!' he laughs. 'What else?'

He goes to wash his hands at the sink. Tiny upward-flying splashes blot clear red words above his head on cardboard. *Keep your mess to yourself, you lazy – yes you!* Naga is not careless or lazy, but he doesn't read the sign. No-one does.

'Why do *you* work here?' he says over the drumming water.

He turns to look at me.

'Are *you* Tamil?' He thinks it's hilarious. He's wiping his hands.

I tell him the truth. 'I love my job. I do nights. It's less trouble for me – personally speaking. And I've got a knack with money, I suppose, like you.'

Naga looks at me seriously for a second. He's dying to get away. His homework is waiting, and his girlfriend.

The computer sings all of a sudden. I check the forecourt. A driver is standing by Pump Number Three with diesel gloves on. A London Black Cab ID medallion hangs low on his gut. He used to be a Ticky Man at the dogs. He used to wear white gloves to make signs across the racetrack to his partners, while the punters lined up itching to place all manner of cash bets. He caught his mate with one hand in the money bag, but he couldn't knock him out because he was a friend from way back when – and he was a gentleman. So he bit him, hard enough to teach him a lesson. Deep into the stealing hand. I authorise.

Naga is by the security door.

'You know, Terry, man, we're good cashiers. It's easy to get this job. It takes only one week: the training is fast, you know. Someone recommends you when you get here: someone from home who knows someone else. If you need money fast, you can work more hours. Every shift if you want! More than other jobs, isn't it? Enough cash to send back – you know, my mother is still in Sri Lanka. And sometimes, like my cousin, people spent all their money to come here, you know, just to run away.'

If you plan to run away from your home, you have to pay people to feed you, hide you, take you as far as possible from the likes of Mr Foster.

'You let me out?'

I follow Naga through the security door and across the shop floor.

'See you, Terry.' He grins.

'See you.'

I bolt the shop door after him.

Outside the taxi driver crosses the forecourt.

51

At my window I take his credit card and feed it through the till. He wants the receipt for his tax. He goes. He keeps a record of all his expenses.

That's the beauty of cash for me, and for Naga. No records. No banks. No-one keeping tabs or interfering.

~

Behind the pumps nearest the main road I can see a man's legs in jeans bending over. I check the security monitor.

00:40

I wait for the cameras to find him. He's leaning over some kind of tin and he has the petrol nozzle pressed into its top. He hasn't noticed that I've already closed the pump. Its lights are off. In any case, I can't authorise. You have to use the right sort of can. He hits the pump as if it's a juke box that's stuck. He's cross.

Now I feel cross and press the tannoy button, dropping my voice into the microphone, like God bearing down on Moses. Slowly I read the official words from the card taped to the bench.

'Fuel can only be delivered directly into vehicles or an authorised receptacle.'

He pulls a face at the booming speaker above his head. There are signs and commandments everywhere. He turns to clock all of them. I stare at him through the glass as he marches up to me.

'My mate's run out,' he says at the window. He holds the empty tin up high and shakes it. The skin on his hand is puckered and scarred. So is the skin on his face.

'I can't authorise unless you've got the right sort of can,' I say. 'It's for Health and Safety. You can buy a proper one from here.'

'And how much profit do you make on that?' He's mad, but he pulls out his wallet anyway. His name is Duffy.

I don't reply. I get him a new fuel can off the shelf.

At Pump Number Four, Duffy nudges the nozzle in and presses the trigger. My computer sings like a blackbird in fright. *Ti. Ti. Ti. Ti. Ti. Ti. Ti. Ti.* I authorise. He fills it up, carefully, doesn't lose a drop. When he comes back to my window to pay, an unlit cigarette hangs from his mouth. I don't say a word. He walks off into the dark beyond the forecourt. I see it all.

52

~

You hear all those stories about petrol going where it shouldn't, about cigarette butts rolling into a patch and catching fire, going up in flames just when you least expect it.

Duffy knew all about the hazards of flammable goods, but some primary teacher (it was Mrs Knight) told him they always got it wrong and the word was *INFLAMMABLE.*

People always read it the wrong way. The Doing Word was 'inflame'.

You could say Duffy wasn't flammable. Which is why he always liked to set his hand to matches. Burned down his father's shed when he was seven and spent weeks in bandages and cream. The scars on his face never went away.

At school it was always *Duffy with the scars* and *Ralph without.* They were best friends, like Siamese twins, all the way through to when they were forty and then things went the way they did. Mrs Knight had a bug about apostrophes, too. They stood for something belonging or something missing, and that was that.

After midnight Duffy walked to the garage in High Street and bought a jerry can and filled it to the top with premium. Careful not to spill a drop, or let it go where it shouldn't. Precious pink.

My mate's run out, he said to the man behind the reinforced glass. And he paid.

Duffy walked all the way to Ralph's house and poured his petrol through the letterbox and onto the luxury-thick carpet inside. Soaking. Ralph was asleep upstairs with his beautiful wife Marie who looked like a model. Their children were straight off the ads – everyone said so.

Duffy used his scarred hand, the one that was burned when he was seven. His other hand still shook sometimes after getting crushed in a robbery, falling off the back extension and running straight into a security patrol car. Ralph got away scot-free and Duffy got six months' probation, which was typical. But even then he said to Gina, *Ralph's my best mate. He never let me down: it was just my bad luck. I would've done the same if I was him.* And Gina sniggered as she always did, and rolled her eyes, which made her make-up crease. She never looked like a model – never would – which caused him no end of quiet grieving. Not that he was God's gift himself.

Duffy poured and poured until his can was empty.

Ah, the smell of petrol. He nearly said the words out loud. *You either love it or you hate it.*

Goes without saying that Duffy loved it. He sat on the doormat just breathing it in while the moon shone down and lit up his scars as he made slow waving gestures with his fingers. They'd turned him down at the council on account of his record, although they never said as much. Couldn't even get a job in permits. And still the penny didn't drop.

Peering through the flap Duffy pointed his torch at the dark inflammable spread inside.

Amazing how much a thick carpet takes in, you'd never think it. He thought of those TV ads with rolls and rolls of toilet paper going on forever and blue liquid pouring onto flying sanitary pads.

Gina didn't hang round long enough to see the penny drop, but that was her loss. He got her phone call while he was at the pub with Ralph and everyone. She broke it off then and there, regardless. He could hardly hear her, but he heard enough. He could picture her rolling her eyes as she always did (especially when she was fed up) and sucking her little finger, flaking nail varnish onto her tongue. Gripping the pub phone, Duffy tickled the scars on his face as if he was thinking something over, maybe planning a holiday. He even ordered another beer across the room in sign language. Winked and fanned his throat like he was parched. From the way he looked you'd be hard-pressed to tell what kind of call it was. There was nothing much he could say in front of the general public, so he didn't.

Soak. Soak.

Duffy thought of pissing through Ralph's letterbox for good measure but he worried about two things. *A weakening of inflammability. Getting caught.*

He lit a cigarette and thought of Ralph, asleep inside, with his hands on Marie's breasts – she was bigger than a page three girl and, Ralph said, more game. Duffy thought of all those times Ralph smiled and charmed his way through everything. Customs: with his bags full, kids loaded up with cases of duty-free and Marie bouncing through the barrier wearing something tight and skimpy. And job interviews, where the bosses wrote in their files: *Looks like Paul Newman. Spotless record. Top man for the position* – whatever the job was, even when he wasn't. As for getting caught, it was never Ralph, simple as that. Girlfriends on the side would take half of him, or some of him – rather *die* than have none of him. Even teachers let him off for all sorts, not just the smoking way back when.

Duffy tapped his cigarette on the doorstep. The ash landed whole, and in his mind it looked like a wart, or a curled-up bug in moonlight, casting a long dark shadow. That was Ralph. The penny had dropped. It was never down to chance. His best friend showed him up, always had done. Set him up. Soaked up all the limelight, took all the takings. Which was why Duffy would never be famous now, not for anything, not at forty. *Let alone a job in permits* – or so he said out loud, breathing smoke through his teeth and blowing a final tiny ring. That's why Gina had sniggered and given him the boot.

Duffy sucked hard on his cigarette and watched cross-eyed down his nose as the glow burned bright in the darkness. He shut his eyes against the smoke. Things were rustling in Ralph's front garden and nothing was quiet. There was a rushing noise he'd never heard before, not on all those nights of football, live and replay, dropping his mate off home and losing his key, falling on the steps with a can of beer in his hand and staying there. Or after all those evenings round the video – men only – only Ralph swore he did all that hardcore stuff with Marie too. Upside-down. Up the bum. On all kinds of furniture. In private. In public. Nothing was still, not a thing, and the rushing noise was like the sudden breath of everything in Ralph's garden.

Duffy looked down on his cigarette and felt the burn come near his fingers at the end, and they were shaking, even though it was his good hand. His fingers were hot. There were ash warts and bugs all over Ralph's steps, casting shadows. Duffy picked the letter flap open and flicked the live butt inside, well down the hall, a little too far. Nothing happened. He could see that. Gently, he let the flap down and the rushing noise of the garden filled his head. He tucked his shirt into his jeans, smoothed out the chest and tweaked the cuffs. He put his torch back in his pocket and tapped the petrol can upside-down, letting the last drops just fall.

And then he smelled it: the singe of hair, knowing it was carpet really. And the rushing noise all around him stopped and two teenagers straggled past on the pavement beyond the hedge, drunk as they get, her shirt half undone in the damp night, him hiccoughing between laughs.

Duffy left his petrol can on Ralph's doorstep and walked all the way home to Cross Street, feeling handsome and bold and full of the delicious smell. You could see there was a new strength in his stride, kind of muscular and straight, like he'd never had before in all his years of Ralph being his best friend, unless perhaps when he was seven.

From the outside looking in, there'd be no way of knowing what he had just been up to. You'd be hard-pressed to find an ounce of worry in his damaged face.

He leaned against estate agent windows and sniggered at how much it would cost to buy a broom cupboard nowadays, never mind a family home with a front garden and porch steps. No-one ever imagined the heights that things would soar to. He looked into closed shops and bars, and saw himself in mirrors smiling so hard he made himself laugh. He rummaged his face with his petrol hands and couldn't get enough of it.

You either love it or you hate it.

He came to the garage on High Street and noticed a security camera looking down on him as he skipped like a lamb up to the window for cigarettes.

My mate's run out, he said to the man behind the reinforced glass. And he paid. The cigarette box was full of warnings. All over the petrol station, there were signs everywhere saying the usual naked warning things and that wrong word *flammable*. Unable to wipe the smirk off his face, Duffy remembered Mrs Knight and rolled his eyes heavenwards. He knew she would be sniggering with him.

~

Duffy has taken his fags and matches from under my window slot. I pass him his change. My hand is shaking. He taps at the health warnings and snorts to himself. *Tobacco seriously damages health. Smoking can be fatal.* He peels the little gold thread off the top of the cigarette box. He lets the plastic wrapper drop to the ground. He pockets his change. He draws off the soft inside foil and throws it away. With his lips and teeth he pulls out a clean new Marlboro. With the cigarette between his teeth he grins. He pockets the pack. The match-box is still in his shaking hand. He turns to go.

My computer sings. I look over to Pump Number Four and there's a girl waiting for me to authorise. Her orange hair is all over the place. She owes a month's rent and all the bills – but tonight she's making a run for it. She's feeling sly and jittery. I authorise.

01:47

Now Duffy is maybe thirty feet away, but he's standing still. There's a tank below his feet. He's about to light that sniggering cigarette.

With my shaking hand, I press the tannoy button and speak.

'No smoking on the forecourt. Do not light your cigarette. No smoking on the forecourt. This area is flammable.'

Ignoring the speaker this time, Duffy turns to look straight at me. He holds his matchbox high and waves it at the nearest camera. He lights a match and throws it. He strikes another match to light his cigarette, and throws it. Blowing smoke, he paces slowly towards me, lighting matches, one after the other, and flicking them, left and right. Then he flicks them at me. He's at my window and he's flicking live matches at the glass, at my face, into my slot.

57

I'm frozen. I can't do a thing. If Naga was here he'd see Duffy off with a baseball bat. I can see fire. And envy. I can see Ralph's burning house. I can smell the singe of hair. I'm paralysed with fear.

All of a sudden, Duffy turns and skips towards Pump Number Four. The girl hasn't noticed a thing. She's twisted, clawing at her hair in the pump's dim reflection. Petrol gushes through the nozzle in her other hand. Duffy gambols past her. She jerks in fright and sprays her car with premium. Her petrol cap's still open.

Before you know it, Duffy's out of my sight. I check the live monitor and catch him jumping, kicking the cage of cylinders from mid-air like Zorba the Greek. Then he strikes a new match and throws it into the open dumper.

Fire bursts up and out – it happens in an instant.

The camera switches to the forecourt where the panicky girl has frozen, gripping the nozzle at Pump Number Four. I can't take my eyes off the TV. The views keep changing: the forecourt, the till, the shop, the forecourt, Siv's dark office – at last the dumpers by the side street.

Duffy's standing there, still as a child, staring at the fire he's made. It's like a huge oven. It's full of rubbish, cartons, piles of fuel-soaked wipes. It's beautiful. Powerful. Better than a bonfire. He flicks his cigarette in for good measure.

I kick the grey padded bar at my feet. The emergency wall shoots up, faster than blinking. Six inches thick. Metal and wood. Everything is invisible. I can't see a thing. I am invisible. Printed on the inside of the wall are the words: *KEEP CALM*. My heart's banging inside my head. There are other words on the wall but I can't bring myself to read them. I feel faint. I sit and hide, sit and stew. I turn the lights off. Close my eyes. What would Siv do? He'd have the answer. Somewhere in the world outside, beyond my shield, there's a huge roar like a jet engine taking off. Something explodes. Louder than a bomb. I can smell the singe of hair and petrol. I sit and grip the edges of my stool, holding tighter than a limpet. My ears are bursting and my heart's beating all over the shop.

58

8: Fortitude

Your average limpet gets covered in weeds because it can't clean itself. Besides, it sits still and does nothing most of the time. Regular work, food and sleep – that's what living is all about. Now and then it tosses off a bit of lust, but then it's back to work, food and sleep.

Your limpet can always find his way home. His home fits snug as an overcoat. He will inch back through the neighbourhood – even when the police have dislodged him from his patch to ask all kinds of questions. Blunt and sharp. It's hard to hear them sometimes through the noise in his ears. Their fluorescent lights hurt his eyes, then tired daylight, when he should be sleeping. There are stories everywhere. The police station is teeming with lives and deaths and pains enough to fill a thousand newspapers.

The boys in blue have snatched up all my security videos, a whole month of them. One of them sits down in a back office and starts watching *Terry's TV*: me with my uneven heart, my bad eyes. Me acting up, stripping off my diesel glove and throwing it like a gauntlet into one of the bins. Me looking guilty. Stolen moments in Siv's dark office.

The police watch old pictures of Mark Register on his short cuts, and the twinless bookkeeper flinching. Siv touching her arm. Moving like he's on wheels. They pore over Siv, my manager, the boss who will sack me because I let him down. I should have cut the pumps off: one swipe on the computer would have done it. I should have called the police. I should have run outside and grabbed a fire extinguisher. I should have taken to Duffy with a baseball bat.

The police find re-runs of Duffy at 00:40 near the main road holding a dead nozzle into his old tin and thumping the pump. Duffy pulling a face. Duffy buying first his can, then later his cigarettes. Duffy at 01:47 lighting up in the middle of the fore-court. Duffy marching at me with his matches. Duffy doing an about-face and heading for Pump Number Four and the jumpy girl with wild hair. Me behind my emergency wall.

Me behind my emergency wall.

Me behind my emergency wall.

Siv will sack me for not doing the right thing.

Beyond my seven cameras there are dozens more in the streets outside. Rotating, recording, red-eyed, peering around corners. The police will piece together bits of other videos to make a proper film. There are pictures of Duffy carrying his heavy load past a council building, the authorised can full of petrol sloshing weight this way, then that. Empty-handed Duffy skipping like a spring lamb up High Street. Duffy grinning into estate agents' windows.

Siv will give me the sack for not doing the right thing. He'll lose his petrol licence. He'll be fined. I'm sitting in the police station corridor and it's all I can do to stop myself from crying into the wastepaper bin. A plastic cup has lipstick on the rim, a ball of chewing gum inside. Yesterday's *Truth* is stained with fat. A blurred man's face is circled by a broken onion ring. My eyes are swelling up with held-back tears. My ears are ringing.

In some office upstairs the police are watching Pump Number Four: the black-and-white woman with the orange hair. As she loosens her grip and lets go, the trigger clicks the nozzle shut. The pump and tank below are cut off for the moment, but her petrol cap's open. She sprays premium all over the place. She's standing in a fresh cloud of vapour ready to ignite. Duffy has a knack with fire. It performs for him. The police can't watch Duffy at the dumper because that camera's blown. But it's a circus back on the forecourt. The woman leaps high into the air. Duffy flies in from nowhere like the human cannon. When the firemen turn up, I'm still behind my emergency wall. I don't know if I've jabbed the two red alert buttons. Maybe the video will tell.

I keep thinking about Siv's idol dancing in a circle of flames. I'm sitting on a bench in the police station corridor and it's just like a hospital. Waiting. Waiting to make my statement. Waiting to sign it. Waiting for them to let me go. The place is full to bursting with stories. People brush past. Phones ring. I wish for the face of my father in every grey-haired crook or cleaner I see. Through the noise in my head, I can hear a mad woman shouting. She's been here before. Her own father's got a lot to answer for – although that's not what she's carrying on about just now. I'm holding onto Siv's painting for dear life. It's the picture from his office, the character with too many arms, with lipstick and curvy hips. I don't remember taking it. My hands are shaking. My chest hurts.

'The third eye,' Siv says out of the blue, 'has the power of destruction.' He's sitting next to me all of a sudden. Grey trousers, white shirt, waterproof jacket. His voice is soft. His ear-lobes are very long – I've never noticed that before. His eyes are blacker than black.

'The sprawling dwarf under his foot is human ignorance. It's the dance of life,' Siv continues as if everything was just normal.

So the idol is a man. I thought as much. I can smell the singe of hair.

'Terry, Terry.' Siv is saying my name as if he's trying to wake me up. His hands are dark but it looks like he's dipped his fingertips in bleach to make them go pale at the ends.

He touches my shoulder.

No-one touches me, apart from Kandy.

It's all I can do to stop from crying.

'I'm sorry, Siv. I let you down.'

'The woman is in hospital. She has shock. The man also. What matters is that they are both alive, isn't it. Both OK. She has whiplash. He has some burns, some fractures and shrapnel wounds. How's your heart, Terry? Did they give you a check-up?'

Siv's not see-through. I don't know why he's asking. My ears are ringing with the blast in my head. I'm waiting for him to sack me. I hold onto his idol picture for dear life. In my inside pocket, the pay packet presses against my chest.

'My heart's irregular.'

'And your eyes?' I can smell his musk now. He's acting like a doctor.

61

'I've always had this trouble with my eyes. There's nothing I can do to fix them. But my vision's 20:20.' – The number sounds like a time on the monitor before my shifts start. It's a score you get in a test when everything adds up and the teacher is pleased with you. It's how well you have to see when you're checking cars and number plates, when people are driving off without paying for their fuel.

Siv must know that I can see properly, that I don't need glasses: I can't lose my job. But I'm going to lose my job.

'You can't go back to the garage now,' he says plain and clear. His head rocks a little, side to side, like an Indian.

I'm staring into the bin. There's an ant on the plastic liner. My hands are trembling, gripping the frame of his picture which I've taken, stolen, for no good reason. Is this the way a man is sacked? In a hospital – no, in a police corridor, sitting next to a bin?

'Terry, I'm going to get back to the garage now. Giri is due any minute now. I should go and open up.'

'For ... for business?'

'We shall see. The Fire Investigation people have been doing their check-up. We were unlucky, and we were lucky. There was one small gas cylinder, it must have been empty, under the big dumper.'

'How did it get there?'

'I don't know. At this stage it is difficult to fathom out. The rest of them were safe. After this one blew up there was a terrific fireball, but it went the other way, towards the street, away from the cage and away from the pumps. These things are always unpredictable, isn't it.' Siv talks as if he's used to it all, as if explosions were just normal.

'The area is roped off until we give everything a check-up, just to be sure, but I think the pumps will be rearing to go.' Siv looks at his watch. 'I'll call you at home in the evening. Terry? Terry?'

'Can I –' (How do I ask it?) 'Do you want me to come back to work?'

'You'll need some time off, Terry, maybe a couple of weeks,

for the ears too.'

I don't know if he wants me back after that.

'And you should have your eyes checked, just to be sure. Will you have your eyes checked?'

'What about Head Office?' I'm a problem now. They'll want to sack me. The cylinder shouldn't have been there.

'I will deal with Head Office.'

They might even want to get rid of Siv. I can't bear the thought.

'Terry, the fire is not your fault.' He stands up to leave. 'You've had a big shock.'

I wish he was porous. I don't want him to go, but I can't speak.

'There's another manifestation of him, you know.' His head rocks as he speaks and he points to the back of his picture. 'The ascetic. Smeared with the ash of corpses. It's a kind of death image. But tonight – I am happy to say – no death!' He claps his hands together once and grins. He has no idea yet what else Duffy got up to before getting to me.

I thought Siv would know everything. But of course he doesn't.

'Bye, Terry. You'll be all right?' He's leaving now, for the garage, as if all this is usual, as if I'll see him again at the next shift. He's leaving and I feel my uneven heart is going to break. I'm all alone.

I keep my eye on the man in the *Truth,* in the bin, with the onion ring around his head. It could be a halo. It could be he's an astronaut. It could be he's a wanted man.

Through the noise in my ears that woman is suddenly shouting again in reception. You'd be hard-pressed not to put two and two together. She sounds just like Michelle.

~

Michelle's boyfriend Aidan was a heavyweight which was just as well for him when he raised the chair and smashed it on her father's head. The stroke felt effortless. Blood came out like a

63

burst pipe and for a second the old man had a look of Michelle in his eyes but Aidan didn't stop. He felt the hardness in his muscles as he raised the chair again and cracked it on the old man's skull, the spray of age spots broken by a line and blood shooting through fast as a sprung leak. The old man tried to speak. Feeble now. There was still a flicker of Michelle like a trick in his watery eyes. Aidan took another breath and this time the crack was in the chair leg but that didn't stop him either. He lifted the chair a fourth time and broke it on the old man's head which put a stop to the talking once and for all. Michelle's father bent into a curl, thin as a wood shaving. He was still sitting.

Aidan remembered for a moment Michelle's set of paintings by Van Gogh with a picture of this very chair. Aidan put the broken real one neatly in the corner and his head was full of sunny colours, like a holiday. Boxing never felt like this.

From the outside looking in, you might think Aidan was just some common kind of thug, the sort of bully that beats people up for a living. But you'd be wrong. It was Michelle he thought of whenever he was fighting. It was her that he was fighting for now. He'd been strong for her, as long as he could remember.

Funny, he thought. *Given how strong she is herself.*

The old man's mouth dropped open in his forward-leaning face and for a moment Aidan braced himself to hear the voice. But there was just blood. Aidan thought of Michelle. And bloodless boxing bags. And rubber torso dummies that bounced back like real men, all agitated. And spurting eyes, real ones, mashed up noses, sweat and cheering.

The house was quiet now. Aidan went over to the other corner without a chair and squatted. And watched as Michelle's father began to dry up, still sitting. Aidan thought of the old crisps you get at the bottom of the packet. The odd brown ones nobody wants. *The old bastard.* Aidan nearly mouthed the words. And then he pictured jail.

Aidan called the police to tell them what he'd done and then he rang Michelle.

He deserved to die, the bastard, was all she could say, even if it was her own father. And then she became so quiet that Aidan thought the line was dead.

Michelle, Michelle, he called at her. His voice was loud in the silence of the telephone. (Anyone who knew him said that Aidan always spoke too softly: you had to crane your neck sometimes just to hear him, like someone who's telling a secret.) And then at last he heard her sobbing – her, the tough one, breaking up into small hard pieces like the best china vase. He had never heard her cry before.

She wouldn't hang up.

And Aidan knew that they were connected, more than ever, him to her and her to him. Both of them just holding the phone. Michelle didn't hang up until the police arrived, which was ages later. She was all blocked up and blowing her nose, trying to say she loved him. But she couldn't talk properly, not at all. Her, the one who could speak her mind in public places. Aidan heard her put the phone down gently.

In the back of the police van Aidan remembered a photo of Michelle and her sister Lisa squinting at the sun. It was his favourite photo. The girls were in their teens and smiling. Heavy eye makeup and junk jewellery. Michelle was already big up top, enough to make her mother jealous. Wearing a leopardskin scarf. Posing like a high-class actress with her cigarette. Lisa screwing up her eyes over sunglasses, smirking at the camera, trying to be grown-up like her older sister.

In the van Aidan suddenly worked out that the old man was interfering with Michelle at the time of his favourite photo. Had been already for years. Broke her into adulthood. Gearing up to move on to Lisa. Both girls smiling at the camera. No sign of the mother – who pretended none of it was happening. Aidan broke out in a sweat as he thought of the old man taking the photo – he who saw only too well the makeup, the cleavage, the eagerness of the little sister. Aidan felt hot and sick in every muscle and ready to kill him all over again. He ground his fist into the seat inside the van, then punched his thigh as hard as he was able. And then he thought of prison again. How did they choose which one? Was it like the doctor choosing you a hospital? Would they let him see Michelle?

Her, the strong one.

Michelle's mother used to smoke forty a day, and drank to match – everyone knew that much. For years she put elastic on tights and stockings at a factory in the East End. Then later she put elastic on chickens and bagged them somewhere near the end of the Northern Line. And for years she pushed a trolley at the hospital which she hated because she had to speak. Aidan knew as well as anyone that she didn't do that part too well. She never talked. And Michelle loathed her for it because of the space it left for the father to fill.

Michelle used to say that she and Lisa left home just to escape the talking. (Mind you, Lisa was pregnant, which helped them get the flat.) Their old man was like a radio on continuous, changing stations without warning, not caring to notice if anyone was actually listening, then suddenly slamming things to make sure someone did, then carrying on forever without a sign of breathing, his voice never cracking or drying up, just the words, endless, filling everything fast as a flood.

Over my dead body, the old man said, sitting square on the chair in the middle of his kitchen. He called Michelle a coward and a slut, but that was typical. He stared at Aidan like he was picking a fight, the usual look, not a bit like anyone. Aidan had come over again to talk about the money and *the effects*. But the old man wouldn't let him get a word in edgeways. It was harder than any proper fight. He lit a ten-pound note with his gold-plate lighter and blew the black bits into Aidan's face. Just to make a point. He ground the rest into the linoleum cracks.

By the time I'm dead there'll be none left, and that's a promise.

You wouldn't think that someone bagging chickens and wheeling trolleys all her life could have mustered up the stash that Michelle's mother had. Her daughters always said their mother had her secrets.

She died without a will, the old man kept saying, but the

66

daughter herself had seen it.

Michelle was never one to remember things – not a childhood puppy or a birthday party, not her first kiss, nor the death of Lisa's baby, and certainly not the business with their father – but her memory in this one simple case was plain as black and white. Everything was made out to her and Lisa, no question about that. She had read it. She had seen her mother's backhand signature, the ink soaked into the form she'd got especially from the newsagents.

That much Michelle could remember.

Now Aidan was at the police station in High Street and they were taping him.

Yes, I think I killed him, he said.

The policemen leaned forward, closer, listening. They made him say it louder, again. It wasn't hard.

Yes, I killed him. It came over me like a big wave. I was going under. I did it for her. Something broke. She's got a picture. The picture of the chair. It was her in my hands making me strong.

And then Aidan listed the things the old man had done, one by one, year after year, working backwards. It felt like something on TV. They had to change the tape. Twice.

Which hospital? Aidan asked at last, a blanket of sleep falling all over him. He meant to say *which prison*. And then they gave him a mug of tea.

It was only because the old man talked so much that Aidan got to hear the full-length stories at last. After all those years of hints and insults. Sitting on that kitchen chair, Michelle's father said things that even a heavyweight couldn't bear. He'd set her back because she was too forward. He'd tied her up because she was too loose. He'd made her sit and beg for it like a dog because in the end that's all she was – still was – just like her skulking mother.

Somehow the words hurt Aidan more than the deeds. The relentless flow of them. Worse than some Japanese torture dreamed up specially to break the toughest trooper. Aidan gagged. Yearned for silence. Yearned for the space to say what he had come to say on behalf of Michelle. To take the old man on and settle the score once and for all. To fix things for the future. But then it hit him: everyone had been knocked out. The wife without a will. Michelle with no memory and a sister in and out of hospital. The old man was going for him too, working on him, looking to get him lying in a heap and cringing.

Aidan was speaking too softly. They turned the tape recorder close to face his face. You had to lean to hear him at the best of times. He was not your typical boxer – anyone would say it who knew him. And he was not a fighting man outside the ring. He left that kind of thing to Michelle.

She spoke up for things in public. At work. In shops. She knew her rights. She never cried. Except tonight.

Mind you, she cried again later on in court. She remembered more stories than anyone could have bargained for.

And when they said the sentence was conditional – that Aidan should not go to hospital *or* prison – Michelle's smile across the room looked younger to him and happier than his favourite photo ever did. He could feel her strength. He had never known a woman like her.

~

I have never known a woman like her. Not personally.

Kandy's the only one that comes close, the only one who touches me. She's got a kind of toughness: she runs a business, she studies all those books, and she doesn't cry all over the place the way girls are meant to do. She never throws a tantrum and she never speaks her mind to stir things up. She listens to my stories. She's always there for me. Faithful. Hard-working. Sexy. She's paradise on earth – and she makes the perfect cup of tea.

Kandy touches me the way I want her to, no matter what.

Siv touched me on the shoulder, just like a father.

~

Back in my flat, everything is where it should be. Nothing moves. The blinds are down. The way I like it. I take my pay packet out and count the notes again. Normal people put their money in the bank. They bet on stocks and shares. But I'm no gambling man. In risky times, cash is king.

A slipper used to be my secret safe. Then it was a pair of shoes. I moved them about to different spots, just to be sure, hiding them in amongst all my old shoes and clothes. Then it was one big biscuit tin called *Tea for Two* with a girl and a boy (like Kandy and me) holding hands in a flowery heart on the top. *Darjeeling. Assam. Ceylon.*

At the kitchen cupboard I remove cans and Cornflakes boxes and heaps of plastic bags. My mother's special blue vanity case is hidden at the back. The leatherette is scarred. The brass buckles are stiff. In the inset mirror I look for her reflection. I try to find her face like a shadow behind my face. *You'll always be ugly. Shut your bloody face.* I don't even know if I look like her. She had dull skin and her eyes were hungry as a cat in spring. That much I do know.

I stuff the best part of Week Seven's pay into the stretchy pocket inside the lid – there's nowhere else it will fit. My life of nights is pressed in the case, wads and wads of notes held tight with rubber bands. It's time to start another safe. It's time to move my hiding spot. My place is small, but I'm spoilt for choice.

My ears are ringing with the blast in my head.

9: Prudence

'You're tense,' Kandy says, as she rubs my back.

A week after the fire, my ears are still ringing and I've gone spotty like a teenager, as sore in the pores as Mark Register – it's an emergency wall I brought down deep inside me. The shock went in and stayed there. Now it's coming out like poison through my skin. This is Kandy's psychological theory. She doesn't seem to mind the way it looks or feels.

Kandy doesn't normally give me massages, but today she had a cancellation and I'm going to pay her extra. I've had my special mug of tea. (I noticed a tiny chip in its lip and wonder if anyone else has been using it. But I don't ask.) Kandy's windows are all steamed up from the kettle. She keeps them closed, I suppose, on account of the neighbours. That's the trouble with flats.

For once I've come to Kandy straight from the Estate, not from the garage. She's amazed to hear it. At home I've rearranged some of my things. I've put on aftershave, and done my hair to the side instead of straight down the middle. I've got to admit she was taken aback when she opened the door. I should say she was pleasantly surprised. Because if anyone knows me, Kandy does – she's your typical head-doctor. And Kandy knows I'm regular, faithful, safe as houses.

I can feel my private parts twitching as she works her fingers across my back. She is squatting on top of me wearing only her robe. I can smell her musk through the smoke. Her left hand is strong. Her right is weak. One of her legs falls out loose to the side. The other is planted firm as a bollard. My stomach prickles and pulls.

'There,' she says. 'There.'

And I feel myself grow hard.

'What now, my love?' she asks. 'Just say what you want and Kandy will give it to you.'

I imagine my mother asking me what I want from Father Christmas, even though she never did.

'What do you want Kandy to give you, baby?' She doesn't stop rubbing for a second.

'I want,' I breathe into the pillow, 'I want my job back. I want my father to … I want to …' I can't even say the words. I'm just about ready to explode.

But Kandy knows without me telling her. She knows best. She always knows. She turns me over like a sausage and eats me up for breakfast. I get her senseless cheek for starters, but then I get her throat – it's like going up a class. (I, for one, can feel the difference.) My wish is her command. All over me, all over her, like spilt milk.

~

'This lot came straight from the home kitty, for once.' I count out the notes, clicking each one like a banker.

I've had more of Kandy's time than usual, a double slot. I've told her all about Aidan's sentence and Duffy's Doing Word *inflame*.

Kandy is lighting a cigarette. Her wrist is buttressed by her stronger hand. She checks the clock.

'We're all capable of whatever shows up in the courts,' she says. 'There's nothing we can't do.' She always says that or something like it.

The money makes a nice little pile.

'I don't believe in banks, do you?' I say, wondering if there's time for another mug of tea.

Kandy shakes her head. She likes her professional fees in cash. She has her income support and her study allowance to consider.

'My personal bank's called *Tea for Two*,' I laugh. I'm feeling happy, silly. 'Well, it *was,* but now it's a special blue vanity case.'

'What makes it special, pet?'

I picture Kandy and me holding hands in the little inset mirror like a painting.

'You're my own true love,' I say.

71

Kandy and I are growing old together. We've lasted longer than most marriages. I pop a tiny kiss on her forehead, avoiding the cigarette. I love her because she's not porous, or perhaps she's not porous because I love her.

Kandy wipes herself with a towel, clips on the calliper and ties up her satin robe.

'You look like Miss Saigon,' I say.

'Or Madame Butterfly.' Kandy smooths her hair, neat as an actress.

When the right moment comes, without a word, she sees me to the door. Her sense of timing is perfect.

The Sacred Entrance serves as the passage to go in and come out of the Temple.

'I'd like you to meet Siv one day. I'm sure he'd approve.' I tickle the ceramic fox plaque by her door.

'Let's take things a step at a time,' she says and blows smoke into the air. It billows into clouds on account of the cold outside.

'You should get a photo of your hair like that,' she smiles.

Then she pulls a girlish face. 'I've got to get back to my homework now.'

And so I go.

~

I take the roundabout way home from Kandy's place and stop at the little chemist's on the corner, not far from Duchess Street. *Free Tests.* I stand outside the door for half an hour.

The eye doctor hardly says a word. She married her second cousin for love when she was still a student, and he has problems with his blood pressure. Some days she wishes he'd cook the dinner. She wears a white coat like they do on TV ads for washing powder, but underneath it there's a sari. I can smell curry on her breath, or maybe it's in her fingers.

I'm feeling hot and faint under her cold stare. The check-up's on account of Siv. He asked me to do it, just in case. You'd be hard-pressed to move me otherwise. It's his duty as the manager.

I've never once seen an eye doctor, except on *Hospital Lives.* I'm nervous in the chair, announcing numbers and letters in nonsense rows like endless registration plates. I want to get out of her sight. She says it's just as well that people come to her before they have an accident. She can't believe what we all get used to seeing without noticing some kind of problem. She's thinking of a book she read way back when, and she's remembering the words. *Only the learned have their faces adorned by two eyes. For the ignorant, eyes are no more than sores.* She says my vision's 20:20, but with this new cream I might control the seeping.

~

Nine days alone in my flat. I haven't been so long away from work in years. Nine nights in a trot, here on the Nightingale Estate. The blackbirds sing to me, so plain they're beautiful. They pour their hearts out from the torn trees and bushes. Their songs run like bubbling water. Sometimes they sound like celebrations.

I take the lift down to the ground floor to throw them currants and cubes of bread, but those swaggering seagulls and pigeons always seem to get in the way, coming from nowhere. And worse still: the magpies. They may be sleek but they're vicious. They've got the run of things. They'd steal the coat off your back if they had half a chance, never mind the babies in a brown mother's nest. That's when the blackbird voice I love turns into panic. *Ti. Ti. Ti. Ti. Ti. Ti. Ti. Ti.*

Here the birds make their dawn and dusk commotion all the time. They're tricked into staying up after-hours, all the hours. They're confused by the security lights that shine down from masts and buildings – outside it's brighter at night than it is during the day. They must be going crazy.

I lie on my bed; asleep by day and awake by night because that's what I'm used to. My mattress is soft and dips in the middle. Like forecourt cement, the gathering of spots and stains tells a kind of story. If you look at it hard enough, you see the shape of me pressed into it, curled up to face away from the light-leaking window.

73

I keep my blinds pulled down, just like my mother.

I keep my head down, counting the hours and minutes till I get back to the garage. Eating food, always plain food. Oven chips, cream of chicken, cheese sandwiches, sausage rolls, tea, lots of tea. Newspapering the furniture because dust breeds. Traipsing up and down the paths worn in the carpet between my piles of papers. Watching videos. *The Blue Lagoon. Miss Saigon. The Fly.* Watching the news on TV with the sound off. Crowds of people shaking signs on their streets. Quiet babies with flies in their eyes. Upset brokers in the stock market. (That's the trouble with betting: it's all too emotional.) I turn the sound on when they talk about Tamil Tigers. That's where Siv comes from. I try to see his home country in the background, but all I can see is tanks. *In places without tanks gods are not present.* Everything is camouflaged.

The reporter talks about explosions, extortions, suicides. A dead drummer by the way.

Pariah, he says, *is a Tamil word.*

It's not normal to want to give yourself up to death. You couldn't persuade me otherwise. There's no getting round that deep-down will to live, to eat, and to make more of your own kind. If you're a normal animal you'll have no intention of dying, let alone killing yourself. Suicide wouldn't even enter your head. Unless, of course, your hand is forced.

Some of the neighbours called it suicide, but my mother died by accident. I know that much. She called me a parasite, but she didn't know that I would live on and on and on as well as any mite. Parasites are the keenest survivors. We sit at the top of the tree. We are the kings of the castle.

Like tape worms, like barnacles, like fleas or cuckoos, blood flukes go to great lengths just to stay alive in this world. When they're tiny, they bed down for a while inside snails. One minute they're chalk; the next, they're cheese. They shy away from sunlight in the water, but when it's dark enough – and safe – they swim out sniffing for the first hint of human skin. Then they drill themselves in. They throw off their tail. They punt through

74

a body's rivers aiming for your liver, where they fatten up on blood, getting huge and strange with private parts. They grow shells. They become a different kind of animal altogether. The ladies and the gents pair off and head for Lovers' Lane (which is your gut) and fornicate all over the shop, guzzling blood into their throats, laying eggs and more eggs. They settle down to a life of drink and sex forever. You'd be hard-pressed to budge them. It's only when the host is all used up that a parasite makes a run for it, no matter how comfortable things get to be. It's the great escape. It has to happen sooner or later.

I've still got Siv's picture. I don't know what to do with it. It stands out here. I rest it on the kitchen bench, I lay it flat on the table. When I come back upstairs after feeding the birds, the first thing I see is Siv's idol dancing in his circle of fire. When I come out of the toilet he catches my eye, distracting. When I wake up I see him in a mirror, or I spot his colours reflecting on a cupboard door. I don't know what to do with him.

The dwarf under his foot is ignorance, that's what Siv said. Maybe I am the dwarf. I still don't know what the idol means. I don't even know my father. If you have no father, you're no-one.

~

The phone rings. The place is full of bells.

'Terry?'

It's 20:20 on my alarm clock. No-one ever calls.

'Siv, yes, it's me.'

'How are you feeling, Terry? Have you had the check-up?'

'Yes. I'm ready for work, Siv. Can I –? Is the camera fixed?'

'The camera is fine, Terry. The bins, the pumps, everything is fine again. We're back in business. We have a new boy training on days: he is my old friend's nephew from Batticaloa. His name is Rajkumar. Naga has his exams now. Giri and Ken are doing your shifts. And me too. It's a long time since I was having to do nights – I've always relied on you.' His voice goes up and down like water through stones. I can picture his long ear lobe pressed against the receiver.

'And Head Office?' I ask, but I'm thinking of that place on the map with the biro dots, where Siv comes from. *In the east.* Batticaloa. I think I could say the word now.

'Head Office is fine. Don't forget: I am the boss. That's why I took up the franchise, isn't it.' Siv laughs. A kind of gurgle. 'We had two cars in one day who drove off without paying – nothing out of the ordinary. Do you miss it?'

'Do you miss Batticaloa?' The question flies out like a dart from nowhere, and I stumble on the name. I can feel myself turn red all over, boiling hot under the collar.

Siv goes quiet now. Perhaps I've offended him.

'I will tell you, Terry, it is the most beautiful place in the world,' he says. His voice is soft. 'We have long sandy beaches. Cashew trees. Mangoes. Coconut palms. But I miss the water, Terry, all kinds of water meeting: we have rivers, and we have the sea, and our freshwater lagoon … There is a special place where you can hear the singing fish, under the famous Kalladi Bridge.'

I've heard Siv wrong because of his accent.

'I'm sorry: the singing –?'

'Singing fish, yes! You heard right! I have heard it myself, like a harp and the wind is playing it, or the lightest violins, but coming from underneath the water. You have to go there in a boat with a full moon. My father used to call it the music of the crying shells. More beautiful than any birds.'

His mystery singers are as dear to him as my blackbirds are to me. For the first time I get a glimpse of where Siv comes from: palm trees and beaches. *The Blue Lagoon.* He grew up in a holiday brochure picture. His home town is awash with water. He had a father.

But water is full of parasites, especially in that sort of place. No doubt blood flukes lurk under the surface. Never mind the shimmer. And mosquitoes prepare like armies for sunset raids, looking for soft black skin like Siv's. Survival of the stillest, I'd say – maybe I'm wrong. Siv has come to a place that's foreign, but here the water is clean and safe. In London you can turn on a tap and drink from it.

'So, Terry, will you come in tomorrow?' His voice is different now.

'23:00, I'll be there.' I nearly call him *Sir*.

'Good man, Terry. I can always rely on you.'

I feel myself go red with his praise as I hang up the phone.

~

I'm out early for my shift. On purpose. I have a special mission. A picture for Kandy.

At this time of night there are still people all over the place. I walk all the way to the overground station, keeping my head down as I go. I pass a designer who's working late again, prime for a nervous breakdown. I'm heading for the photo booth. Passengers are coming off the escalators in clumps. I take the stairs. A homesick Scot steps on my toe by accident. A cleaner drops her tissue to the ground and doesn't pick it up again. She's on her way to her first bank for the evening. Her eldest son is at home looking after the baby.

On Platform 2, past the big railway map, I find it. I have the coins ready. There's a comb in my inside pocket. I'm going to do my hair on the side for the photo, just as Kandy wanted. It's funny: me doing things to please her. I suppose that's the meaning of give and take. We've lasted longer than most marriages, and she'd be the first to say it suits her. I'm what you might call *solid*. Compared to the others that enter her temple, I know I'm the best behaved. I don't go around smashing things like some people.

Choose your background, the sign says. I didn't ask to be born, let alone the rest of it. I was a fluke. My mother said I bled her dry. I kept what I could: her lucky charms. But my father? Sometimes I think I have many, I'm spoilt rotten with fathers – breeding and commanding and taking over the place – not just *one* like ordinary people. The man with slippery eyes, the man with the temper, the man with the string of other children, the ginger man, the passerby ... no-one knows which one. I never did ask the questions that needed asking. My mother let go of this world, and me, before I had the chance. She was all used up.

I swivel the stool down to the proper height. It's cosy in here, like a cocoon. There's a McDonald's drink bucket on the floor, a newspaper shoved into one corner and a strip of old passport photos with tread marks all over it. A girl called Eve. Her freckly faces are deadly serious. Her lips are pursed. Four times over. She's thinking of something ambitious and grand, as final as Napoleon. I pick her up. I can't help myself: she's here and I see right through her.

~

Eve's bedroom walls were bare. No pop-star posters. No soft kittens. Just a picture of Napoleon and a calendar with the days struck off.

Eve's diary started when she was thirteen, along with the bleeding. It wasn't the way she'd worked it out. She was feeling the fat on her hips when she bought the blank book at the newsagents. There were no cartoons on its cover, not even the word *diary*. She had always been a skinny child. And then, some smoking girls in the shade of the flats in Lordship Road called after her, taunting. There was blood on her school tunic. She hadn't noticed. Her first loss.

It's nice for a girl to keep a diary. Anyone would say it. It's a secret place to keep your stories, your pets, your hopes and heroes. But you have to lock it up, so no-one finds it. Mind you, that's what girls do with themselves anyway. It's in their very nature.

A fine way to practise self-expression is what her parents said. Not that Eve needed any practice. She was brighter than most and she was going to be a lawyer.

Dear Diary, she wrote on the first page. And then she crossed it out.

You're not dear to me at all. I hardly know you. And you didn't cost much either. Eve liked the crossing out. Did it specially in red pen. Then back to blue.

Besides, this is all a fiction. Not a letter. Not a friend. Just an empty book. Until I turn the book into My Diary. Which is

Me. Eve chewed her pen, then chewed the other side to make it even. From the outside looking in, you'd think she was doing algebra, or some test.

Dear Me. She wrote with certainty.

That's how the whole business started. For two years Eve did her diary – but it concerned her that the word was singular when in fact it filled up several books. Writing felt like looking in the mirror which she (frowning) did from time to time, but not as much as other girls. Eve kept her books tucked out of sight, just as you'd expect. Not that anyone would ever go poking about in her things. There was one drawer in the cupboard with a tiny lock and she wore the key on a chain at her neck.

It made her father smile and ask who held the key to her heart. He was always one for winking. And Eve would smile back, especially in company. Grown-ups would pause for a while and Eve could see the fondness in their faces as they remembered back to when they were in their teens and all the world lay before them like brand new carpet. Just ready to walk on. With bare feet.

Eve wore glasses and bled every month neat as a calendar. She had red hair which was really orange. And she had freckles, even on her eyelids. Looking at her speckled arms she thought of gazing at the cosmos. Her life was a pendulum.

Your life is a progressive line, her mother said. But her mother had been trained to be a Christian. She believed in human advancement and repentance. She played tennis at the local club.

Your life is a spiral, moving upwards, Eve's father said. But he was a godless architect who let himself be married in a church. When Eve thought of life in his way it was coiled and dwindling, like a steeple.

Dear Me, she wrote, and laid out the arguments. *Life is a pendulum. Where I start, and where I finish, is arbitrary. I keep returning to where I was. Only each time I am bigger, I have new teeth, I lose blood, whatever. I am stronger in some ways, but the trials grow more complex too. And so each new battle is really the same. Repeats. No rest. Always the swing of the pendulum.*

Eve had read about a man who rolled a boulder up a hill and then it rolled back down again. His work was endless. Pointless.

Why was I created? she wrote on her fifteenth birthday. And all through dinner in a restaurant she thought of ways to ask her parents, but she knew they wouldn't have a satisfactory answer.

I was born in the middle of a major strike. Tools down. Unemployment, poverty, pollution, divorce, population up. Always up.

Eve's friend Christine was in love with some boy she saw at the station on Platform 2, and sometimes at the supermarket. Christine filled her diary with him and read out the safe parts over the phone.

Christine still didn't know his name, so she called him Paul. She wanted to let him know how well she had done in her exams. He had fine hands, she had noticed. And she knew now that he was musical: she had seen him carrying a violin case. His shoes were always scuffed and mucky, which she loved. He always stared at her on and off until his train came and she felt her whole body melt inside. She had nearly got run over brushing her hair outside the station. She'd been checking her little mirror and didn't see the car. *What price love!?* She didn't like his smirking friend at all. She suspected that he knew about her and Paul. Perhaps he was jealous. Perhaps he wasn't even a friend.

Eve knew that Christine didn't dream to think 'Paul' had a penis. Christine had never even heard his voice. Eve wanted to discuss the life of animals that all humans lived, and the contradiction of minds and souls.

Dear Me

In the midst of loving people, people everywhere, Mother, Father, Christine, the girls, the family, school (especially school), netball, choir, orchestra, anywhere – I am alone.

Eve mapped out a life where she made the grade, each time, each year, but all she saw were boggy stretches – exams, work, friends, marriage, babies, sickness, ageing, dying – it was all like wading. On and on. No. She crossed that out. Backwards and forwards.

Dear Me

Napoleon got everything he wanted but he was never content. And he was one in a million. Every genius is unsatisfied. (Everyone else has to slop them out.) Sometimes they turn to Evil. Sometimes they turn to God.

Eve turned to God and found him missing. No-one could prove he existed, unless they cheated in the argument. And it worried her that he was always *him* – she knew he couldn't have a penis. It made him biological, living the life that animals did. And this, she knew, ruled out the chance that he was some kind of floating soul or mind. So God was just another diary. People wrote *Dear God* but what they meant to say was *Dear Me*.

When the passport photo booth appeared next to the railway map on Platform 2, Eve's friend Christine thanked her lucky stars. It was the perfect excuse to get near Paul. If things went well, Christine might just give him her photo. She wondered if she should put her phone number on the back. She would take a good pen just in case, and a pair of scissors. He could keep her portrait in his wallet. Whatever happened, she would get to hear his voice. Perhaps his friend would call out his name. Hard to believe he would be anyone but Paul.

Christine phoned Eve the night before, with instructions. *Wash your hair and don't wear your glasses. We'll both go over and pose together. For the photos we'll just hug or whatever.* It was all worked out. The extra time, just in case. A purse full of the right coins. Christine confessed to practice-runs in the mirror, widening her mascara eyes and sucking in her cheeks. Clean hair. Freshly shaved legs. No dinner, so her stomach would be extra flat. A special devil-may-care laugh. She wanted to be heard (sounding fun) despite those thick grey curtains. *If we all end up talking together, maybe you could talk to his friend – I know it's a big favour.*

Eve did all her homework and practised for choir. For Christine's sake, she washed her hair and shaved her legs, just so. She wrote in her Diary late into the night. She wrote, crossed out, and kept on writing until the first waking birdsong.

Dear Me.

When Napoleon took his soldiers to Egypt they moaned and bled like women. He laid his healing hand upon them as Jesus might have done to lift a curse, but he was out of luck: it was a case of the flukes. There was no getting round the parasites' homicidal lust for life.

I've weighed it up like an argument, life and death.

I've read back over two years of My Diary. That's 24 months crossed off the calendar. I've re-read my list of pros and cons. My philosophical proof and my formula of probable outcomes. I've rated my personal feelings, day to day, and worked out an average. I've done the religious arguments. Statistics. You can't be thinking I'm a typical girl going through an ugly phase (no phase lasts forever, and all that), and you can't dismiss me as some weird emotional teenager. But anyway, who are YOU? You're me. I'm talking to me, no-one else but me. You know as well as I do that my very existence in this world is an excess. Each new life is surplus to requirements.

On balance – that is, taking all things into account – life is not worth living. I've weighed this up: I'm not in the business of making rash or impulsive decisions. I hope that's perfectly clear.

From the outside looking in, writing all through the night like that, you'd say Eve was the last word in staying power. She put her diary in the drawer and left the key sticking out of the lock.

And in the full light of morning she obliged her friend with the best hairstyle she could muster and her glasses in a pocket. A clean shirt. Her nicest underpants. You could say it was a kind of selflessness, no matter what some people might say afterwards.

Eve met her friend on time. Christine was in a kind of heaven. Her face shone. At Platform 2, the boys were waiting for their train and Christine jangled her purse of coins as she walked past. She laughed her careless laugh – at nothing – and Eve felt herself blush down to the last freckle. They fell inside the photo booth and giggled behind the curtain.

Choose your background.

They hugged and kissed for the hidden camera and squealed each time the flash went off.

Now one set each of singles. Christine pushed Eve out and started to brush her hair.

Outside, Paul's friend was smirking and Paul was in the middle of a mime, riding a horse with reins pulled high in the air. Eve heard coins drop into the slot inside the booth. Christine was babbling. Caught, Paul froze for a moment where he stood but then started again. This time his face was mean as a bull. Eve felt the flash go off and Christine faked a groan inside. Paul was raping the air, grasping some invisible girl's hair from behind. The flash went off again. Paul was looking Eve straight in the face, cock-sure and jerking. Another flash. The two boys laughed. Eve took her glasses out of her pocket and put them on. She stared Paul straight in the face, without emotion. The final flash. It was her turn to pose alone. She was satisfied that she had finished her diary once and for all. (You could see the satisfaction in her photos.)

I know I must die, she had written in blue pen.

That's a certain fact to balance with my birth, my one remaining certainty. But isn't it better if I do it myself? Surely it's the only thing an intelligent person can do, to take control and not be messed up by this life.

Tonight I prepared my body. No more vacillation. I am not afraid at all, although the blood when I nicked my shin nearly made me faint. Christine will get to talk to her boy, I'm sure of that. After school today I will hang myself on the cloakroom hook. This is the best method I can think of, in terms of neatness and efficiency. I can't get this wrong. Here at home I'll leave the key in the lock, so that everything will be explained afterwards. Sorry. The birds are going crazy out there at the start of my big day, at the end of My Diary.

~

A bird is going crazy out there on the platform. The sound is so clear it's only now that I realise my ears have stopped ringing.

Below the curtain of my cosy booth, there's a pair of dancing shoes. A lady's shins. Tonight, after dinner, she came to a decision. It's now or never. She's made up her mind to get a passport so she can fly off somewhere foreign. She spent almost twenty years waiting for her sweetheart to leave his wife. Longing years, without so much as a night with him to keep her going. He finally saw the light, but he died of a stroke two days before his divorce came through. He'd promised her they'd have a life together.

I'm still gripping my money in one hand, Eve's photos in the other. I comb my hair to the side, just as Kandy wanted it.

The birdsong stops and the Whistling Woman clears her throat to speak. I don't know how long I've kept her waiting. She taps the booth.

'Hello,' she says. 'Have you finished in there?'

I drop the coins into the slot. 'I'm sorry, I've just started.'

I forgot to choose my background. It's too late to do it now. Eve didn't ask to be born. She didn't ask to die – she just went ahead and did it. Unnatural, maybe, but she had her reasons. I authorise.

The flashes fire and freeze my face. Once, again, again, again. It hurts my eyes, brighter than daylight, harder than fluorescents.

Eve was wearing her glasses in the booth, so her vision was 20:20. My eyes are looking sore. The rims are wet and puffy. They've seen better times, but Kandy has seen worse.

Beyond the curtain the Whistling Woman has begun again. I'd say it was a blackbird if I didn't know better.

'The birds are going crazy out there at the start of my big day,' I say to myself in the mirror, and the Whistling Woman stops to listen. My reflection blushes.

When I step outside she smiles at me. She's done her hair specially for the photo, and the lipstick on her thin mouth is fresh and shiny. I wonder if it helps her whistle.

84

'You sound just like a blackbird.' I say the words without thinking, like a foolish darting question.

'Turdus merula,' she replies. It's some kind of insult.

I'm speechless.

'It's not the nicest name, but they're my favourite.' Now she's embarrassed. She's blinking a lot, remembering some old poem.

'What's in a name?' she says, but she doesn't wait for an answer. Before you know it, the Whistling Woman has hopped inside the photo booth and drawn the curtain closed.

I'm waiting for my pictures and I can see her shins and shoes next to the rubbish on the floor inside. She's quiet now, and concentrating. I can't see her face but I know she's smiling – better still, she's grinning ear-to-ear as the flashes fire. Inside her head she's repeating the words, over and over:

Life begins at forty-something.

~

The petrol station wears the usual spots and stains, but there's a huge black shadow across the concrete. The cylinder cage has been moved to the other side of the forecourt, leaving rusty scab-lines on the ground. There's not much sign of Duffy's damage. I can pretend nothing happened. There's even a car filling up at Number Four. I'm like a winner returning home. It's V-day.

22:53 on the camera, the start of my new shift, and Ken is getting ready to go. He laughs by way of greeting.

The changeover float adds up.

'I've kind of missed you, Terry,' Ken says. 'You know I hate the night shift. Messes up my body clock worse than jet-lag!'

Ken laughs at everything, but I know he's worried about things back home. His daughter has been washing her face with special bleaching soap that gives you cancer. His mother's losing her wits and his wife misses him like mad.

'What's the news, then?' I ask him.

'The glass was fixed. And the camera is totally new. There have been lots of investigations, you know. But we didn't lose our licence.'

Ken points to the notes stuck on the inside of the window. His fingers are two-tone: dark chocolate on top, white chocolate under.

'There have been two runaways: a jacked-up black Mini. I did not get the registration on him. A beige Jaguar with personalised plates. The driver was a wealthy lady. Your firebug has gone to hell or somewhere like that. I heard he burned a house down.' Ken shakes his head. 'Women and children inside!'

He reaches under the bench and pulls out a baseball bat. 'This is from Naga – for next time – but I know you turn the other cheek.'

He smiles all of a sudden and nods his head towards the door. 'You let me out? I'm going back home soon, you know.'

'Home?'

'All the way! And I'm not talking about Leyton.' Ken lets out another little laugh. 'Oh – there's a new code. I nearly forgot to tell you.' He whispers the numbers into my ear. I can smell garlic on his breath. Personally, I stay away from the stuff if I can help it.

I let Ken out and lock up the shop. At the security door I swipe my ID card and tap in the new code. I'm back inside my glass box. The windows are new – I can see that, though it's impossible to say what's different.

Life has returned to normal, but not – things have changed. Like the chip on the lip of my *Terry's Mug*. Or the door code. Or that new boy of Siv's I haven't seen – I haven't even got the knack of his name. Or the photo I took to please Kandy, still fresh in my pocket. Or Ken leaving. Or the empty shelf in Siv's office where the month of videos usually lives. Or the gap where his garish idol used to be before I took it. Or the new security camera over the dumpers, the new glass in my windows, flashing reflections, lights, tricks, all over the shop.

Everything has changed in no time.

Here: foreign and dangerous.

86

10: Temperance

It's worse than I thought. Siv's done a spring-clean in his office, only it's not spring. Everything is in a different place. The video shelf is nearly empty, but there are nine new days and nights to catch up on by way of consolation. I can't see his work diary anywhere.

I hear the computer sing beyond the door.

A health worker stands by her Beetle. She's on her way home from a West End play. She's seen too many stuck-at-home housewives who injure themselves on purpose. Today's been no exception. I authorise.

I feel the surge of power in the stroke of my fingertip. My body's getting back to business as usual. Soon I'll be firing on all cylinders.

At Pump Number Six I spot the familiar pizza delivery boy with another black eye. His boyfriend hits him on account of jealousy. He says it's love. I authorise.

At Pump Number Three, a hairdresser holds back her morning sickness, but the name is wrong because she gets it at night. She doesn't know who the father is. I authorise.

I wait to take their payments before going out back at 00:00. Through the hum of the fridges and the air control system, I'm sure I can hear church bells toll in the distance. My mother took me as a baby to some clergyman or other. She asked for a blessing, but all she got was a lesson.

Siv's office is dark, quiet. The camera switches onto me, but I don't care. Siv knows I wouldn't steal anything. I wouldn't bite the hand that feeds me. I wouldn't show disrespect. Especially not now. I'm as grateful as a butler. And he knows I'll bring his picture back.

I see by the light that seeps in from outside. The place smells of detergent. All the current forms and papers are in neat-edged piles. Correspondence with the Council. Health and safety. Insurance. Letters from the Metropolitan Police. *With reference to the incident.* An airmail envelope addressed to Siv, but no stamps. He must have left it for me to read. That new cashier must have brought it with him. I weigh it in my hand. There are photos inside. Siv's full name looks like a spell.

Sivalingam Easwaran.

I prefer to call him Siv.

I've got all night to read his letter. I suspect they're trying to marry him off – at his age! Or perhaps they want his English wages.

The noticeboard is tidy. His map of Sri Lanka still hangs in the middle of everything. I thought of it as a water-drop, but now it looks to me like a lady's belly. My heart skips a beat. The navel is labelled *Kandy.* I press the strip of photos in my pocket. It's only me that calls her that.

The computer sings.

Back in my glass box, I check the pastor standing next to his demonstration Ferrari. He's got it for a week to inspire the congregation: all things come to those who work hard, pray hard. Nothing is too grand, and no-one is too weak or small. The meek don't inherit the earth – or much at all, really – ask any cuckoo. I authorise.

My heart's all over the place.

The only note I can find in Siv's office is a piece of paper taped to a milk crate. He's written nothing personal for me.

Help yourself or throw away.

Inside the crate, there's an old phone, the sort you have to dial. A tartan scarf. Notepads. A shop-soiled teddy bear. Esso coasters with the tiger. Last year's *Tamil Pages,* which is like a normal phone book, only smaller. I put it to one side for later. A hardbound desk diary, unused but out of date. Another one, blank except for the dates and the Nestlé logo on every page. (It's a nest of birds, maybe warblers.) And glossy calendars from way back when. Photographs of vintage cars one year, young girls the next. On behalf of the garage, in the days when Bob was manager (before Bharathi, before Siv) caramel-coloured Verena smiles her calendar smile and holds a trail of jasmine at her shoulder. Her hands are beautiful. She was a virgin then, and men didn't have one name.

~

Verena went to church a lot. At home she prayed with her beautiful hands in a tight ball. She always kept a Bible next to her bed, just like they do in hotels. She had high standards.

When there were three children to look after, and no husband all of a sudden – except for the photo on the fridge held in place by a ladybird magnet – she prayed more than ever. In the picture they were all together. Verena believed Matthew would come back. It was only a matter of time. He was chasing the wind. From the outside looking in, you could tell that God's word mostly gave her comfort.

They might be called John or Mark or whatever, but all men have one name – that's what she said from time to time, even in front of the boys. They were young, so maybe they didn't make the connection.

Jasmine was the eldest but she never plucked up the courage to ask her mother what the 'one name' was. In that one name she felt her father would come undone. And she wondered if chasing the wind was the same as chasing skirt, because he certainly did that.

Matthew had always been weak at the knees for pretty women. He called it his Achilles' knee. He would argue again and again that his heart was bigger than your average *homo sapiens*. (Jasmine remembered pressing her head against his skinny chest, his heart so big it bulged out beating through his soft skin.) Her father loved women more than anything in this world. He said there was something wrong with God if loving too much was deemed a sin. His way of feeling was – and here he stopped each time, as if to search for some new word or meaning – *original*.

Original sin is what you mean to say. Just read the Bible, Verena used to argue back. But that was in the early days, when she was in a strong position. When she knew that the very sight of his boys could bring a quivering to his lip and lure him home.

89

When she was able to persuade him to abstain. That was before he gave in and left her.

Afterwards, she was philosophical. She went to church more than ever. She took out the family photos to be anointed by the pastor. But sometimes, in the middle of nothing in particular, tears climbed up the whites of her eyes and then settled back down again.

Like onions – Jasmine thought. *She's got pickling onions in her sockets.*

When Jasmine was little she liked food in general but she loved sour things in particular. (That became one of her excuses later on.) She got a taste for filling an empty soup bowl with vinegar and mopping it out with bread, careful not to miss a drop or leave a crumb.

You'll turn into a sour sop. Her mother wagged a finger. Verena's hands were soft and smooth, even though she worked in a hotel kitchen. Jasmine could have stroked her lacquered fingernails for hours.

What's a sour sop?

That's a white fruit. Falls apart when you eat it.

Jasmine was light-skinned, but that was not her mother's meaning.

Your stomach will go all sloppy and rot.

Jasmine sometimes found her mother staring at the hallway mirror, holding in her belly and squeezing her thighs. Pushing up the sallow skin around her eyes.

He didn't leave because I'm fat or ugly, her mother said – too often. *Because I'm* not *fat or ugly!* – *But don't you give them the excuse, either. When I was your age I learned fast enough to look after what God gave me. You don't have to be a model to make the most of yourself.*

Verena had done some modelling when she was younger, before her babies. Product catalogues. A garage calendar. There was still a picture of her on a card in the hairdressers' window. Anyone who saw that card would say for certain she was a beauty. She curved in and out like a double bass.

90

Matthew had been gone more than a year when Jasmine started to see herself properly in the mirror, staring as she held in her belly and squeezed her thighs. Peg legs. The flesh joined all the way down to the knees. Her stomach would not go in. Bun face. Bulging armpits. Nipples the size of plates. She was fat and she was ugly.

Jasmine didn't care about getting married or men in general because they all had one name, but she did want to work in the airline business. She was ambitious. So she decided to make the most of herself.

She bought a book with each calorie laid out like a price-list. Everything that had fat in it was out of the question, that much she knew for starters. Fiddly as a princess, she learned to cut the crust off bread and the outer skin off chips. (She wished thighs could be so easy.) She checked her book over and over. In no time at all she knew by heart the value of every mouthful. She got to know her calories better than she knew her chemistry tables, better than her history dates, better than her geographical features. She kept a record of all her additions. You'd have been blind not to notice the way she turned up her nose at dinner.

You've gone off my food? Verena would plead in the same quiet voice she'd tried with her husband, the begging voice that was bound to fail. She looked for reasons in the leftovers.

And sometimes Jasmine was touched to spare her feelings, nibbled and chewed just to please her mother, knowing that smooth things, starchy things, creamy things, were the best to bring up afterwards because they hurt the least.

Jasmine began to devour the special features. Extra weights in the school bag. Not enough clothes on cold days. No-one was allowed to distract you from your mission – especially not parents, friends or doctors, who all wanted to wear down your willpower and impose their views on you regardless. Cooking steam carried tiny bubbles of fat, which was why chefs grew plump just by breathing. Toothpaste had to be spat out, and phlegm or mucous could not be swallowed – it was all down to starch. (The same applied to semen, for what it was worth.) Cider vinegar in boiling water, four times a day, cleansed the system. Acids burned up fat. Lemon juice was good for breakfast. Lettuce for lunch. Water if hungry. Jasmine took single ideas – the best, the hardest – from each regime and put them all together.

I've always loved sour things, she burst out before her mother had a chance to speak her mind. Jasmine was learning a new defiance, instead of being quiet and helpful.

Verena got to dreaming of hell. The pastor had shown her a technical drawing of the earth with its burning heart. A geologist – a non-believer – had drilled down through the earth's crust and found a cavern of shocking heat. His microphones picked up millions of human voices screaming. Verena had done science and geography, so she knew better. But then there was the famous diver on TV who quit his work on account of the cries he heard in deep sea caves – and he was not a Christian either. They were cries of agony.

What if the father of her children ended up there? Verena didn't know that hell existed, but you never could be sure. Matthew was chasing the wind, Jasmine was thin enough to blow away, and prayer was the only answer.

Verena fasted every day until noon. She worked from five in the morning through to lunchtime and sometimes she did split shifts. At the hotel she breathed in all kinds of vapours – boiling soups, frying bacon, coffee, pots of gravy – and she wondered if that broke the fast in God's eyes. She went to church every night. She took Jasmine's belt on Tuesdays to be blessed before the Medical Chain of Prayer. She took Jasmine's school bag on Wednesdays to be anointed along with everyone else's Hopes and Goals. On Thursdays, which were Nights of Love, she prayed for Matthew to repent and return. And on Saturdays, Family Days, she held and rubbed the photo from the fridge. It wasn't long before she started to take the ladybird magnet too, as it held the photo in its place.

And in the end, the praying worked. Matthew came back timid as a household pet, pressing his big heart with his hand and saying he'd felt a change. He stood at the door for an hour in his new suede coat and Verena wouldn't let him in. Jasmine was in her room. The boys were watching TV.

This time is for good, he said, looking pitiful as Jesus. He'd been chasing the wind. He'd fathered a baby and it died at birth. His girlfriend had kicked him out. He'd been to hell and back.

Verena said a silent prayer. It was a Thursday and she was going to be late for the Night of Love. She wouldn't let her husband in, but she invited him to God's house instead. When he said yes she had to pinch herself.

She could hardly hold herself back from smiling when they got through the church doors. The two of them looked like new lovers – she, gripping his skinny hand, and checking for the pastor's nod. She prayed like she'd never prayed before. She let herself go. Nearly everyone there was single.

Verena and Matthew stood before God, while at home Jasmine stood before the hallway mirror. Her father's voice at the door had made her catch her breath – and it hurt. Her teeth hurt. What would he see after all this time? The veins stuck out in her legs, which made her calves look fat and ugly.

Yesterday there had been the faint taste of her mother's lipstick, a fine slick in her glass of vinegar, perhaps even a tiny rainbow on the surface. Lipstick was pure fat and certainly not to be swallowed. Perhaps her mother was trying to thwart her.

Jasmine's interview was coming up in less than a month, so she had to put on a good show. Like an athlete, or a ballerina, her body had become hard and dry. She stood on the scales. She caught her breath. It hurt. She'd put on weight since the morning.

~

The computer sings. I go to obey, smooth as you like. Totally professional.

There's a pizza delivery boy at the nearest pump. No black eye. This one can't speak English yet. I authorise.

Back in Siv's office, I put the calendar back into the box. I don't want it. Young Verena (before the husband or the babies) floats above a row of ads. She's the local printer's full colour showpiece. She's a mermaid for the fish shop. She's Lady Luck from the betting shop (the one with the dogs on the door.) Her lipstick shines. She's a guardian angel courtesy of the undertakers. I feel sick with the smell of dying jasmine. My teeth hurt where the enamel's stripped off.

If you tear a tissue into fronds and tickle your throat, everything comes up. Your lunch. Your dinner. Your past. It's like a spring clean – but I'd never starve myself to death. No matter what things look like.

There's a parasite you breathe into your lungs and it tickles you on purpose. It flies up with the hurl of an itchy cough to your throat for the chance to get down to your gut – that's where the real job begins.

I put the first video on to play. *Day One of Terry's Absence.* I watch the mothering book-keeper. The mouthing alcoholic. The lady in the Jaguar with the personalised number plates who drives off without paying. In broad daylight. Naga's last shift before his exams. Siv at night, doing my shift – that's the downside of being a manager: it's like being on call. Sometimes he disappears in the darkness. The pictures are rough at the best of times.

I sit through all the videos, one by one, in between live customers. I press *play* and *fast forward*. I authorise. I empty the bins into the new dumper. Beyond it, I can see a burnt tree at the road's edge. The ground is blackened. I can smell the singe of hair, the stink of chemicals. I return to Siv's nice dark office, the flickering record of my lost nights. Black and white policemen making follow-up visits. Businessmen from Head Office. Repair men, delivery men, inspectors who look like other people's fathers. The new dumpers come into view at last when the replacement camera joins the circuit. The safety tape is torn away. I authorise. I run through the familiar faces on days. Giri, Ken, Siv, taking turns to do my nights. And that new fellow under training, whatever his long name is. Siv shows him how everything works. Silently he talks to him, laughs with him – no doubt they've got a lot in common, because they're both

94

from Batticaloa. I count up the till money, doing regular cash drops into the floor chute in between live customers. I make the proper notes in the register. I check the week's roster for that new cashier's name. I find it: *Rajkumar*. No doubt he's fresh off the boat or whatever, on account of the troubles back home. I authorise. I'm missing from all the goings-on, nowhere to be seen. I see panic in Siv's eyes when two strangers visit him at the office. Maybe it's a trick of the light. The view shifts to the forecourt, to the shop, the usual rounds, and when it comes back the men have turned and Siv is giving them huge wads of money from his pocket, and more from the till. My heart's beating like a broken clock. Outside, in real life, the computer sings and I press *pause* again. It's driving me mad. More customers. More deadly sins. More deadly virtues. Petrol, chewing gum, Coke, cigarettes. I authorise. Lottery tickets – I don't ask for that extra sale. I press *rewind* and there's Siv again, with the rough light catching his fear as he looks up at me in a darting glance, as he meets the eye of the roving camera. The skinny bearded man does all the talking. The other man takes Siv's money. Dark as Siv, perhaps the same age as Siv, but his jutting teeth are crooked when he smiles. I've never seen him before. Not once. He's not from Head Office. His mate isn't either.

I check the date and time. It was *Day One of Terry's Absence* when the men came and made Siv give them his cash. I try to count how much, but it's impossible to tell. It's thousands and thousands. Enough to fill a small case. It's blackmail, or protection money. They're friends of terrorists. I see fear in Siv's eyes. The time was 14:00. Broad daylight. I do not authorise.

The *Tamil Pages* and the tiger coasters fit into my coat pocket. For later. My heart's a mess but I've got to tackle Siv's letter – it's the only thing he's left for me to read.

11: Justice

The envelope is made out to *Sivalingam Easwaran*, care of an address in East London. The top has been torn open, carefully. The security camera may or may not be spying on me. I don't care. Siv doesn't watch the videos on playback like I do. Besides, there are no other notes from him in the office. He's read his letter and he's left it for me to have a look at. It has something to do with those men.

The photos are black and white. There's no writing on the back. No explanations. Some family standing stiff and upright, too blurred to see their faces properly. And a tiny portrait of a young couple. It's as formal-feeling as a wedding picture, but they're not touching. The woman is wearing a sari.

The letter seems to begin in the middle of things. There's no name, no date either.

At last I write to you, and I know exactly how much time has passed. It was very hard to forgive you; I knew very well when you left that you were washing your hands of everything (politics was never your strong point). Forgive me now for my silence. It is no wonder you became silent too. I met one fellow (visiting like a rich tourist now!), he was very committed to fundraising, he used to work for you there, so I know you are doing well enough, and I am happy for you. Living in London must be so fine, the freedom to go to work and Temple without fear etc, even though the price is great. You have one kind of Freedom. I am making another kind. Life carries on as normal here from day to day but you must know the situation is always serious! We remember the big massacres by their dates and numbers (you should have read about them), but who is counting all the others? Which newspapers in England will be interested about the cashew seller who was killed by chance just because he was standing in the street at the wrong moment? Or one local girl shot in both legs (still living, but now she is not able to walk). Even you with your healing hands could not help such a person. Any time of day the SLA can round up Tamil boys for any reason, big trouble for them if they have banned goods (batteries, kerosene, paracetemol, bicycle spare parts etc) and we still have curfew, etc. (How many bribes!) You cannot hear your Singing Fish because the SL Army is there with their encampment at the Bridge. They're scared of what will come out of the lagoon!

We have not been to Colombo for a while. I remember when Central Bank had more than 150 Tamils working in banking jobs. N. says now no more than ten, thanks to Sinhala chauvinist policies. And on top of everything the regime is spending money through their Tamil lackeys to bribe our people, to keep them quiet and fool the outside world. You will be shaking your head and asking why I write to you about these things so I will also tell you (personally) that our uncles and aunts sold nearly all the family land five years ago. I don't know how many acres. There are three new houses there, and in the main house garden the guava tree is still going strong, also the seven mango trees and of course the well that never dries.

I gave this chap Rajkumar this address (I don't know if it is where you live), he worked at the prawn farm (Irrigation Engineer). He went out with his friend to get some booze for the office party and when they came back everyone was massacred. This was three years or thereabouts after you took off. So he is material witness, you know about that. He went to live (disappear) in Colombo but not far from here he gave two hitchhikers a lift to hospital (they were Tigers, one was wounded), so he was interrogated by police for LTTE connections and his name went on the blacklist. I told him you could help him, you must know the system inside out by now.

I dream that one day everyone will come back but I know life there is too good with all the material comforts you could wish for, as everyone says, and parents with children want to give them a future, and of course we cannot expect to see the dead again in this life. Thambi, I'm shedding tears now for your wife and children. I found these photos, it is best for you to have them. I wonder if I will see you once more. You must have all your British papers in order and a great deal to be proud about after all but still you never come back. I am sure the checkpoints do not put you off. Thambi, how much time is left for us in this life? N. always has nightmares but he is fine and always good to me, his work is good, he is needed. My work is also good (I am conducting education programmes in training centres, in suburbs and villages, etc). My health is so-so. Best wishes from a Bird of Freedom.

~

The computer has been singing for some time, I realise. My hands are shaking. My eyes are prickling with the smell of petrol. I fold the letter back into its envelope and head for the till in the bright light of my box. I need to read it again before the night is out.

A man stands at the nearest pump, holding onto the nozzle with a white handkerchief to protect his hand. He's checking his watch. He's a stickler for time. I authorise.

One of the girls from Customer Care is sitting in his front seat, playing with the gadgets. He has the works in his car, a computer to do everything short of drive. If it's summer he can make it winter. If it's fast he can make it slow. His list of special features and customised adjustments is like a speech he can recite. His car will steer him through a foreign place and tell him what's for dinner at the end of all his searching. *Your mother sucks more cocks than I've had hot dinners* – he hates graffiti, and he hates this kind (the kind you find on High Street) more than most things, but he's got ideas to fix it. If you're the king of building materials, you don't just sit by and watch while louts and hooligans deface every building in your sight. And there's no forgetting the power of your Abrasives Division.

Graffiti abrasion: there has to be a patent in it. That's what he's thinking.

The girl wonders if dinner cost him enough for her trouble, if it could have been more pricey, if she's made it too easy, if her boss has VD – but then she remembers how he disinfected

98

himself before and after. And how he criticised the stubble in her armpits.

Not tidy, not feminine.

When he comes to my window, he tells me off for keeping him waiting at the pump.

'It's not as if you've got any other customers,' he snaps at the slot.

He doesn't know about my letter and I'm not about to tell him either.

He pays by credit card, making sure not to touch anything if he can help it. It's a grubby business. Public handrails and door furniture are bad enough, but counters, where money changes hands, are the worst for germs.

Actually, he's annoyed because he hates being taken by surprise more than most things. He can't stand all the clumsiness of self-service, especially not with a pretty girl inside. Someone in the office should have seen to it.

I'm thinking about Siv's letter. That line about his wife and children. They're dead. As far as I'm concerned, they lived for a second. They died as soon as I heard them mentioned. I'm thinking about that word *fundraising*.

'I'm sorry I kept you waiting.' I pass the receipt through the slot for the man to sign.

Keith Harrison.

His signature reads like handwriting, clear as day.

'By the way,' Keith Harrison says, glancing up at my CCTV, 'the time on your monitor is out.' He wipes his fingers on his handkerchief.

'I'm sorry,' I say.

He's right. I'm beginning to feel annoyed, like he is. The police must know when crimes actually happen. The more you know the less you need to ask. Cheating, murdered wives, stolen deposits … if justice is going to be served, you need the facts. And I must know exactly when those men came for Siv.

'It's inexcusable!' I say, feeling the anger in my throat.

I pass Keith Harrison a promotional voucher. Free points for every litre of fuel.

His face relaxes.

'You'd better get it fixed,' he says, as if he owns the company.

I want to tell him the place belongs to Siv, my manager, the independent owner of the franchise, the man who loves listening to the Singing Fish and the Bird of Freedom, the man who washed his healing hands of everything.

'Thank you,' I say, polite as a secretary.

And Keith Harrison returns to his car with the automatic girl on the front seat.

~

Just behind Hatt Street – you'd never know it was there unless you were looking for it – there's a little cul-de-sac. The cobbled part is not much wider than a bus. The terrace looks huddled in the space, but you'd be hard-pressed to find higher house prices for miles. You can tell by the cars. And the door knockers. None of your usual stack of buzzers and bells making a mess. Not one council flat or cheap conversion in sight. And from the outside looking in through the windows, if the shutters aren't closed you can see right through to back gardens big as a park.

That's where Keith Harrison lives. Lived. His house went up for sale and the estate agents wouldn't even put a figure on it. *Price on application* is what they said in their window, like some special fish on a menu before it goes on the scales. And someone applied. And the sign came down, and there was nothing in the street to give you the idea that anything bad had happened there.

If she'd called me bald or ugly, that would have been different, Keith said in his defence. He was talking about his wife.

Keith had a bathroom fit for angels: all the nozzles and taps were gold and the mirrors were heated from behind so they wouldn't steam up and interfere with his shaving. The toilet had a grinder in it that made a buzz like a dentist's drill instead of the coughs and hocks of your typical London plumbing. (His wife

100

thought it was mad, and the plumber agreed, because it meant you had to be picky and choosy about what you put down there, but Keith was in love with the neatness.) Then there was a path of white carpet thick as you like, set into a floor paved with some rare pink marble. You had to go in with bare feet or socks. Shoes carried germs in off the street.

And it doesn't take long for that to show on a white carpet. Keith and his wife agreed on that much at least. *Germs do not discriminate. Germs are blind.*

There was an antique-style gold clock on the wall, which made old-fashioned ticking sounds just for show. Keith had all the clocks in his house, and at work, synchronised to the same last fraction of a second. Just like in spy films. At board meetings – and Keith was the boss – everyone had to have their watches timed to the same moment, or else. It was the little beeps he didn't like, squealing out all over the place. Drove him mad. Everyone knew about his temper, but they said that's how you get to run an empire. *You have to have a temper.* People have a reason for everything.

And back in the cul-de-sac, there wasn't a neighbour that didn't have a polite word to say about Mr Harrison – the way he tipped the dustmen at Christmas and so on – he was nothing if not fair.

That's how he talked about all the business that happened with his wife. She had said the wrong thing. It was tit for tat. They never did have children. Something to do with one side being out of kilter in her organs. It never bothered him that much. In any case, he had his model trains, two floors of them, no expense spared. It would all have been so different if she'd called him stubborn, or whatever. But she didn't.

She was lying on the bathroom floor, still as a stone on the line of white carpet, in between the shiny pink. Keith got back to his new train. He had to test it. The delivery boy who'd flown in on the first morning flight from Austria was still waiting in the porch downstairs. The little locomotive was wrapped in tissue, then cotton wool and bubble plastic, all nicely bedded with foam shapes inside a reinforced box. It had survived the journey. It was fine. The gold-leaf trim was perfect. It was better than fine, it was heaven. Then there was the detail of the motion – all sorts of tiny particulars you'd be hard-pressed to know about unless you had this kind of hobby. Keith was so pleased he reached for his wallet to sort out a tip, but it went straight back into his pocket: the boy's watch was six minutes off the hour. Inexcusable.

It was time to go to work. At the office, Keith noticed the new receptionist's shapely legs and like a cat she curled towards him when he entered. He could nearly hear her purr.

One for the in-tray, he smiled to himself, *along with that other one in Customer Care.*

The Board met at noon, and Keith timed how long it took from the first man through the door to the last one sitting, and it was too long. Three and a half minutes. He made them do it all over again, like rehearsing for a show. And then they had to synchronise their watches, only the Head of Sales and Marketing must have done it wrong because his watch started beeping in the middle of Keith's speech about the takeover and then everyone sat bolt upright in their chairs to see the famous temper in action.

But for once he didn't lose it. He just took a breath and carried on – you could hear all the noses letting out their relief at once – carried on in the full knowledge that his company was about to be twice the size it was the day before and that this was the smoothest takeover in the history of the building materials business. Not to mention the growth of the Abrasives Division. And then the new Board Members were let in on cue and Keith noticed that they wore lighter suits than was usual and that Jan, his personal assistant, had hairs poking out through her clear skin-colour tights and he made a note of it in his diary.

The deal was done.

Clinched, he said. *And it was fair play on both sides.* The way Keith liked it.

In the afternoon he signed more than a hundred cheques and took two headache pills before calling Jan into his office and pointing out the business of her leg hair. When she burst into tears because (she said) she was having a hard time at home these days, he told her to take the rest of the day off and get her legs waxed, which was such a surprise you could have picked her mouth up off the floor.

No-one can say I'm mean, he thought.

Jan was so thankful she might have kissed him, only Keith wasn't like that. He always made the first move, or else. That much was certain.

She cleared off and left him to his own devices. He buzzed Reception and had that purring girl put all his calls on *divert* and then he gave his scaled-down office railway a run for its money: ten metres of electric track and one each of his favourite intersections, all tucked away behind oak cabinet doors so thick you'd think it was just your typical corporate headquarters wall. But when he noticed his remote control was feeling sluggish, he made an irritable note.

Sticky keys. Telephone hygienist.

And then he called the Chief Inspector and booked an appointment with the police.

It was all because of that apartment in the Alps. As if one home was not enough. Who else had a bathroom to match hers? His wife was always going on about something. Sales staff (idle housewives) who let her down – he did warn her about pyramid selling but she didn't listen. She visited all kinds of charlatans. She was constantly following some awkward regime or other, and lusting after absurd hotels in remote locations. Her wants were endless, until push came to shove in the bedroom. (Is that what happened to all the pretty girls? Perhaps all those receptionists turned to frost on the marital bed.)

Suddenly there was this apartment in the Alps, out of nowhere, because the Weills had one, and because it wasn't good enough just to visit, and because she needed some ridiculous course of treatments ... *et cetera and so on.*

And just because he'd denied her, rebuffed her reasons one by one, kept things fair and square and unemotional...

There's a fellow called Ken Senior. He manages Regional

Distribution and, for the record, he's exceeded his productivity targets by more than two per cent for five years running – we're not talking about some corporate jester here.

Ken has a notice stuck on his door: 'It's a woman's prerogative to change her mind ... and ALL MONEY into ALIMONY.'

Do you get my point?

Keith had said all this to his wife, just like that, off the cuff, to redirect her train of thought. (It tickled him pink.) But she was too caught up in herself to see the bigger picture.

She was in the flesh, in the bathroom, preparing her face, courtesy of the steam-free heated mirror and the daylight-balanced lamps. Surrounded by hand-selected rose marble. Her feet on bespoke white carpet. Working herself into a state with this new craving of hers. Her Adam's apple going up and down like a chicken. Her neck straining, pulling, going pink, blue.

If she'd called me something else, that would have been different. But she called me MEAN. After everything I've given her. From Day One. You can check the records. Check the house. She had no right, absolutely no right, to say that.

Besides, there were other pressing matters at the time. That business of the long-awaited Austrian locomotive, made to order with gold-leaf trim and adjustable bogeys. *Imperial Princess.* Not to mention the last details of the takeover and the formal blessing of the new Board. It was a big day.

Just like a wedding was how Keith put it.

He didn't need or want a lawyer. He was going to represent himself. Of course he would admit that he hadn't expected things to go as far as they did. You can't account for absolutely everything. A child of ten knows that. But if Keith Harrison didn't know about being even-handed, then no-one did.

~

The computer sings. I don't know where I've been, or for how long. I check the time: 02:40. It's out by a minute. At Pump Number Three there's another company man in a bank-blue shirt, but he's alone and he's not bald and he would never put an end to his wife, not for anything. His tie's undone. He's been working late and stuffing himself with chips. Starch. Salt. Fat. In the beginning Jasmine cut the oil-soaked outer skin off every chip. My heart's all over the place. There's tomato sauce all over his face. He's sucking on a box of Ribena. I authorise.

02:43

The computer sings again. At Pump Number Five is a pink woman with psoriasis. Underneath her clothes, secretly, she bleeds at the edges of her bra. My back is sore with pimples from the inside shock of the Duffy explosion. I authorise.

I want to read Siv's letter again. I have to wait. It was written by a woman. Keith Harrison killed his wife. I don't know what Siv did with his – he's not porous.

Thambi, I'm shedding tears now for your wife and children.

It's strange the writer calls him Thambi. Perhaps the letter is not Siv's after all. Perhaps it's for someone else. A man called Sivalingam Easwaran. But there's all that business about the Singing Fish.

'Pump Number Three,' my customer announces at the window. He sounds like a son of the Royal Family. I've got half a mind to tell him about the tomato smears like blood across his face.

When the pink woman leaves, part of her doesn't. There are flakes of skin in the money tray beneath my window. She makes a trail wherever she goes, just like children in a fairytale.

Thambi, I'm shedding tears now for your wife and children.

Siv never mentioned having children. I've never thought of him as a father. I think of his wife lying dead on the bathroom floor. The stain of blood on the white, white carpet.

In his spring-cleaned office (no messages, no musk) I read the letter from start to finish again. And again. The camera may be watching me, but the idol's at home keeping an eye on other things. This can't look too good, but Siv doesn't go through the old videos like I do. No-one does.

I'm in the middle of reading his letter when the phone rings. I jump at the noise. It's as if I've been caught.

03:15

No-one rings, especially not at this hour. I think of those two men: the skinny bearded one, and the one with crooked teeth. It's possible they've been watching me. Beyond the blazing forecourt I see nothing but darkness, the stream of traffic, the winking of lights. There's no-one in a lit-up phone booth. No-one standing on the other side of the road. No-one leaning against the burnt black tree. My hands are shaking when I pick up the phone by the till.

'Terry? Terry, it's me,' Siv says, as if he always calls in the middle of the night. My face in the reflection on the glass looks weird, distorted.

'Do you have any customers? Is it OK to talk?'

'The coast is clear, Siv. I'm all ears.' I can feel my voice catch in my throat. I'm thinking about his wife and children. The Singing Fish. Silenced because of some army. Siv's wife is lying dead on the bathroom floor in Keith Harrison's house.

'It's just that, Terry, I think I left something in the office, but I'm not sure about it. I'm wondering if you could have a look for me and call me back?'

'What are you missing?' I ask the question (it pops out neat as a dart) but I know full well what he means.

'It's just a letter, Terry, with an airmail envelope. The name on the front is Sivalingam Easwaran. That's me. Perhaps you have seen it?'

'I'll have a look for you and call you back at the end of my shift,' I say. 'When you wake up.'

'No, any time, Terry, as soon as you find it – that's *if* you find it.' His voice stops for a moment. It's like someone has turned the water off. 'You haven't seen it? It's possible that I have lost it. We did a spring clean. You could check the inside bins too. And there's a milk crate full of things, isn't it.'

'I'll give the place a good once-over. I'll do my best, Siv,' I say. 'Was it important?' – Another dart from nowhere.

'It's from my sister in Batticaloa, in Ceylon. Sri Lanka. She doesn't usually write very often. She has sent me some photographs.'

106

I can picture his head rocking from side to side. His long earlobes.

He changes tack. 'Everything all right at the garage, Terry? Business as usual? How is your health keeping up?'

I can't quite bring myself to thank him for sparing me. He could have sacked me, but he let me off.

'It's good to be back on the job, Siv.' I gulp.

'They gave us the all-clear, Terry. No penalties, no fines. And next time you'll be prepared, isn't it – but I am hoping there will be no next time! You call me if you find the envelope. I'll leave you to it.'

'Good night, Siv.'

By 06:30 I've learned his photos, his address and his letter by heart. There's a constant stream of nuisance customers.

At 07:00 I call Siv to say I've found what he was looking for. I know he's been up all night like I have.

12: Faith

There are tigers everywhere. A billboard campaign to save them from extinction. Those Esso coasters I salvaged from the milk crate at work. When I think about the dogs painted on the betting-shop door in High Street, baring their fangs and straining to win, they've turned into tigers. Under the bed of Mary Sturgess, the panting beast is a tiger. *Put a Tiger in your Tank* – Siv had written that in his diary. Then there's that letter from his sister: *He gave two hitchhikers a lift to hospital (they were Tigers, one was wounded), so he was interrogated by police for LTTE connections and his name went on the blacklist.*

There's even a tiger on the cover of some psychology book that Kandy's reading for her exams.

'Do you know about the Tamil Tigers?' I ask her as I sip my tea. I'm sitting on her bed. My tongue teases the chip on the mug's lip – it bothers me. I take a coaster from my jacket pocket and place it carefully on the bedside table. Politics was never my strong point. That's what Siv's sister said.

Kandy shrugs. 'They blow things up, don't they?'

'Are they terrorists?'

'Depends on your point of view, my love, same as everything.'

She's sitting at the end of the bed. She's wearing my favourite satin robe, light catching the curves of her. No bra. When she shrugs, her breasts move up a little with a sideways twitch. I like it.

'Better to die on your feet than live on your knees. I can't remember who said that, but it's a good line.' Kandy's waiting in ambush, taking her time – our time. When the moment comes, her dream and mine will match exactly. We're nothing if not soulmates, and her timing is always impeccable.

I remember I've done my hair to the side again to match the photos.

'Look,' I say, pulling them out of my inside pocket: four of

Terry's Faces in a row.

'Oh look, it's you,' she says.

'I did them especially for you.' I hand them to her. It feels like I've been hanging onto them forever, keeping them under wraps, waiting for just this moment.

'Thank you, baby, I'll keep them in my drawer.' She's touched, but she hasn't read the back yet.

Your body is my temple.

That's what I've written. It will make her blush.

Kandy slips the strip of pictures into her pocket. Now I notice her nipples poking points in her robe – I knew she'd like her present. I can feel myself go hard, but I haven't finished my tea yet. I'm thinking about the way her breasts move underneath the satin, that animal twitch of her woman's muscles. My own parts start to move. It's a kind of twin action. I'm thinking of tigers mating, one behind the other in the wild, and Kandy reads my mind, taking the mug from the grip of my fingers and placing it bang in the middle of my tiger coaster, leaning across me as she does it, so my face is full of the smell of her, musk and cigarettes, and her breasts brush against mine by accident.

'Get your kit off,' she says with a growl. 'You're not allowed to play with your uniform on, and I haven't got all day.'

I'm just about ready to explode.

Kandy gets onto her hands and knees. She keeps her calliper on and she doesn't take off her robe. She's in the tigress position. With her good hand, she flicks the satin up like a curtain over her rump and it's all I can do to get myself unzipped and ready. My heart's jumping. I keep my clothes on, but before you know it I'm undone and I'm letting myself go, I'm ramming her gate, her Sacred Entrance, the passage to her Temple. I'm lost in the gape, the gape of the lady, I'm lost, I'm lost, I'm lost, destroyed. Spilled and scattered. All over the shop.

The third eye, Siv said, *has the power of destruction.*

~

If I didn't know better, I'd say Kandy has a special kind of insight.

109

I don't tell her much, especially if it's personal. I keep myself to myself. I'm locked up like a diary. But I always tell her what I've seen. I'm a tapeworm taping. Today I tell her about Keith Harrison and his murdered wife.

Someone always dies, Kandy says when I get to the end.

She's probably guessed by now that I learned to expect things and see through things before I knew how to walk. If her exams go well, she'll be a proper psychologist soon. She's got a head for it. But there's more to it than meets the eye: with Kandy it feels as if I'm see-through, in the way that so many people are see-through for me.

She thinks I make a good tiger.

I'm padding home in the soft light of early morning and the birds are making a racket in every tree and hedge.

MR Stinks

LUV U 4 EVVA

Mark Register gave his life for those words, died of a deodorised heart attack.

Graffiti shouts from the walls on High Street.

GO HOME

Your mum rang

ROBS a twat

Rob is missing his apostrophe – Duffy would be full of scorn, worked up, inflammable.

Christine 4 Paul

Hitler woz right

Words hiss from the back of bus-stops, whisper from padlocked wooden hoardings. From Siv's letter.

I told him you could help him, you must know the system inside out by now.

I want to ask Siv a hundred questions.

How much time is left for us in this life?

I can't get those men out of my mind's eye. The skinny bearded one. The dark one with the crooked teeth. Siv is in danger but he's not about to tell me.

There's a song and dance at the Nightingale Estate. My black-

110

birds are twitchy, hungry, moody. I feed them as best I can before going to bed in the cold light of day. I kick the pigeons and magpies out of the way, but then *all* the birds take flight. My Birds of Freedom. My Singing Fish.

I follow the paths in my carpet, in between the piles of teetering papers, low walls of *The Truth* like a crooked model city. My hoard. In bed I curl up and sleep uneasily, fitting myself to the shape on my mattress.

I make myself tiny, neat as a mite.

~

After Maureen, my first foster mother, there was a run of them, one after the other, year after year, until I got my first proper job.

The mothers were fine hosts. Some of them made sacrifices out of pity. They all earned their allowance from the council. They bought me books and clothes and toys. They walked me to school. They listened to my stories. They washed my sheets and cooked my dinner. They took me to the supermarket or the park.

Sometimes we passed by the shallow house where I was born, where me and my real mother lived and the delivery men came and went like there was no tomorrow. The blinds were replaced with net curtains after the shop floor became a living room – I don't remember when. So if it was newspapers you needed, or milk, or whatever, you'd have to go somewhere else. I never breathed a word about any of it. Some foster mothers would write about that in their official foster diary.

Today we went past Terry's birth home. He didn't seem to recognise it. There was no change in his behaviour.

In the end it was always the Mr Fosters that got to me. I couldn't put my finger on it. The social worker would ask the usual official foster questions and I would give the usual official foster answers.

He made me feel bad.
He shouted and broke things.
He drank so much he changed into another person.

He treated me very differently from his own children.
He hit me.
He touched me in ways I didn't like.
He called me a monster, a spooky little bastard, a cunt, a pariah.

A pariah is an outcast. A pariah-dog is a low-breed vagabond. A pariah-kite is a scavenger bird. *Pariah* is a Tamil word.

He called me a bloody parasite.

For all the Mr Fosters and me, it became a fight over territory. No give. No take. Regardless. You could say we were looking for attention.

The way I see it, we all live on a kind of island. One type of worm moves into the eyeball, and one sort gets the run of the retina. Some wigglers take a shining to tear-ducts, others colonise the whites, and others go for the lashes. We'll do anything to survive. And if by chance we end up on some microscope slide, we might look up – but the stare of the doctor in the white coat is huge. Too huge to take in.

In the bathroom mirror my eyes seem worse than usual. I put some cream on. The parasite that lives inside the mirror looks back at me. I should say he looks down on me. *The Other Terry* has total condescension written all over his face. *You'll always be rubbish.* In the living room, Siv's idol keeps watch over everything, keen as a hawk guarding my hoards, day and night, its third eye narrowed.

~

When I get to the garage I'm out of breath.

That Rajkumar is finishing up. It's the first time I've seen him in real life. He's small, built like a boy. His teeth stick out like that man who takes Siv's money, but his skin's a kind of mushroom colour.

We do the changeover float in silence.

'Do you know those men who came for Siv?' I ask. The question's out of the blue, but it's the best way to get an honest answer.

112

'For Siva?'

'Those men who came to visit Siv – Siva. He gave them money. Do you have to give them money too?' It feels like I'm breaking and entering, but I'm grabbing the moment for what it's worth. *Have you asked for that extra sale?*

Rajkumar knows how to cash up with his eyes closed, he's got a gift with money, but English clearly isn't his strong point.

'Fundraising?' he asks. He shrugs and gives a feeble smile.

'Are they Tigers?' I'm pressing the point home. For the moment there are no customers. 'Do you know the Tamil Tigers?'

'Yes, Tamil Tigers, yes,' he says. I see panic like a flicker in his eyes.

He gave them a lift in his car, of course. One was wounded. They were fighting for some place where Tamils could be happy again. He took the hitchhikers to the hospital. They drove through holiday brochure scenery, coconut groves and fields of rice, a cashew-nut seller at the roadside. When the two men got out, Rajkumar saw blood on his seat. He left them at the door to Casualty.

Five boys pile into the shop. The door hasn't been locked yet. For a moment it looks as if they're wearing pyjamas. Striped shirts and baggy track-pants. It feels like an invasion.

'Where'sya bread, mate?' One of them shouts in my direction across the floor. He clocks Rajkumar and sniffs for show, as if he's hit upon a bad smell.

One of the gang finds the bread shelf and shouts back. 'What sort ya want?'

'White.' The leader helps himself to cans of soup, and Coke, and magazines, and dog food. His arms are full. I check the monitor. The camera's got the measure of him.

'There's only brown. And more fucking brown.'

'But I want white.'

Rajkumar glances at the screen. It's 23:00. He's ready to knock off. The shop door should have been locked by now. I've run out of time.

The pyjama boys unload at the counter. I'm not used to this.

113

I'm happier with the outdoor slot, the barrier of glass. The shop door should have been locked by now. The leader pulls out a wad of notes and pays. I pass him his change and some plastic bags. He stands there waiting. He drums his fingers, just where the slit for the emergency wall cuts a line across the counter. His knuckles are big and bent.

Please do not lean across this line, the sticker says for his benefit, but he's not reading any warnings just now. He's feeling insulted.

He looks Rajkumar straight in the face and says, 'I thought *you're* supposed to bag up.'

His mates snigger behind him.

He gives me a darting look – it's smug, one white man to another.

I'll teach this Paki a lesson if he doesn't smarten up quick – is what he's thinking. He's leaning over the line. He's ready to jump over. They all are.

Next to me, Rajkumar has his hand on the baseball bat underneath the counter.

Ti. Ti. Ti. Ti. The computer sings. There's a policeman waiting at Pump Number Five. And another one inside the patrol car. They haven't the faintest idea. *Ti. Ti. Ti. Ti.*

'Look who's at Pump Number Five,' I say to Rajkumar, as if we're making conversation, as if we know them personally, as if he'll understand.

The pyjama boys glance sideways out to the forecourt.

Ti. Ti. Ti. Ti. Ti. Ti. Ti. Ti. I give the plastic bags a little forward nudge. Then with a slow swipe of my finger on the screen I authorise and the computer goes quiet.

The leader bags up in a sulk and he's the first to kick at every shelf and cage and bin before he marches out the door. The shop is full of thuds and clatters.

'Saved by the bell,' Rajkumar says suddenly, fluent as you like.

My pulse is banging inside my head and I'm sweating from head to toe, but Rajkumar is acting as if he's not bothered, as if he's seen it all a thousand times before.

'Coast is clear,' he says.

'I'll lock up after you.'

~

05:00

The dead of morning. The shop is locked, of course. I've rearranged the toppled goods, put the old merchandise towards the front, and binned a leaking bag of sugar. Just like my mother. Business carries on as usual. Fits and starts, serving night-clubbers through the slot. Coke. Cigarettes. Roll-up papers. Water. Bottles and bottles of water.

Ti. Ti. Ti. Ti. The pizza delivery boy with the black eye is at Pump Number Three. His boyfriend has gone further than usual. He still says it's love. I authorise.

On *Terry's TV* all the black-and-white characters come and go like actors in a Hollywood thriller. No sign of those men for Siv. But at 17:00 on the video a lady in a light-coloured Jaguar pulls up by the shop door, steps out and heaves a bag of coals into her open boot.

Her registration plate says *1 ABOVE*.

She's been to the hairdresser and she's putting on a barbecue for her husband's friends. There's a parcel of fresh fillet steak on the front seat and it's seeping blood into her upholstery (she hasn't seen it yet) just as a wounded Tiger does.

Her husband doesn't talk to her unless he has to, and he hasn't had to for a long time. She wants to leave him on account of her deep-down loneliness but she hangs on to the notion of how things used to be. She can't let go of all their comforts. On the sly, she enters every lottery going. Every raffle, bet and competition.

I check the inside of my window, and there it is, just as I thought, the note Ken wrote about the cream Jag with the customised registration plates:

'1 ABOVE' – DO NOT AUTHORISE FUEL

On video the lady driver struts right into the shop, pays

115

Rajkumar for her bag of barbeque coals and buys herself a lottery ticket. There's no fuel to authorise. Technically speaking, Rajkumar hasn't missed a trick. But I know for certain that she has.

I want to call her. I'm going to warn her.

Gail, they're after you, I'll say. *The men. They want the money. I see it all, the blood on the seat, I've seen it all –*

~

Hector gripped his Big Idea like betting men cling to Lady Luck. It was set in his face: in his mouth, his poker eyes, his glasses. He had waited and waited. He carried on for years as if things were just normal. It was like a religion, every day, in the way that someone else might do prayers. Even at work there were comforting signs, as if everything secretly revolved around his plan. A small hard grain of faith was enough to move a mountain, let alone a wife.

He and Bill went on holiday together, just the two of them – it was nearly like the old days. Greece. No ties. No women. Bill hadn't taken a break for years, and certainly not since Susan won the divorce and custody of his children. Hector's wife Gail was back home. Out of sight but not out of mind, not for one moment.

Hector and Bill had a terrace overlooking the sea.

Out of the blue, beer in one hand, cigarette in the other, squinting behind sunglasses, Hector sat upright on his sun-lounger and made Bill a proposition.

If you rub Gail out I'll give you thirty grand.

It sounded like a line from a film, and it gave him a little kick in the belly, but it wasn't out of the blue, not a bit. He took an inch off his lager, gulped it down and focused hard on his friend.

Bill tried to laugh and helped himself to peanuts. He'd been Best Man at their wedding, lost a lot of hair since then, but he still had a face like an open pie.

Hector swung his shades up and stared to show he wasn't making a joke. (Bill was blurry now, but that didn't matter.)

I wouldn't pay for anyone else's holiday, Bill.

It was true. And Bill was the last word in gratefulness. Until now. This was the moment when he would think about the money mixed up with the sunshine and the way things never worked out the way he wanted.

This was all part of Hector's Big Idea. *Thinking outside of the box,* he liked to call it to himself. He could rely on Bill.

What Hector wanted more than anything in this world was a new life with no Gail in it – without her taking him to the cleaners, as wives were prone to do. Divorce was a non-starter. The system was rigged to wreck a man's whole life: all those years of hard graft, your worth, your peace of mind. Hector only had to look at Bill to see how an ex could bleed a man dry and still carry on pulling the strings. That's why he was making the proposition.

Bill could do with the money. Obviously. He swallowed his peanuts the wrong way and coughed, but he gave Hector a *no* for an answer, which was to be expected.

Hector slid his glasses back down and twirled a black curl of hair in the middle of his stomach. He was determined not to say a word about The Photograph. Yet. You don't look a gift-horse in the mouth. You don't give it away in a rash moment, either. You bide your time. You cover things off slowly, bit by bit.

Gail's let herself go, Hector said.

Bill was wiping salt on his chest. And little bits of dry peanut skin catching like brown confetti. From the outside looking in, you could tell he was out of his depth.

One thing after another, Bill. One thing leading to another. As bad as the worst leak you'll ever see. Where it'll stop, I have no idea. She spends more money than all the tourists in Greece put together. She was at me for ages to get that swimming pool. And you know she still can't even swim.

Hector lit two cigarettes and passed one over to his friend.

She always says you got what you deserved, Bill. She sides with Susan, of course. Not to your face – I never told you – but behind closed doors. She says it's a stroke of bad luck you get to see those kids of yours at all. Your own kids.

Bill had come close to breaking laws and jaws before now, with less to stir him. But Hector knew you needed more than this to lead a horse to water. He was saving The Photograph for the right moment.

Let's forget about all that, Bill. I fancy a lobster.

When they got back to London, their eyes in white sockets where the sunglasses had been, their noses still peeling just like they did in the old days, Hector brought it up again. They were standing by his pool.

At the other end, Gail was poking at coals in the barbeque and Belinda was telling her how she and Bill had met even though it was all a secret. After stoking the coals, Gail was using big tongs to turn things over, and feeding slivers of steak to her cat like an only child. The sky was white and dull.

Bill, Bill! Belinda called, pointing to the cat. *You've got to get me one for Christmas! Its name is Slater. Isn't that cute?*

How many G&Ts have you had? Bill called back. And Belinda put on a face and went back to telling Gail how grateful Bill was to Hector for taking him on that holiday, his first proper one in years, but how he couldn't stand pets.

Bill had never seen The Photograph before. He didn't have a clue it existed in the first place. Not an inkling.

Hector had asked him over to see the new holiday snaps fresh from the chemists: dozy grins under the beach umbrella; every Tom, Dick and Harry lined up at Zorba's Bar; sunset from their terrace. And then – as if it was just another funny bikini shot – Hector showed his friend the old unheard-of photo. The one of Bill from way back when. Greece. More than ten years ago.

Bill's upset was written all over his face. His sideways cough shot out a pellet of phlegm that hit his shoe.

Where did it come from? He could hardly speak.

It was in my camera. You borrowed it one night you went out on your own and got plastered.

Back home after that trip, Hector had been more surprised than anyone to find The Photograph in amongst his own. And then he'd kept it safe for years and years, never knowing when or why it would come in handy, but keeping faith that maybe somehow it would. He knew to hold on until the moment revealed itself. You'd

118

be hard-pressed to find more patience in another man.

He was on a roll now and announced the project's code name. *Holiday Brothers*. On the planned weekend, there was a Roofing Expo in Birmingham. It would be his alibi, although he wasn't about to call it that. People in the trade would recognise him there. He had reserved a double stand. He would hand out business cards. *A tiptop roof is the 1 Above.* (The company slogan went across a whole spread in the Yellow Pages.) He didn't have two Jags and a swimming pool for nothing.

Some of the paving tiles were loose near the deep end of Hector's pool. As he ambled around with Bill at his side, heading back towards the girls and the barbecue, he stopped to point out the hollow sound that tiles made as they shifted underfoot. He would have to pull a lad off a job to do the repairs one day – but maybe Bill could make use of a stray tile to see Gail off. A quick start on the head. Something to knock her out before getting her under water.

A tip from the top, Hector snorted.

And then Slater trotted over, all skittish and full of steak. Purring and rubbing up to his legs, like a sign.

Gail would do anything for this cat, Hector said. *You know what women are like about animals. Remember Susan with that whining mongrel? No offence, and don't take this the wrong way, Bill, but she treated that mongrel better than she treated you.*

All Bill had to do was drown Slater and everyone would know that Gail had gone in after it, with all her clothes on. The fact was – even after all these years with a pool in her own back yard – Gail couldn't swim half as well as a blind kitten in a bag. It would be the end of her, if Bill started her off right.

I can't do it, Hec. Bill's voice wobbled.

Hector took off his glasses and gave them a shine, before explaining the situation. There were more prints in a vault. One for Susan, one for Belinda, and one for Bill's mum. Addressed and ready to go out on the first Wednesday after the Roofing Expo – unless Hector himself got the bank to stop them.

He thought, not for the first time, how unlucky Bill had always been when it came to women. He watched as his friend clocked the consequences. (He could kiss his kids goodbye for starters.)

There's no-one else I can turn to, Bill. We're like brothers. He slipped The Photograph loose into his front pocket and waved the fat envelope of holiday snaps at the women for them to look at if they felt like a good laugh. Pressed against his brown nipple, he had the picture of Bill being held and buggered while a third nameless man took the shot. Hector knew that the mountain would be moved at last.

~

There's a mountain pressing on my chest and it's all I can do to stop from fainting. The computer sings but it's at a distance. The computer sings like a blackbird in fright, the way a mother screams for her babies when the magpie is lurking, hopping, searching, claws twitching, beak hungry to snap and kill.

Ti. Ti. Ti. Ti. Ti. Ti.

I'm in Siv's hot office and the TV is playing fast-forward re-runs of the days I missed. The forecourt, the shop floor, the till area. I can't seem to get the video to stop or pause. There's a mountain pressing inside my chest and the computer outside in my glass box keeps singing. *Ti. Ti. Ti. Ti. Ti. Ti.* There's someone at some pump or other, maybe more than one, maybe each and every pump is rearing to go, but I can't authorise. *Ti. Ti. Ti.* It's all I can do to grab the phone and talk, but I'm out of breath.

'Help me, Siv,' I say.

'Terry? What's up, man?'

'My heart –' I try to talk but it's just like trying to call out in a dream.

'Terry? Are you there? Terry?'

'My heart –'

'Take an aspirin, man, take an aspirin straightaway and chew it.' Siv calls down the phone.

'Terry, Terry.' He keeps saying my name to wake me up.

I think I'm chewing aspirin and the foil is hurting my teeth.

The phone goes dead, and so do I.

§

Punching between my ribs. Siv has a third eye, smack in the middle of his forehead. Red and white. Staring. Drown. My name, saying my name, waking me up. My shirt undone. Chest exposed. Siv sees the woman's breasts on me. Punching me. My sad cleavage. Nothing I can do.

~

Stretcher. Bumping. Bright lights hurt eyes. Other people. Engines.

'The garage –' All I can say.

'Giri is there already. Don't worry.' Everything organised. Siv holding me like a child. Stroking my eyeless forehead. No-one touches me like that. I'm untouchable.

'We're nearly there now.' – Siv talking like a doctor.

Driving to the garage. Computer singing its head off.

~

A tube in my leg. Something else into my arm. Arms hurt. I'm wired up. On a microscope slide. Looking out. Looking up. White coat stare too huge to take in. Chest hurts. Wearing some kind of nightdress. I'm on video. *Terry's TV*.

~

Day. Light floods dormitory. Women with cleaning machines. A new big TV showing graphs, just like on *Hospital Lives*. Head down, Siv is sitting on a chair at the end of my bed. With two eyes he reads a newspaper. His third eye is watching me. I'm dying.

~

Hospital forms ask for name, address, occupation, the usual suspects.

Next of kin?

There's no answer to that question.

Siv is leaning backwards, with his eyes shut, but the eye in the middle of his forehead is unblinking. I know I'm dying.

~

'Myocardial infarction,' Siv says, as if he's speaking English. His three eyes are staring me in the face now.

'You had a heart attack, Terry, isn't it. You were unconscious when I got to you. I could kick myself. I could see it coming.'

How could he see it coming? I'm trying to make sense of his third eye – it looks swollen, spreading like a sore across his forehead, red and white. My chest hurts. I close my eyes.

'You saved me, didn't you?' My voice comes out in a puny breath.

I couldn't open my eyes again if I tried.

Siv doesn't say a word. Perhaps he hasn't heard me.

~

'Who is this?' Her voice is sleepy.

'This is Terry from the garage. I'm calling because –'

'Do you know what time it is?'

'1 ABOVE, you didn't pay for your fuel,' I say.

It's enough to wake her up a bit.

'But that's not why I'm calling. I want to save you...' And then the words fail me.

'I think you've got the wrong number,' Gail says, but I know she's not about to hang up.

'They're after you,' I say. It's hard to speak. 'The two men. I see it all, the blood on the seat, I've seen it all –'

She hangs up. I'm just some telephone crank. I become an extra in her nightmare.

But this is my nightmare. I'm not at the garage.

'Will I be able to work again, Siv?' I say out loud.

'You are strong, Terry, but even elephants with great tusks will tremble before a tiger.' He's talking in code. He's trying to tell me something about the Tigers, before it's too late. He's in danger. But I'm too tired to feel the worry of it. The third eye has disappeared into his forehead.

'Your other eye –' I try to touch the space on my brow by way of explanation.

Siv laughs suddenly and the sound is happy, ridiculous as a fountain. He rubs his forehead as though he's cleaning it.

'I went to Temple last night. I forgot to wipe it off.'

I don't know what he's talking about.

'Now tell me, Terry, if there is someone I can call for you.'

I'm thinking of that form to be filled in. *Next of kin?* Thinking of my dead mother. My runaway father. A statue of The Unknown Soldier. Maureen, my first foster mother. Social workers, cuckoo mothers, hand in hand, making a line as far as the eye can see, disappearing into the sunset. And all the Mr Fosters.

'There's no-one to call, Siv.'

'Now, Terry, I should be going back to the garage shortly – but there must be some things you need from home. You will be staying here for observation, maybe three days, depending. Tell me what I can gather up for you.'

The blackbirds will be singing their hearts out at the Nightingale Estate. The lift will be stinking. The numbers will light up red for each floor, every floor except thirteen and fourteen. The doors will grind open at fifteen. There are three locked locks for him to open. Then he'll see inside my hermit shell: blinds down, papers spread about, paths in the carpet, cupboards full of soup. The secret case packed tight with my earnings. His idol picture which I stole without meaning to, which I kept planning to return. Which he knows I have, but doesn't ask for. Which an honest man would give back. Which was not a theft.

No-one ever goes into my flat. It's like being stripped, searched, exposed in public. But Siv has seen my half-hearted woman's breasts, my shame. He's seen me nearly naked. He saved me. Twice. If I let him go, he'll see what kind of place I live in, and feel sorry for me. If I let him go, he'll give me my job back. He'll look after me forever. Even if I am wearing a nightdress.

'My pyjamas. Some things to wash and shave with.' *Now wash your hands you lazy – yes you.* I remember upward-flying splashes from somewhere. Someone nameless and white flinching at Siv's touch.

I don't notice him leaving.

~

A nurse appears, fairer than the Virgin Mary. She jiggles things, writes things, asks all kinds of questions, pumps my arm and takes my pulse, touches me all over. I'm not used to this. I am untouchable. She picks up the blank form, taking a pen out of her pocket.

Next of kin? she says.

It's taunting like a photo booth. *Choose your background.* No-one asks to be born, let alone the rest of it, but some people choose to end it all for prudence, or for politics, for better or for worse. Come to think of it, they choose their foreground. Not me. I've been face to face with my end, and I'm hanging on like a hookworm.

Next of kin? the form keeps asking me, silently, like a question on a sticker, like a question on a lottery till, endlessly repeating. *Have you asked for that extra sale?* Like dogs racing around a track, stuck on a betting shop door. *Next of kin.*

I clear my throat and spell out his name: 'Sivalingam Easwaran.'

Sister Mary takes dictation. The form speaks through her, more questions.

Relationship to you?

'Foster father.'

Her eyebrows go up and then she moves on to another question. 'Do you know if heart disease runs in the family?'

And then I remember the little fox plaque, the redhead that turns to look at you, through you. Through me.

'Next of kin,' I say. 'Kandy.'

Sister Mary's pen hovers. She's waiting for the surname, but I don't know what comes next. I don't even know Kandy's real first name. Just wondering about it wears me out.

~

Siv returns from the Nightingale Estate with a Safeway bag in his arms. He takes my mail out and places it on the trolley by the bed. He needn't have bothered. I don't get proper letters like he does. Just bills and fliers and offers. People only want my money. Siv puts my keys down like a paperweight. He looks inside the bag.

'Pyjamas. Change of clothes. Toiletries. Some apples and some grapes.'

The fruit didn't come from my fridge. I never touch the stuff if I can help it. In any case I don't feel like eating anything just now. I feel like dying, like everyone in the world is dying. Rotting. Crumbling. Giving in. This ward doesn't fool me, not for a second.

My heart is on *Terry's TV*, making patterns, drawing conclusions.

'Can I call Kandy for you?' Siv asks out of the blue. He hasn't met her. I don't know how he's heard of her. Maybe what he's got in mind is that town on his map. The navel. He puts the bag on the lower shelf of my trolley.

'Terry, would you like Kandy to visit?'

Imagine Kandy limping into this place. She'd look like a patient. Or wearing her satin robe and nothing else – the front of it would blow apart, revealing her private parts, like hospital curtains in the morning. Or Kandy in a nurse's uniform with a plunging neckline. Sheer black tights. Not a shred of underwear. All kinds of examinations. My heart beats a little faster on *Terry's TV*, making jagged mountains.

I tell Siv her phone number. She'll be asleep now, unless she's staying up late to do her homework. I know she's got exams.

'Kandy works nights, like me,' I say, and it hurts. I don't tell him that Kandy is my one true love.

~

I don't know where Siv's gone, but when I wake up there's a

nurse pulling curtains around me. She's the spit of Verena. She curves in and out like a double bass. The bed is my desert island, but the world is suddenly inside the soft green booth and I'm not exactly feeling cosy. A man who talks like the star of *Hospital Lives* checks my charts and asks rude questions. He doesn't look me in the eye. To all and sundry (the actors who wear white coats or uniforms) he announces the story of my body and the failure of my heart. He calls me a classic case. When it comes to personal details, he doesn't hold back. If anything, his voice gets louder. Everyone takes their turn to prod me. Two of the students put their heads together and whisper. I'm sure I hear them say *she-male*. They get told off for having a poor attitude. Verena is staring at my chest. Then she pulls the green screen back. The curtain rings rasp and catch, rasp and catch, louder than a tetchy thieving jerking magpie.

~

'Look, it's you.' Kandy is standing at the end of the bed. At least I think it's her. She looks different.

'Miss Butterfly!' I sigh. 'You look different.'

'So do you, if you don't mind me saying.'

She seems fairer, redder, smaller than my Kandy, as if the big space here will swallow her up. She's wearing a fuzzy pink jumper and black army trousers.

'What time is it?'

'Way past my bed-time – and yours,' Kandy says, half-smiling. She looks at her watch. 'Three thirty, just about. You've been in here all day.'

'And you? – I've been sleeping.'

'I just arrived.'

'How long have you been here?'

'Don't worry, pet, this one's on me. No charge. No clock-watching, all right?'

Kandy grips the bars at the end of the bed and makes her way over to the bedside trolley.

'Think of it as your loyalty bonus.'

127

She picks up my mail with her strong hand.

'You never said you lived at the Nightingale Estate,' she says. 'I know a couple of your neighbours.'

I don't. I can't say I know a single one.

'Lucky you've got that boss of yours.' Kandy clips her calliper into the bend-position for kneeling. She rummages through the Safeway bag. She helps herself to some grapes. She's going through my folded clothes, my pockets, the trolley drawer. Then she clicks her calliper into upright and hoists herself to standing.

'Someone's looking out for you, then.' Her eyes are green. Or grey. She spits grape pips into her good hand. Her front tooth is chipped. Like *Terry's Mug*. I'd never noticed.

Kandy strokes my forehead with her weak hand. Her bracelets jangle and clash. Her fingertips feel cool. With her long pink nails, she tidies my hair, combing it slowly, carefully, to one side, just like in the photos. It's as if she's dressing me.

'So tell me, baby, tell me everything.' Her voice is soothing.

I'd keep myself to myself. I'd tell her about the see-through people, the deadly sins, the deadly virtues, the usual suspects – but all I can think of is the story of the baby born in the corner shop with all that muck in its eyes.

Nightmare, you are. You'll never amount to anything.

I've never told that to anyone.

'For her it wasn't love,' I start. 'Not at all. I know that.'

~

Kandy's gone.

Siv's gone.

I'm lying on a giant sponge, ungiving as the gut of The Brown Sturgess. Slowly but surely it's sucking out every last drop of me, bleeding me dry. Everyone is lying on their own sponge. Releasing spots and stains, seepings, leakings. Leaving shadows of their bodies when they die.

128

~

I dream of the Whistling Woman. She's dancing her way through palm trees around the big lagoon, like Julie Andrews in *The Sound of Music*. Her song is making crazy mountains on the monitor. She's the woman from *Brigadoon*, waiting all her life for just this moment. She's so happy her heart wants to sing for love. But something terrible is lurking underneath the water. The Whistling Woman is in danger. She doesn't know it and there's nothing I can do. I'm stuck. Paralysed. Wired up to *Terry's TV*.

~

I try to press the shape of me into my sponge. Plastic squeaks far below me. I've never slept anywhere but my own bed. I'm trapped in purgatory. I know I must wait. The patient has to bide his time, watchful as a tick.

~

When the guinea worm inside you has had enough, it simply has to get out. Its head pokes through the burning skin in your thigh, coughing up babies, looking for water. You have to take things slowly. Try pulling it out too fast and the worm will break. Then you're in big trouble.

You have to get a winding stick. You have to lie still. Inch by inch you turn it, coil it, spool it, wind it, day after day, week after week. Until at last the parasite is out.

§

It's broad daylight when I get back to the Nightingale Estate. I can't remember the last time I saw the big security floodlights turned off. It's way past my normal bed-time. Two boys sitting on a broken wall go quiet as I pass. A foreign woman (disguised in a headscarf) parks a car. An old man appears to be dozing on a bench. I can't see what he's been up to – come to think of it, I haven't seen through a single soul in days. Did the doctors notice? Did they add that to their list of symptoms?

On the home stretch, a clutch of prams rolls past me, pushed by whispering mothers. Not one of them is porous. A gust of wind slaps a newspaper against my shin. Apparently another little girl is missing. I kick it off. A man leans out of a first-floor window, shouting some kind of garble in the direction of the second floor. Doesn't anyone have a job to go to? Out of nowhere, a pizza delivery boy overtakes me on a whining scooter. He turns back as if he wants to tell me something. I don't recognise him. I don't know his name. I don't know what hurts him.

Someone has been feeding my blackbirds. There's a fresh scattering of diced bread and currants on the scabby lawn beneath the trees. Raisins too, if I can believe my eyes. There's more than enough for everyone, even the magpies.

My birds don't seem to have missed me. You'd be hard-pressed to say they ever knew me. They just carry on pecking at the ground as if I wasn't there. As if I'd become a different kind of animal altogether.

The doctors told me to change my life. *The Body in Question.* They've given me tablets and all kinds of instructions. More of this, less of that. *Don't be straining your heart all over the shop.* They're not fond of my limpet ways, even if I am. I've left my shadow on one of their sponge beds. I've left my stories on *Terry's TV.* The sun is shining, bright and cold, and it doesn't hurt my eyes.

~

Thirteen and fourteen fail to light up as usual: at least I can laugh at that. The lift grinds open at the fifteenth floor: there's comfort in the sound. But trouble lurks below the surface of things, I can feel it. I know it before my keys are out. My door's not locked. Since when? My door's not locked. Did Siv forget? Has someone broken in? Just as well I hid my savings. The door smells faintly of musk and smoke. Is Kandy in there, waiting for me? Of course she knows where I live now. She said she even knew my neighbours. She could have let herself in. Free of charge.

'Kandy?' My voice sounds small at the threshold.

The living room blinds are up. I always keep them down. I can barely see on account of the sunshine crashing through the windows, lighting up the smoke – or is it dust?

'Kandy?' I'm like a husband coming home after the war. Who knows what his wife's been up to?

But there's no reply, and nothing is where it should be. All the sorry sons, all the dead wives, the problem fathers – all my newspapers have been gathered into straight-edged piles, making space on the floor. Someone has stuffed the wastebasket with free pizza offers, takeaway menus and fortune tellers' fliers. There are plenty more somewhere – I can't remember where they normally should be. In the clearing on the carpet, I see Siv and Kandy making love like tigers. Behind me a blackbird is singing its head off – not the *ti ti ti* of fright, but a happy song that echoes up and down the public stairwell, full of disregard and teasing.

Of course, I am alone. I'm standing at my doorstep, totally alone.

Then I see the note. It's tucked into a bowl of fresh fruit.

To those who cannot smile in the face of misfortune, the wide world will be full of darkness even during day.

I'm standing there, reading Siv's message over and over, looking for clues. He's in some kind of trouble. He hid the note, but he knew I'd find it, just as he knew I'd spot his third eye before it disappeared back into his forehead. Has he taken his idol back too? It's his, after all. He'd have every right. If only I could remember where I hid it. I bet – but then again, I'm not the betting type. The more you know the less you bet, and I'm not about to get emotional.

But then I do. My tin is empty. *Tea for Two*. The happy couple, me and Kandy holding hands, my life's savings – I'm throwing tea and biscuits all over the kitchen floor. All over the shop. But it's my mother's vanity case I should be looking for. My blue leatherette case with the mirror inside.

Plastic bags. Cornflakes boxes. Empty jars.

It's gone.

Soup cans are rolling.

Gone.

The front door was left unlocked. Of course it was.

I've been robbed.

How much money? I start counting in my head.

Everything.

What else is missing?

Gone.

My life. I don't throw things away.

They gave my heart back with one hand, and stole my vision with the other.

Gone.

All I had to show for my life.

They chose their moment: as I lay dying, clinging on for more time – gasping for it, gagging for it in a hospital nightdress.

Gone.

Everything. They took their chances. They took a gamble, all or nothing.

Gone.

They played me for a fool.

Who?

§

'Your eyes look better,' Kandy says to greet me. I can't say the same for her. There's a dark lump and cut above her temple. 'I half expected you to cancel.'

'Kandy, let me in.'

She stands back, prompt as you like, and closes the door behind me. Her flat is hazy blue with smoke. There's a kind of tea-coloured dew all over her ceiling. I've never noticed that before. It's like a special paint effect, although in some places the drops have gathered into hanging beads.

'I think you smoke too much.' I'm trying to count the drips.

'I'll quit, baby, if it bothers you.'

Is it that easy?

She goes to put the kettle on, same as ever. Then she sets about washing my *Terry's Mug* at the sink. Through her kaftan, the cheeks of her buttocks twitch and dance in time with her jangling bracelets. I've never seen cloth so thin. It catches like gauze on her calliper. She's dressed for a harem. No wonder the heating's always on.

'I don't suppose you're back at work yet. How's your heart now, baby?'

'Everything's under control,' I say.

'Lucky about that boss of yours being a doctor.'

'Which boss?'

'How many have you got?' Kandy teases.

'You mean Siv?'

'Who else, pet?' Kandy turns to look at me, through me, just like her painted fox. She smiles but the chip on her front tooth steals the show.

Siv's a petrol station manager.

'What kind of doctor? Who told you that?'

'He did. Back in Shangri-La, where he comes from –'

'You mean Sri Lanka.'

'Yes, of course I mean Sri Lanka.' If I didn't know better, I'd say Kandy was sounding a bit tetchy.

'What do you mean *of course*?' I ask. 'What sort of doctor?'

'I don't know what sort of doctor. But you know he might have saved your life.'

I can't forget the picture of Siv and Kandy mating on my floor. All I can hear in my head is the sound of my fright. *Ti. Ti. Ti. Ti.* I know it's not exactly real, but the odds are beginning to swing again. The two of them are thick as thieves now. He's impressing her – what kind of doctor? If he was a proper doctor, he wouldn't be working in some garage, would he? Same with Kandy: if she was a proper head-doctor, she wouldn't be stuck in this place getting knocked about by all and sundry.

I'm sitting on the bed, as usual, when Kandy brings me my tea.

'Who else has been using my mug, then?'

'No-one, pet. It's got your name all over it –'

'So who put the chip in it?'

'We can get another one made, brand new.'

'And why did you have to wash it just now?'

'Of course, I use it sometimes. You don't mind, do you? I haven't got much crockery.'

'And who did that to your eye?'

'Oh that was just a silly accident. Everything's under control. Besides…' Her voice trails off. She doesn't finish her sentence.

Besides … she knows not to say too much about herself, especially if it's personal. She's not porous and she's nothing if not professional.

Kandy lies down behind me on the bed. Her kaftan is rucked up around her thighs. She doesn't smooth it down. Her nipples make me think of big flat coins under gauze. I don't want to look at them.

I turn back to face the wall again. 'Has Siv been here?'

Kandy's quiet. If I didn't know better, I'd guess she was sounding guilty.

'No, Terry. Of course not.'

Since when does she use my name?

134

'And have you been inside my flat?' (I'm thinking of my missing tin, the hint of smoke. She hasn't got much crockery.)

'Why do you ask?' Kandy says after a while.

'Because things were … moved around. Tidied up a bit.'

'Terry, you know I haven't been to your flat. And I don't do housework, not for anybody. Better to die on your feet and all that.'

She's taking a stand, making points. It's not like Kandy. Besides, she loves it on her knees – you'd be hard-pressed to persuade me otherwise.

'Don't you like your tea?' She's changing the subject. She knows she's overstepped the mark.

I nod and take a slurp. It burns my tongue. She didn't come clean about my mug. She's too clever for that. She's a prostitute. All kinds of men have slobbered over it. I put it down on the bedside table.

Behind my back, Kandy untucks my shirt on cue and her long pink fingernails creep round to tickle my stomach.

'Can I nurse you better, baby?' Her voice is sweet again, like someone's mother. She's stroking my belly, making circles. There's no action in my private parts, not yet.

I stop her hand.

'Kandy, maybe not today. The doctors said I should take it easy for a while.' I pat my heart by way of explanation. 'Would you mind if we just talk?'

'Of course not, whatever your heart desires, my love. D'you want to tell me one of your stories? I'm all yours.'

I lie down beside her, looking up at the tobacco dew that makes a film across her ceiling.

I'm thinking about the way her nipples looked for a moment through the kaftan, and I tell her my secret story about the time I took the coins from the curtain, and how I hated Mr Foster, and how I never did run away, even though I always wanted to. Now that I think of it, running away was the only thing I ever had ambitions for.

135

∫

So Siv's some kind of doctor. Who says? Kandy says. But who's Kandy? I don't even know her name. She's Miss Butterfly, a limping lady who smokes too much. She's got bruises. Now I've told her things I wouldn't tell another soul alive. She knows me from the inside. She'd call herself a doctor.

I'm sitting on my living room floor, going through all my old newspapers.

Has Kandy been here?

She could do with the money. How does she pay for her college fees? She doesn't even have enough crockery. Who wants to be a prostitute when you can put on a white coat and charge whatever you like without having to undo one single button? She was saying all those things about standing on her feet and making a stand – her, with the calliper.

I'm sitting on my living room floor, turning my hands black with each and every page of *The Truth*. Sins are on the march from cover to cover, a man smothers a woman, happy-go-lucky faces smile in the days before getting twisted up forever with pain, more flies crawl across more baby eyes, a boy is bullied to death, a few men have all the money and win the best bets, a few men wish they did, some dress up in dynamite and go for broke. I wonder how it feels when they bring themselves off. Does it hurt? Can they have a change of heart? Maybe it feels like Duffy's fireball. (That jumpy girl got whiplash.) I'm looking for clues, looking for Tigers, looking for customers I recognise, looking for stories, but nothing joins up. Where Siv comes from, a little report says, hundreds of people die because there's an election.

Newspapers are all over the floor. The blinds are still up. *To those who cannot smile in the face of misfortune, the wide world will be full of darkness even during day.* That's what Siv wrote. A blackbird is singing its heart out in the stairwell – of all places.

My money's gone. I should call the police. That's what they do in *Cop Shop* and *The Bill*. But what would I say? That I'm

136

the one who saw what Duffy had in mind and gave him all the ammunition he needed. That I'm the one who sat skulking behind the emergency wall instead of acting like a man. I'm the one Siv saved, but now I'm saying he's taken my picture – that is, *his* picture, which I stole from him. That Siv, my manager, who saved my skin, has been into my flat and given me fruit for my heart and taken Kandy aside and told her things in hospital (the two of them thick as thieves) and meddled with my papers and left the door unlocked for all and sundry to take away every last penny he gave me to satisfy my craze for saving…

Ti. Ti. Ti. Ti. Ti.

What's a blackbird doing inside the building? Blackbirds aren't stupid like pigeons, and they're not as brazen as magpies. They're clever, but they know their place.

It must be trapped.

From the public landing, I peer down the middle of the stairwell. Fifteen floors in a coil, tightening at the end, neat as a guinea worm on a winding stick.

The song changes from panic to sweetness and back again.

There's a hand (I think it's a woman's hand) moving along the handrail in the middle storey somewhere, getting smaller with each step, fingers picking up all kinds of germs. No sign of any blackbird, and I'm not about to climb down fifteen flights on the off-chance. Nothing moves except the little hand that nearly dances as it shrinks, step by step, foot by foot, like a singer's hand on a staircase in *The Sound of Music*.

Siv must be trapped.

~

'Who's that?' I say into the phone. (Whoever it is took an age to answer.)

'Naga here. Is that Terry?'

'Yes, it's me. Is Siv there?'

'Terry, man! You all right? I thought the baseball bat would see off anyone, you know. But not the doctors, right?'

'Is Siv there? Naga, I need to speak to him.'

'Siva is not here today, you know. D'you want me to check the roster? I thought you were having some time off. You must be taking it easy, man –'

'Where's Siv? When's he due back?'

'Man, I don't know. I've just come back after my exams. Giri's on night shift tonight. And tomorrow…' Naga's voice trails off. 'Tomorrow there's Rajkumar. Me the day after –'

'And Siv?'

'It was Giri who called me up. I don't know about Siva. Maybe he's on holiday.'

'Holiday? Since when?'

'Rajkumar said something about it, you know, but I can't remember. Is there a problem, Terry?'

'No. No problem.'

'Hey, I've got to go – call me back when it's quiet if you want to leave a message.'

~

'Rajkumar?'

'Rajkumar speaking.'

'It's Terry. Is Siv there?'

'Who shall I say is calling?'

'It's Terry.'

'And to whom would you speak?'

'Is Siva there?'

'No. Siva is not there.'

'Is he coming back today?'

Rajkumar is tickled at the thought. I don't know why. He doesn't answer my question. I think of his crooked teeth.

'Rajkumar, is Siva coming back today?'

'Not yesterday, not today, not tomorrow. Book-keeper is here today.'

'Can I speak to her?' (At least the flinching cuckoo-mother makes some kind of sense.)

'Book-keeper is out to lunch.' Rajkumar laughs. '*Out to lunch* – that means *crazy*, isn't it! One moment –'

138

He puts the receiver down. I can hear the computer singing in the background. He's authorising fuel. The shop sounds busy. He's taking payments. He's handing back change. He's pointing someone north and south, giving directions. He picks up the phone.

'Terry, man, I'm spinning plates – very busy today.'

'Do you know where Siva is?' I try again, slowly this time.

Rajkumar lets out another chuckle. 'I think Siva is in his favourite Temple now. Very happy. Giri is Manager. Possibly you should call Giri for information. OK?'

I can't say it is.

'Bye. Cheerio. Bye-bye,' says Rajkumar. And then he hangs up on me.

~

Not today, not tomorrow, not yesterday.

Why is Siv not working, all of a sudden? He never takes holidays, not at all, just like me. He's just like me. Siv's the same as me. The third eye – but mine has gone. I don't see into people like I used to, and every time I remember it, my stomach ties up in knots. What's he doing in his Temple now, when he should be at the petrol station? What kind of secret doctor? He's in trouble. In my mind's eye, I can still see the video of those men who came and threatened him.

Living in London must be so fine, the freedom to go to work and Temple without fear etc, even though the price is great –

I call the garage.

'Rajkumar, which temple?'

'I beg your pardon.'

'Siva: which favourite temple does he go to?'

'Murugan Temple. Or Sri Mahalakshmi.' It sounds like someone talking with their mouth full. He's poking fun.

I can hear the smile through his teeth. Whatever he's saying, it's unsayable. I think of those long names on the map in the office.

'He's making beeline for Lord Murugan. Or Lakshmi.'

139

'Can you spell that?' I say.

Rajkumar spells the names out slowly, as if I was a child.

'OK?' he says. 'Bye-bye. Cheerio.'

This time I hang up before he does.

He doesn't know I've got last year's *Tamil Pages*. Temples don't move in a hurry.

I find *Churches*. Methodist, Baptist, Protestant, Catholic. *Mosques*.

Hindu Temples. Pages of them. Lists and full-page ads.

I find the Murugan Temple faster than you can say *Cock Robin*.

§

Dislodge a sucker from his spot and take him to the edges of his territory. He doesn't like it, not one bit, he doesn't feel ready for it, but he's got a mission on. He's going, going. He forgot to change his slippers for shoes but he couldn't go back or stop the going now if he tried.

I'm heading north. Past the betting shop door with the dogs. Past the private doors you wouldn't normally notice with the black filth like a tide climbing up. North London. Big roads. Old shops. I can't remember the last time I caught a bus. Upstairs it smells of farting, mildew, garlic. But the view from here is good. Peering down, I see a phone book on top of a bus-stop roof, an oblong pond of rippling water. The lonely ribs of a radiator. Thirty-four security cameras in five minutes. Busy roads. Dirty shops. A beggar gets up from his squat near the underground station entrance, leaving the shape of him in a fixed shadow on the wall. Seven more CCTV cameras.

There's a copy of *The Truth* on the floor. We're going uphill. An empty Coca Cola can rolls against my slipper. We pass a hospital. Is this where the daughter of Elizabeth Sturgess gets unplugged by accident, making a murderer of her mother? Where Jasmine comes to die of anorexia, or one of her father's hopeful ladies delivers a miscarriage? Where Bill arrives with a police escort and Gail arrives by ambulance?

The bus gets stuck in traffic next to a little park. Someone has sprayed the welcome sign with swastikas. Heavy raindrops start to fall out of the blue. Each leaf, all the leaves, bob down, spring up. The park is a green pianola. We move on. The next bus shelter has a plastic bag on top, spilling piles of pizza offers and fliers for curry. Under a fortune teller's awning an old woman tries to keep dry. Her hair, soft and white, catches in the wind like candy floss.

A passenger across the aisle from me has his head bowed. He starts to cough in his sleep, short chokes without a noise in

141

between. Tears jump out of his eyes onto the inside of his glasses. He wakes up.

We pass a cemetery. Maybe this is where Ray, forced into the outside world at last, feeds himself to clumps of violet roots. Where Mark Register smells sweet to thirsty worms and scouring beetles. Where Beatrice and Adam lie in the same bed forever.

I wonder.

Another run of shops. I look for numbers. Look for Siv. Another bus-stop roof, laid out with a drowned condom and the carcass of a chicken. Houses now. Terraces. Net curtains. Hardly the spot for a temple. I'm nervous when I press the button for the bus to stop. Am I too early or too late?

My bus-stop has caught a shoe.

The rain is pelting from all sides now. Gutters are full to bursting. I'm on the wrong side of the road, judging by the numbers. My slippers are soaked in no time. There's a plain brick building with a giant neon sign inside like a curly ear burning red in the rain. No pagoda or Taj Mahal. It's an age before I can cross over on account of the speeding cars and lorries. I run through the roar.

I climb the steps to the big doors. My heart is all over the place. *The Sacred Entrance serves as the passage to go in and come out of the Temple. This is the most important part of the Temple and we should offer our prayers here.* I pray for the doors to be open, but they're locked. Rusty hinges. Always closed. I clock the CCTV camera. Someone is watching me. I guess if your people blow things up left, right and centre, you've got to be on your guard. All kinds will be out to get you.

Down the steps and round the side I find a small wooden door, like a servant's entrance. Also locked. Rubbish blown and gathered into a line. Rain is running down my back. Into my pants. Another camera peers around corners. There's no way in. Maybe you have to be a Tamil Tiger.

Next door there's a block of modern flats like Kandy's. I press the buzzer without a name. I don't know what will happen next. I don't know if someone lives here. I look up at the security camera staring me in the face. Who am I looking at? Nothing interrupts the howl and rumble. Do people abandon temples? I'm ready to quit when the door opens and a half-naked witch-doctor type appears, looking me up and down as if I'm the odd one out. His black eyes are all over the place.

He's got no clothes on, except for a cloth around his middle, beads and cords hanging from his neck. He's painted white stripes all over his brown arms and forehead. He opens his mouth to speak, but he doesn't say a word. His splayed teeth remind me of the man who took Siv's money.

'Is this the temple entrance? How can I get into the temple? I'm looking for Sivalingam Easwaran. I've been told he's here. Or he was here just now.'

The Door Man looks at me cock-eyed for at least a minute.

'You want?' His English is going to be worse than Rajkumar's.

'Siva. I need to see him.'

'Please?'

'Sivalingam Easwaran.' I say the name slowly, carefully. I even put on something of a foreign accent.

He looks me up and down. I'm wet all over. I'm wearing house slippers. I might be some kind of spy in disguise. I don't think he's keen to let me in. He's got goose-bumps from standing at the door in the middle of this weather without proper clothes on. As it happens, he's dressed for the tropics.

'Sivalingam?' He parrots back at me.

I nod.

'Please.' He stands back and I'm in.

143

§

The Door Man points me down a gloomy corridor where shoes
are spilling out of a room. Inside, it's like a school hall. Some
men are fussing over huge cooking pots on plastic tables, fiddling
with gas burners, tasting food. They look at me as if I was some
kind of alien. The Door Man is waiting for me to take off my
slippers. In a way, it's a relief. My socks are soggy, making wet
prints on the floor. I peel them off. I follow him upstairs. He
looks like a young woman from behind. Black hair in a bun. A
proper waist and hips. My nose is full of incense, sickly sweet,
and the smell of curry. Bits of lint stick to my soles.

He leads me to another corridor where pictures with cobwebs
hang off a rail along the wall. There are human bodies with white
faces, black faces, blue faces, merry-go-rounds of painted faces,
animal heads, big breasts, lipstick, smiling midget dolls, curvy
bodies wrapped in snakes, covered in eyes, sprouting arms like
crabs. All the eyes are looking at me. Gazing at me. Siv's idol
is not here.

The Door Man points to a dull picture in a frame and makes
to go.

'Lingam,' he says, as if he's trying to make some point.
'Sivalingam.'

It's a photograph of a stone like a thick bollard with yellow
stuff smeared all over it, maybe mustard. There's some misunderstanding. Time is slipping. I have to find Siv. Save Siv. My
money. This fellow doesn't get it. Bells are ringing.

'The temple?' I ask.

'Pooja,' he says, as if he's speaking English. He turns on his
heels and disappears through a door.

We should offer our prayers here. I pray to find Siv. I don't
know why, any more.

Inside the big hall there are more characters just like the
Door Man: painted brown flesh, half-naked, necklaces, hips.
They could all be brothers. Some of them are sorting out plates

144

of fruit, like mothers at playtime. Others are lighting candles, one by one. Bells are tinkling. Incense is smoking everywhere. Cloths are being taken away to show idols who look smug and cosy in their fancy booths: a huge china human topped with a smiling elephant's head, a throne of three characters with hats like bandstands, a busty black doll who has the look of a devil. More people, more priests. Praying families walking in circles around a statue. Children traipsing about as if they're here for a picnic.

Out of the corner of my eye I spot a glass case with my idol dancing inside. He's made of shiny brass or gold. He's raised on a platform so he can look down. There's the familiar hoop of burning flames, the smooth body balancing on one leg, the squashed dwarf, the third eye. For all that extra seeing, he hasn't got a care in the world. He might even be having a secret laugh. *The dwarf under his foot is human ignorance. It's the dance of life.* Siv told me that much, but I never asked him for his god's name.

My Door Man is singing to a four-armed brass character in a fancy frame. It's a she-male inside a tear-drop shaped like Sri Lanka, only upside-down. The Door Man chants, throws flowers, lights an Aladdin's lamp. He's not bothered about me now. Come to think of it, no-one is. He's in some kind of trance with a whole family praying in front of him, putting their hands into the flames and whisking it back to their mouths and chins, making wishes. He puts the flames out, takes their pieces of paper, gives them each a flower and dabs white ash onto their foreheads, moving just like a priest. They put money in a safe box and then he spoons something into their hands. They touch their necks. They dip their fingers into his brass bowl, adding mustard to the white eye in the middle of their foreheads.

I went to Temple last night. I forgot to wipe it off. This is what Siv does when he's not at the garage.

But he's not here. I scan the place, peer into the dusty corners. He's nowhere to be seen. I see the huge neon ear symbol from behind. I find myself another priest. One who doesn't look too busy.

145

'I'm looking for Sivalingam Easwaran. He's my boss. I was told he'd be here. Do you know him? Siva. I need to speak to him.'

You couldn't say it plainer than that.

'Lord Siva?' the priest asks. 'All Siva. All Siva.' He makes a sweeping gesture, as if he's just cleaned out the whole temple with his arm. But then he takes me back to Siv's idol.

'Nataraja,' he says. He looks at my fat white feet, my bedraggled clothes.

I'm feeling ashamed now. 'Is this … Siva?'

'Certainly he is divine Lord Siva. Manifestation is Nataraja.' His head rocks gently from side to side like a no. It feels familiar. It means a kind of yes. 'God is dancing. To make less suffering. You pray to Siva?'

I think it's an invitation.

'Is this the Murugan temple?' I ask.

He points to another shrine, the threesome, but the male statue is a crowd all by himself with six heads and twelve hands.

'Lord Murugan,' the priest says. 'Son of Siva has two wives.'

One wife is whiter than me. The other is blacker than the priest or anyone.

'Day and night,' he says.

And I remember the time. My hands are deep in my pockets. Everything feels clammy. The *Tamil Pages* are damp. If I get moving I might be able to find Siv at that other temple. Besides, I'm not about to start saying my prayers. It's like betting. You can hope your head off. You can wish your heart out. The more you know, the less you pray. I've lost my insight, and my money, but I haven't lost my wits. As far as I can tell, I haven't lost Siv.

146

§

I've changed from the black line to the green line. Bank. Monument. Bow. Ham. Barking. No, that's too far. The tube train takes an age. It's night forever underground. Here the birds would sleep all the time. It's getting late. How long does a man hang around a temple? Overground now. Dark outside.

Opposite me a builder with filthy boots is reading *The Truth*. His sweatshirt says *Sex Machine*. Two seats away a fish-faced woman is painting a line where her left eyebrow should be. The train screeches to stop. She holds her tiny brush in mid air, then starts on her bald right brow. A gypsy gets on, with a baby strapped to her hip. She whimpers and tilts a McDonald's cup at me. My hands are not moving. My fingers are gripped on the damp *Tamil Pages*. My slippers are staining dry on the outside, feet moist as clay on the inside. I'm counting the stations. Too many. She rattles the cup. I close my eyes. We're hurtling into black space. We're all dying, slowly, every minute, every second. The universe is like a clock winding down. The more you know, the less you beg. Maybe Siv is standing in front of his idol right now, saying his prayers. Maybe he's putting all my money in the safe box. No. Not that. Those men are caught on video. That's evidence enough. I can save him, save my savings.

It's night. Real night. The rain is cold, slaps me in the face, smells like another country. I zip up my jacket to hide my wet shirt clinging to my breasts. I ask for directions.

'This way, this way.' A man guarding piles of chillies and lemons and nameless fruits points up the high street. He glances at my feet. I don't know what he's thinking.

I'm walking as fast as I can, tripping sometimes. My slippers are slowing me down. I'm hot, even if the weather isn't. The shops are lit up and open for business as if it was broad daylight. *Sounds of Ceylon. Madras Restaurant. Haq Halal Butcher. Lakshmi's Jewellers & Silk. Islamic Centre. Marriage Liaison Bureau. Specialists in Immigration.* I pick out names. *Siva*

147

Accountancy. Sivakumaran. Sivanathan. Sivaratnam. Sivarajah. His name is all over the place. But so many of the words are in unreadable scripts. Foreign. Dangerous.

In between the awnings, water pisses through in trickles and sudden buckets. Eskimos are supposed to have a hundred different words for snow. You'd be hard-pressed to find a Londoner that didn't have as many words for rain. But some of these people look like they're straight out of the desert, judging by their costumes. I bet they'd know a hundred words for sand.

The temple is on a corner in amongst all the shops and lawyers and restaurants. It's some kind of hall at the end of an old terrace, and instead of a neon sign to give it away, there's a fancy entrance like a wedding cake stuck on the front. Layers and layers of carved white, looking ghostly in the dark, maybe twenty feet high. Lights catch in the rain. I'm squinting for water. The wind is whipping cold. The rain is snivelling now. People are going in, not through the front, but an ordinary side-street door. When it's closed, you wouldn't even know it was there. I wait and watch for a while before I cross the road. My heart is running ahead of me as I pull the door open and step inside.

Shoes. More shoes than I've ever kept. A flood of them. All sorts. Used. Like mine. I keep my head down and take my sodden slippers off. And my socks. My feet are white as dough.

And beyond the shoes (I look up) another bobbing sea. Black heads of hair. Slick like Naga's. Thick mops like Giri's. Shiny plaits and buns. Salt and pepper like Siva's. Grizzled grey. Nearly everyone is watching some kind of play. I look for Siva. This time I know not to ask for him. Besides, who would I ask? There's a pot-bellied man in a business suit sitting behind a card table, a book of raffle tickets by his hand. A gang of boys standing near a wall of coat hooks. A clutch of mothers on the stairs. Cherry, peacock, emerald, gold, tangerine, pink. Through the hot press of people I sift my way in, damp as a sponge. I suck up the smells of incense smoke, oil, sweet flowers, skin that breathes out coconut, perfume, curry, sweat. Siva's musk.

A girl and two boys in fancy dress and make-up, prettier than any calendar picture, are dancing out a story in the middle of the temple. They're covered in bells, so every time they move they make a kind of music. Some invisible woman's voice is beating out foreign words with drums and cymbals. I guess it's singing, but it drones on like a spell. It's as soothing as a barber stroking your head, or watching someone draw a careful picture. The children quiver and fall, they swoon and die, they get up again and go round in circles, they make patterns with their hands and feet. I don't know how they can remember all the steps. Who is their real-life mother and father? I wonder if they'd dance like that for some Mr Foster. I try to spot the proudest couple. I can't see Siva anywhere. Everyone looks as pleased as a parent.

You'll always be rubbish. You'll never amount to anything. Shut up. Shut your bloody face.

Past the crowd, there are more half-naked priests painted in spots and stripes. Two of them are fussing over something behind a red hospital screen. Statues huddle to walls, all the way down to the end of the hall. I look for Siva, but all the faces are strangers.

The droning voice stops and everyone starts clapping. I feel as if I'm waking up. I'm clapping. I never clap. I feel happy. My hands sting. The dancers bow and bow. They're more beautiful than religious pictures. They're smiling now, like children. Everyone is clapping. A man makes a speech. I guess it's in Tamil. Everyone claps again. The crowd starts to break up, heading in different directions. Piling up the stairs, queuing for the Raffle Man, wandering off towards shrines. No sign of Siva. The air is close and muggy, hot as summer, sweet, confusing.

'Terry!' A hand grabs me by the shoulder.

I spin around. I see the crucifix first.

Giri is looking more amazed than me.

'Are you here to pray to Lakshmi?' he laughs.

Mahalakshmi. That was the name of the temple. I'm distracted, slapped flat as a mosquito caught in the act.

Giri's face turns serious. 'Is something up at the garage?'

'No. Not at all. Actually –' I say, but then a woman appears at his side. She's wearing a crimson sari with gold borders, but she wouldn't look out of place in jeans. She says something to him in Tamil.

'This is Terry, from work,' Giri says in English. 'My wife, Saratha.'

'Hello, Terry.' She's got questions all over her face but she keeps them to herself. A little boy tugs at her arm. She bends over and he whispers into her ear.

'Excuse me, I have a mission!' She smiles and takes her leave.

'Hey, let me show you Lakshmi, goddess of money. We can *all* pray to her!' Giri tries to lead me towards the screen.

Behind it, two priests are bed-bathing and dressing up a black statue. They're taking their time, as if they've got all day to play with their flowers and frills.

Should I say I'm looking for Siv? How can I explain why I'm all the way out here? Giri will know if Siv is somewhere in the building.

'Are you feeling OK now, Terry? You're looking better than I've ever seen you.'

I nod. I wonder if it's true.

Giri checks his watch. 'I'm on your shift tonight.'

What's he doing here anyway?

'I thought you were Catholic,' I say.

'Yes, yes I am. Taught by the Jesuits. But Saratha was brought up a Hindu. She still loves Ganesha. You know, the one with the elephant's head. He removes obstacles from your path. In our place he's doing a job-share with Saint Christopher.'

I could do with that sort of help. And from Lady Lakshmi.

'Tonight is a bit of a social thing, really. A good excuse to catch up with people. And the food is always nice.' Giri stops. 'So are you going to tell me what you're doing here?'

'I'm looking for Siv.'

'Siv? You mean Siva from work?'

'I couldn't track him down at the garage. I went to the other – Rajkumar told me he'd be here.'

150

Giri rolls his eyes and stamps the carpet. 'Rajkumar told you that?'

'Yes and no –'

'But you should have got the message. Siva's in Sri Lanka. On leave.'

'On leave?'

'First time in years.'

All of a sudden, there's jazzy music coming from the back. It soars and swoops like a wild bird. It sounds as if something exciting is about to happen. The priests move the red screen aside for people to see the goddess of money. She's all done up now. I guess she's ready to take on the banks, the insurance companies, the loan sharks, the crooks and the shady men who come to steal your savings.

Siv's gone and left me, just like all the fathers.

'Why did he go away?'

'Something cropped up,' Giri says. 'An emergency back home. I'm holding the fort, so if you have any –'

'So you're the manager now?' I feel like Duffy for a moment, on the losing side next to Ralph. Would Siv make me his deputy? Not after the fire, not after the heart attack. Perhaps not ever. *You suck me dry, but you'll never amount to anything.*

Giri stops to think before he answers, 'For the time being.'

'So when is he coming back?' I've got the feeling I'll never see him or my savings again. Now, even if I wanted to run away, I couldn't. Even if I wanted to chase after him, all the way to Sri Lanka, I couldn't. I feel trapped.

'Two weeks, maybe more. I think he's got an open ticket. He said he'd get in touch. Is there something…?'

'I think the Tigers are after him.' I don't know why I say it. Maybe Giri's one of them. I've done it now. I've got nothing more to lose.

'Why do you say that?' His voice is hushed.

'They came and took his money.'

'They took money from Siva?'

'Well, he handed it over. Wads and wads of it. From his pocket.

151

And from the till.'

Giri shakes his head from side to side. This time it means no.

'I think you are mistaken, Terry.'

I wait for him to say more, but he doesn't.

'Why do you think I am mistaken?'

'I think the Tigers are into big business these days. Computers. Shipping. Proper companies. I don't think they'd bother with –'

'I saw them on video.'

'And were they wearing their cyanide neck-chains?' Giri tickles at his crucifix. He's trying to be humorous. 'You know, their head office is just around the corner, up the road. You can go and check them out for yourself!'

Personally, I don't see the funny side. 'Aren't they like the – don't they do extortion?'

'Who says that? Word would get around. They'd lose the people's support –'

'I read it in the papers.'

'Terry, you can't believe everything you read in the papers.'

'No? Then who can I believe? Who can I believe?' The words break out of me. Too loud.

Giri looks around. Two priests are staring. I feel like a freak. The wild music has stopped. The crowd is pressing up the stairs. I catch a whiff of food. Curry again. It smells good. I'm feeling weak and hungry, but that's beside the point. If I'm not mistaken, Giri is looking sorry for me. I can't be sure.

'Terry, you can believe my mother-in-law. Shall I tell you –?' He looks at his watch.

'Tell me what?'

'She was the last one left and she sold her property to emigrate. The Tigers came to see her. They knew everything about her family. She was scared. She had no cash, so she gave them her jewellery. But she held back the wedding stuff for her daughter. They asked her, *Why don't you give us that?* She told them it was wedding jewellery for her daughter in Canada. And you know what they said?'

152

'No.' Of course I don't. *The dwarf under the foot is ignorance.*

'They said: *If you don't want to give us your jewellery, don't. Keep it. We're asking for a donation, no-one is forcing you.* Terry, I can believe my mother-in-law.'

Giri checks his watch again. He starts moving in the direction of the stairs. 'I'm going up to get some food. I'm on your shift, remember? Come and try some Sri Lankan home cooking – it's on the house.'

'Thanks, but I'm not hungry,' I lie.

'Well, since you've got your shoes off, why don't you make a prayer to Lakshmi? You can buy a ticket, over here,' he points to the Raffle Man. 'You write your name on it and give it to the priest. He'll pray to God for you. And you think of your prayer. See you, Terry. See you soon? I can't wait to get back to days again.'

Giri shakes my hand, as if we've just done some kind of business deal. The stairs are empty now, and he bounds up, two at a time.

I don't know what to do. I creep up after him. It's like being in the back of someone's house. Children in their Sunday best are teasing one another on the landing. The floor is littered with squashed lentils. Soft rice sticks to my feet. It's hotter than mid-summer. The smells of curry and perfume drift out from noisy rooms where everyone is talking. I don't know what to do.

I go back to the Raffle Man. He's rubbing his belly as if he's just finished a good meal. The business suit stops at his waist – he's wearing some kind of skirt below.

'Can you tell me where the Tigers' office is?' I ask.

He frowns. 'Please?'

'The Tamil Tigers. Their office. I believe it's near here –'

'No politic here!' He shuts his eyes and waves his hand in the air, as if he's moving on traffic.

A limpet doesn't let go. A leech doesn't quit until he's filled up.

I notice a little boy dawdling on the stairs. I recognise him from the play. He's still in costume, made up like an Indian princess.

'No politic here!' The Raffle Man says again.

'Is that because they take money?' I say, as if I know the answer.

'They kidnapped my uncle for money!' The boy pokes his head through the banisters.

He gets a scolding in Tamil, blushes all the way down his neck and runs back up the stairs.

Did they kidnap Siv?

'Here is temple.' The Raffle Man looks me in the eye. He's upset. 'No politic. Only grace of God.'

My stomach rumbles. I feel guilty. I don't know what to do next. The more you know, the less you bet. The more you know, the less you pray.

'Could I have one, please?'

His face breaks into a smile and he rips a ticket from his book, leaving a stub behind with a serial number. God is counting. *Have you asked for that extra sale?* I pay. The ticket says ARCHANA. I head for the exit, slipping the ticket into my pocket alongside the *Tamil Pages*. The Raffle Man jumps up behind me, touches my elbow and points me back to Lakshmi.

'This way! This way!' It's as if he wants me to use all the facilities. He leads me to an idle priest.

'No, it's all right,' I say.

But he won't stand for it.

'Put on tray,' he nods. 'Say name. Also family name. Think prayer.' He smiles broadly, lets go of my arm and returns to his little table by the stairs. He keeps on encouraging me from a distance.

My priest starts chanting and I think I hear my name in amongst the foreign words, but I can't be sure. He takes the tray with my ticket into a huge altar. It's like a white marble house, decorated all over with gold creatures and lucky charms. When he comes out again, still praying, he pours water into my hand and signals for me to drink it, to touch my forehead with it. I suppose it's a kind of baptism. His hands are busy working charades all over the place. He cups my whole head in a moment with a metal pot. He gives me some fresh green leaves. A clear plastic packet of peanuts, raisins and white crystals. Another plastic packet inside, a powder redder than blood. And all the while I'm thinking of my prayer.

Dear God.

Give me the answers.

Please God help me find love.

§

The security light turns on when I come near. For a moment I'm blinded. It's the Tamil Information Centre. The place is covered in wire mesh. CCTV cameras are staring at me. It's dark inside, but I can make out a shabby office upstairs. Perhaps that's where the lawyers work. *Specialists in Immigration.* I try the buzzer. There's no reply. It's late. The traffic thunders. I'm doing the buzzer and shouting into the letterbox, my fingers pressing through the flap in the door, my lips in the space calling his name.

~

Their head office has no name, no sign. It's worse than a prison. Bars and shutters and cameras everywhere you look. I guess if you go round kidnapping people, you've got to watch your back. And front. There's a light on inside. I press the buzzer. I don't know what I'll find. Nothing happens. I'm cold and hungry. I've been walking all night, barefoot since the temple. Traffic growls past. I press the buzzer again. What will I say if one of those men comes to answer the door? If I was someone else I'd have a proper plan, smart enough to move a mountain. I'm on their videos now, just as they're on mine. If I was someone else I'd hide behind a headscarf. But I'm no-one. And no-one comes.

~

Two columns of buzzers at the main entrance. The third one says his name. The last one says *Tradesmen* – I press it and there's a little click. I push the door open and follow the signs into the yellow gloom. The caretaker's arrow points to the right. Siva's flat number is to the left. This building must be as old as me. The floor is clean, cold, hard. My grimy feet make no sound. The stone turns to lino after the fire doors. He lives next to the storage room. There's a glass eye above the letterbox flap. I tap, tap again. No reply. I peer through the slot into darkness. Softly,

156

I call his name.

I hadn't planned this far ahead. I half expected him to be here. Lying low for a while, even hiding. Giri might have got it wrong. Or maybe he was telling stories. Someone's television is turned up to full volume. I feel around in my pockets for tools. The *Tamil Pages*. A tiger coaster. Something loose like moist skin rolling in my fingers – the herb leaves from the temple. My wallet.

My garage ID card slides through Siva's lock smoother than a wire through cheese. For someone in his position, his security is wanting. No wonder he left my flat without locking up. My heart's hammering. It's time I took those tablets. But not now. I close his door and sift inside, invisible as a fluke in water. I sniff for a hint of human skin. But all I can smell is old musk and curry. It's warm, as warm as Kandy's place. My breaths sound like the roar of traffic.

'Siva?' I call. 'Siva?'

I feel my way into the first room off the corridor. I turn the light on.

There's a bed with clothes in a mess all over it. An empty travel bag. Shoes scattered on the floor. A mug of coffee with mould on top. Papers. A window onto a lightwell. A hospital screen across a corner table, with a shrine behind it. My idol, Siva's god in miniature, dancing in his brass flames to an audience of wilted flowers and spent incense sticks. Notes stuck to a mirror behind him.

There's a wall of pictures, hardly a space between them.

A young woman's face printed up to nearly life size. A gem in the middle of her forehead, black hair, black eyes, beautiful. Then she's holding flowers, she's holding a baby, she's wearing a graduate's outfit, she's part of a family portrait, she's wearing a sari, she's wearing another sari, she's wearing a suit, she's standing by a monument, she's standing with some old people, she's in a line with school children, she's sleeping, she's sitting in a boat and smiling, she's looking sad, she's on a big bridge, she's walking a toddler, she's in the photo sent by Siva's sister. *Thambi, I'm shedding tears now for your wife and children.* She is the

157

woman in the formal-feeling couple, not touching. The young man with her is Siva.

I lie on his bed. I keep my dirty feet off the edge.

He lies in his bed and looks at her. Every day and every night.

Warm now and past hunger, I stare at the beautiful woman in the bright light and cry myself to sleep for Siva.

§

1 Creation
2 Preservation
3 Destruction
4 Veiling
5 Grace

His list of things is stuck on the mirror above his shrine. I draw back the screen. I light a lamp for dancing Nataraja. It's morning. Sun is leaking sideways through the window. I'm eating fruit from his fridge. I've sat on his toilet. I've made myself some tea that comes from where he comes from. His home is quiet. It makes me think of cotton wool. I read another note, one of his familiar biro scrawls.

There are 3 realities: god, souls and bondage. Through grace a soul can move from bondage to intimate communion with god.

I empty my pockets and take off my jacket. My armpits stink. I unbutton my shirt and peel it off. I go to fill the bath. I sink into hot water and scrub my filthy feet with his soap. I wrap a towel around my waist. I look in the bathroom mirror but it's all steamed up like Kandy's windows, so I go back to the bedroom.

I sit at his shrine and read more notes. I've missed his messages. I recognise the last one he left me: *To those who cannot smile in the face of misfortune, the wide world will be full of darkness even during day.* His handwriting is worse than a doctor's. *The best and most precious of all knowledge is not to return evil for evil.* They're like prescriptions for getting well. What kind of doctor runs a garage?

I sit and stare at my face in the mirror. *The Other Terry* looks back at me. His eyes are not sore any more, or puffy, or seeping – but he only has two. I pick up last night's plastic packet and split the top open. I dip my finger into the red powder and draw a spot on my forehead, big and bright. I close my eyes, knowing that the third bloodshot eye is still there even when I'm not looking. I open my eyes again. I light another lamp. I dab at the burnt incense ash. It's pale grey, soft as talcum powder. I drag a line from my shoulder down my arm. Another across my front. I

159

smear my face. It's like finger-painting. I point at myself, making spots. I'm a trout, a clown, a half-naked priest.

Non-killing is the highest virtue, but the taking of life will bring all evil in its wake. I know about deadly sins and deadly virtues. The suicides and murders. I write a note to Siva, just in case he ever makes it back alive.

I came looking for you. The more you hope, the more you gamble.

I've broken into his home like a common thief, but he knows I wouldn't steal. His life is in danger. Trouble is, I can't actually see it. I never could – and then there's the question of my money.

I search for clues. He must have left in a hurry. On the bed I find an empty ticket folder from a travel agent. *Ganesha Travel. Sri Lankan Airlines.* At least Giri got that much right. Cashew trees, coconut palms, waters meeting. The most beautiful place in the world. I find that envelope from his sister, but not the letter. I trip on some shoes. His things are all over the place – he had a nerve, tidying up my flat. I put his shoes away – but first I try them on for size. They pinch. In the back of his wardrobe I find a certificate in a frame. The glass is cracked. *Perdenya University.* A royal crest. *1970. Sivalingam Easwaran. Faculty of Medicine.* So Kandy was right.

And then I find another one. All the details are the same, except the year: 1972. And the graduate's name. I've heard it somewhere before.

Archana Sivalingam.

I imagine his wife in a white coat, testing my eyes, hooking my heart up to the hospital TV, appearing on an ad for washing powder. But the stare of the doctor in the white coat is huge. Too huge to take in.

I make his bed and hang up his clothes. He doesn't have many. I shuffle his paperwork into a neat pile. I read the lot, but there are no clues. Not even a tell-tale bank statement. I wash the mould out of his mug. I throw away the dead flowers from his shrine. In the kitchen bin I see his face. A strip of passport photos, with tread marks all over it. His faces are deadly serious. His lips are pursed. Four times over. He's thinking of something

160

ambitious and grand, as final as Napoleon. He's here in my hand but I can't see through him.

And then I find the drawer full of newspaper cuttings stuffed in so tight that they fly out before I get the chance to catch them. Decades of blockades. Election fatalities. Sri Lankans top refugee lists. Exodus of a million. They flee. They fall to the floor like bank notes. Some of them are in English, some of them in looping Tamil script. I don't know if Siva had them in order, but I've already made a mess of things.

There's a picture of men in uniforms with guns. I look at all the photos. I try to recognise someone. Siva. Rajkumar. Giri. Or those men from the security video. But all I see is mob riots. Rape. Murder. Suicide. People I don't know. Falling apart in my hands.

Siva has been finding and keeping all these stories ever since he left. I'm rifling through his hoard of white and yellowing paper. The more I look, the more the headlines seem to shout. Cuttings drop to the floor.

Batticaloa remembers massacre. I look for signs of Siva in there. It's his home town, but he's been away for years and the talk is all of army checkpoints and demonstrations. No holiday brochure scenery. Coconut plantations have been deserted. Fishing is banned in the lagoon. Every night there's curfew.

You cannot hear your Singing Fish.

Is he there right now?

The open drawer is full of death. It's happening now, yesterday, last year. Bombs in Colombo. Bombs in villages. Fields of mines. Army camps attacked. Navy ships blown up. Civilian boat massacres. Commuters killed. Rajiv Gandhi killed. Thousands of soldiers killed. Thousands of Tamils killed. Roads closed. Embargoes of fuel, food, medicine. India arms guerrillas. Indian troops go home. Schools burned. Temples destroyed. Women fight for Liberation Tigers. Tigers gun down Buddhists. Buddhist monks fight peace talks. Peace talks fail.

The third eye, Siva said, *has the power of destruction.*

I wipe it off my forehead. My fingers are red.

He's not here. I want to go home.

'Kandy?' I'm knocking at her door. 'Kandy?' There's no answer.

I'm wearing a pair of Siva's shoes and they hurt, but it's better than nothing.

'Kandy?'

She must be home. I know she is. She's always home.

'Kandy!' I knock louder, harder. I press the bell. The little ceramic fox is smirking at me.

Her door squeaks open. I can see her eyes in the narrow space. They're green. Or grey. There's another bruise above her temple.

'You didn't book,' she says. Her breath stinks of smoke.

'Kandy, let me in!'

'You never come on weekends. I've got someone here.' She smiles and all I can see is her chipped front tooth.

'Who? Who's in there with you? The one who hit you?' I'm furious, jealous. I want to throttle him.

'Look, Terry, it's my day off. I'll see you Thursday, pet, same time as usual.' She shuts her door. It's like a slap in the face.

'Kandy! Kandy! Let me in.' I raise my voice. I hit the door. It will bother her. It will bother the neighbours. That's the thing with flats.

The door opens an inch. This time I catch a whiff of perfume. I push hard and the door gives way, never mind Kandy's good hand trying to hold me back. I stumble in.

I look for the man, but there's no-one inside.

'What the fuck do you think you're doing?' Kandy's making a scene. I've never heard her swear before. She's standing up to me. She's got army trousers on, the same ones she wore to hospital.

I don't know what I'm doing.

'Well? And what's with the war paint?' Now there's a sneer in her voice.

I touch my forehead. I thought I'd cleaned the red off. Then I remember the ash. I wipe my face on my sleeve. I'm sweating.

'Siva's disappeared. My money's disappeared. His life is in danger. I've read the papers. I don't know what to do. I don't see into things any more, ever since – Kandy, please help me. '

'Have you called the police?' She asks the question, but she doesn't sound too interested.

I shake my head. It means no.

'Why not?'

I don't know where to start – and then I notice the steam coming off the kettle spout. My *Terry's Mug*. Another mug next to it on the bench. He must be lurking in the bathroom. There's nowhere else to hide in Kandy's place.

'Kandy, who's here?'

'So it's you,' a voice announces out of nowhere.

A woman is standing by the bathroom door. She's wearing dancing shoes. She looks familiar, but I don't know why.

Kandy makes her way towards the kitchenette. As if everything is just normal.

'This is my friend Terry,' she says with her back to me.

'What's in a name?' the woman says, as if she's making sense.

Kandy continues. 'And this is –'

'We *talk*.' I say it loudly. It sounds like a lie, but these days it's not. I'm feeling ashamed.

The woman is eyeing me up and down. She's piecing two and two together. I guess she's not convinced.

'Well, *I* talk. Kandy listens.'

'Psychology.' Kandy lights a cigarette. Her bedsit is already blue with smoke. 'But perhaps you can help him more than I can. He's in a spot of trouble.'

'It's time to choose your background,' the woman says. She's still by the bathroom door. She smiles. 'Sometimes we forget.'

I remember the sign inside the photo booth.

'Now, in despite of your trouble, I have an appointment with my young friend here, but if I can be of any usage, do please give me a call.' She holds out a card but she doesn't budge.

163

I cross the room and take it.

CLAIRE. Her name is Claire.

No, it's *CLAIREVOYANT*. She's got the spelling wrong.

Her name is Miss Flood.

'It's a mobile number,' Miss Claire says. 'You can leave a message if there's no answer.'

'Floodie's got a gift,' Kandy says. 'And you couldn't get more local.' Kandy's mopped a clear space in the window steam. She's looking out. I think she's cross at me.

'I'm sorry I didn't book. I'm sorry, Kandy. I wasn't thinking.'

I add Miss Claire's card to the filth and nonsense in my pocket.

'Whatever,' Kandy says to the window pane.

'Thank you. I'll let myself out,' I say, and I go.

On the outside steps and in the slit between buildings I hear the faint sound of a blackbird singing. I'd say it was one of mine if I didn't know better. On Sillwood Street all I can make out is the television in someone's flat, turned up so loud even a deaf man could hear it. The sun is so bright I can barely see.

$

How long since I was home? It's hard to tell. It feels like I've been wandering for days. Siva's shoes – another theft. As if he needs it. I have his passport photos in my pocket. He'll hardly miss them. At least they were in his bin. My head is crowded with pictures of men in camouflage. Lurking under my bed, waiting. Ready to bite, or shoot, if my feet touch the floor. Some nights I can't sleep. Some days I can't sleep. I dream of Siva and he's plain as a blackbird, singing to me and flying away. He tells me to make a shrine to Nataraja but I can't because my idol picture's missing. I wake myself calling out to him without a noise. My things are all over the bedroom floor. All over the kitchen floor. I don't eat. The apples Siva left in the bowl are going soft and brown. Tiny flies turn up out of the blue. The pears are fuzzy with fur. I get up to feed the blackbirds by daylight or floodlight. But I'm not the only one. Someone else is leaving out dried fruit enough to make a pudding, and yet I never see the hand that feeds them. Kandy said I should call the police. I pick up the phone and dial.

'Miss Claire? It's Terry here, Kandy's friend. We met at her flat.'

'So it's you.'

'Could I make an appointment?'

'Yes, of course. I make house calls, as I do with your friend, or I do readings from home. After hours and weekends. Pacific or general. Tea or cards or eyes, whichever you prefer.'

I might have gone into her line of business. Made a living from other people's fortunes. The more you know, the less you bet. The less you guess. The less you pray. The less you wish.

'Your place,' I say.

'You'll need to have something with you that you wear – always or usually.'

I tickle the lucky charm bracelet round my wrist. The Four-Leafed Clover, the Lucky Clog, the Three Gold Monkeys who

165

Hear and See and Speak No Evil. The Golden Rabbit's Foot.

'What about tonight?' she says. 'I have a cancellation at seven.'

'Where do I go?'

'The Nightingale Estate. Block B. Twelfth floor.'

'But –' I gulp. 'That's three floors below me, where I live!'

'Yes. I know it. You don't have to go very far, then. You've fallen flat on your feet.'

I suppose I have.

'And don't forget to bring your special something.'

~

I get into the lift. The corners are damp with the usual stink of piss and disinfectant. Fourteen and thirteen fail to light up, like floors that don't exist. Then the number twelve comes alive, a bell tings and the doors scrape open.

It feels wrong to get out. I don't know any of my neighbours. Her landing is just like mine: you'd be hard-pressed to tell the difference. Only her flat has a wire mesh door and it makes me think of silver fishnets.

I press the buzzer and wait.

'Who is it?' a voice says from inside.

'Terry.'

'So it's you.'

I hear the jangle of keys.

'I knew it.'

The first door opens.

Dear God, I pray. *Give me the answers.*

Her flat is full of knick-knacks. Pictures of Arabs and swans and French cafés. A curly dagger. A ceramic dog. Dolls in national costumes. We pass the kitchen and the fridge door is swarming with magnets. Her living room is dark because the curtains are drawn, so she switches on the main light. Souvenirs everywhere you look. Horse brasses. Photos. Clocks on the mantelpiece.

We sit at a card table covered in green cloth.

'Pacific or general?' she asks.

166

'Specific.'

'Tea leaves, cards or eyes, whichever?'

I think of my old savings tin. *Darjeeling. Assam. Ceylon.* My *Terry's Mug.*

'Tea,' I say.

'I knew it. It's in the pot. And have you brought the special something that you wear?' Her eyes are bright and round.

'I've worn this ever since my mother –' I stop before I give away too many clues. Kandy said this woman has a gift, but Kandy isn't always right.

'Ah, yes,' Miss Claire says. She pours tea into two old-fashioned china cups. Tiny swallows weave in amongst rose garlands.

'Ceylon, the best,' Miss Claire says as I take my first sip.

It goes down the wrong way. I cough.

'But before we take things further, I'm going to ask you some questions.'

And then she asks me what month of the year it is, and how many freckles are on her back, what was the last thing I ate and what do I secretly wish for.

'You see…' She holds up a piece of cardboard from nowhere.

She's drawn cartoon eyes in felt tip all over it. One pair of eyes is looking straight up. Another pair looks up left. Two eyes look up right, and two look down.

'You see?' She shakes the cardboard. Then she talks so fast I feel breathless just listening.

'I asked you four types of questions. What month? Of course you know that already – your eyes went straight up to get the answer off the shelf. That's *certainty.* My freckles? Of course you can't know, so your eyes moved up and left. That's the *unknown,* the *no.* What you ate, you know, but you have to think a while before you get the answer.'

She raps the eyes that look to the right.

'That's *doubt,* but it's short-lived. Then it's *agreement.* And what you secretly pray for, you try to hide from me. *Inner truth.'*

167

She shakes the eyes and throws them to the floor.

'*That* is what the impostors rely on: your body language. To know when they're getting somewhere. They make it up as they go along. Guesswork.'

I'm thinking the more you know, the less you guess. Her hair matches the wallpaper, a kind of cinnamon colour. She's wearing a thick green cardigan. She must be forty-something, but it's hard to tell.

'You must appreciate that I am not – and I quote – I am *not* going to cook the books. My mother had a gift. She passed it on to me. I reach out and touch things with my inner eye. Like an invisible finger, I'll pick up for you what you can't see with your own two eyes.'

It's like a speech. She rattles through it.

'Sometimes I make mistakes – we all do in this life. To err is to forgive. But what I *can* tell you is that I average ninety-eight percent accuracy.'

She takes my hands in hers. Her fingers are cool and smooth.

'Now, if what I'm saying is not your cup of tea, you can leave at this junction, and there'll be no hard feelings and no fee – I don't do this for the money.'

She leans forward. She's still holding my hands in hers.

I don't want to let go.

'Or you can pass me your special something, and we'll begin.'

I unclasp the bracelet and give it to her. I don't know what to do with my hands after that.

'Good,' she says, smiling. 'Now, don't say a word.' Miss Claire fondles my lucky charms and closes her eyes.

I hear minute after minute, clicking loudly from all her clocks.

Her eyebrows are two perfect half-circles, high above her unseeing lids.

'Mmm,' she hums. 'Mmm.'

Her hair is a cloud of cinnamon curls. Her skin is like a peach.

168

There's a spray of freckles on her forehead. I wonder how many are on her back. She reminds me of somebody.

'She misses you,' Miss Claire says suddenly, like a woman talking in her sleep.

'Oh, how she suffered! – but now the ball's on the other foot, isn't it? It's *you* who have suffered. Yes, I can see that. – Are you feeling the old pain now?'

I clear my throat to talk but Miss Claire holds her hand to her lips the way librarians do on TV. Some shiny coral lipstick ends up on her finger.

'Mmm. She didn't mean some of the things she said.'

Nightmare you are, with all that crap in your eyes.

'Mmm. She loved you – loves you still. Mmm. She did her best, in the way that she knew how. Her hands were tied.'

I think of my mother in the corner shop with the blinds down, her head in a wax paper bag. I don't remember her hands being tied. I think of the man who slipped away just like all the fathers, quick to close their zips until another time. The sundries man, the shouting man, the married man, the stranger delivering nothing, paying for nothing, taking nothing away. I've seen a shadow of him in every man.

'Mmm. There's a man. I don't know his name. Mmm. She can't tell me.'

Miss Claire suddenly opens her eyes and they're shining wet, as if she's been crying.

'You can talk now.'

But I've got nothing to say. Her clocks tick through the silence.

I finish my tea.

She takes my teacup and turns it slowly around in her hands.

Why does she have so many clocks?

'I still see a man. He's like a father figure to you. Do you know his name?'

I shake my head. It means no. I thought she was supposed to tell *me*. My heart's thumping. I wonder if she can see that much.

'In any case, he's gone. Gone. Gone for good, in one foul sweep,' Miss Claire mutters. 'He took a gamble. Life's a lottery. He made his bet. He was very important to you, but he's not important now. The wheel has come full circle. You will never see him again. You must let go of him. You must choose your background. He's gone for good.' She spreads her hands wide and flat on the green cloth and then she wipes them in mid air, just like a croupier quitting the table.

Who's gone for good? I'm thinking of Siva, but maybe she means my unknown father. I'm wondering if Miss Claire sees stories the way I used to, if she has my sort of insight, enough to call a sickness, if she lives inside people like I did, like a tapeworm taping.

She said I must let go. The most important step in a parasite's life is that final journey: leaving the host.

She's still staring into my cup. 'There!' she says. 'You see?'

All I can see is clumps of brown in a soggy jumbled mess. That's the thing with loose tea.

'You see the ups and downs? I see travelling. Long distance. I see a ship. Someone is making waves. Is it a cruise? No. But there is desire. Someone yearning to go to sea. But remember the Jumblies. They went to sea in a sieve.'

Did she say his name? Did Siv go by boat? Is that what she's seeing?

'I see a palm tree. Oh yes, a palm tree. It must be hot. And foreign. It's in a holiday brochure. But what's that?' Miss Claire is startled.

'I smell baby powder. No. It's suntan lotion. No. It's perfume. A woman's perfume. A peach. Yes. And flowers. No. And spices. Nutmeg. Yes. No. And cinnamon. Yes. Yes.'

I want to hold her hands again.

'Ah yes.' She looks into my eyes. 'A cinnamon peach. She has soft hair. She has waited for ... for such a long time.'

She might be thinking of Kandy. Her hair is the right colour.

'Do I know her already?' I ask.

'You know her, yes. And yet you do not know her. There's a

170

block. Some kind of obstruction.' Miss Claire pats her heart by way of explanation.

'Do you have another question?'

'Yes.' I think of my questions, one at a time.

Miss Claire's eyes are shining with expectation.

'I've thought of my questions,' I say.

'You need to say them.'

But I don't want to say them out loud. She should know my questions from the inside looking out. She should know the answers. She peers into my cup again.

'You have questions about money. About love. About someone you've lost. About your work. – But what's this? I see fire. Yes. Flames. Yes. A flaming fire. Yes. A ring of fire. It's a circus. No. It's a hoop you have to cross. Yes. I see the signs of work. And reward, yes, there: the hoop of fire becomes a crown. You are working very hard. It's dark. It's night. You're managing things. You are in charge. Yes. No. You're not there now, but you will be. It's just a matter of time. You will be. Not now, but then. After. Yes, after. I see people listening to you, a small circle of people listening. You're on a pedestal. No. A stage, a kind of – what's the word? – a podium, a sort of booth. Yes. I see light. Yes. Bright lights. You wear the crown. The people are listening to you. You're not famous, not like a pop star walking down the street, or a Hollywood actor. No. Not at all. But you wear the crown. Mmm. Be careful! Someone wants your money. Yes, someone wants your money. Don't just give it away. Hold onto it. Yes. Hold onto it.'

She stops to take a deep breath. She looks into my eyes. I feel naked. She reads eyes.

'My life – my question is – where...?' I can hardly say the words.

'Have you looked below your feet? Perhaps you're standing on it. Sometimes the thing you are looking for is just there before your very eyes.'

I am lost in her eyes. Her shiny button eyes with the looping eyebrows high on top. Her eyes are full of questions. Hazel. Or brown. Disappointment. Unfinished business. I wonder how eyes become windows to a body's soul. I don't mean the surface flecks or spots and stains. I mean the look inside that comes outside. You'd be hard-pressed to explain the physics of it to a blind man.

'What thing am I looking for?' The question flies out before I can hold it back.

Miss Claire puts my teacup down on its side. The saucer clanks. The dregs spill onto the green cloth. I notice other marks, old spills. Miss Claire checks a clock. Another clock. Her watch.

'Some questions have no answers,' she sighs. 'And I'm afraid that's the end of your session, now. Readings can be so … so draining! The gift comes from deep inside. One needs time to refill. Like petrol. If you know what I mean.'

'Yes, I know.' How much has Kandy told her? My heart feels like a bird trapped inside my rib cage.

Her eyes are downcast. 'I've been doing this since … since I was literally green behind the ears. And you know …' She sighs again. 'It never gets easier!'

'Next time I want you to read my eyes,' I say. The words pop out of me. As if they were waiting inside my mouth.

She looks up and she takes the answer straight off the shelf.

'Of course, yes, of course. Tea leaves, cards or eyes, which-ever.'

I pay her and I go.

Her door shuts behind me, making echoes. I press the button for the lift and the arrow lights up. I hang over the edge of the public stairwell and look all the way to the ground floor below. The handrail winds down twelve floors, getting tighter and smaller in the distance, as neat as a half-free worm wrapped around a stick.

A bell tings and the lift doors grind open. I change my mind. I take the stairs. A door slams somewhere. I hear a voice behind walls shouting out some foreign garble. Muffled televisions. Something hard dropping and clattering. The faint carefree whis-tling chirruping tricky pretty song of a hidden blackbird.

I have another appointment with Miss Claire next week. She doesn't have the gift at all, but you couldn't get more local.

S

On top of all the old familiar spills, the forecourt concrete has fresh streaks of diesel. New drops of oil shining like rainbows in the fluorescent light. I try to see a palm tree or a boat, a lost man or a cinnamon woman, but you'd be wrong if you found any rhyme or reason in spots and stains.

'Long time no see,' Rajkumar says. He's doing the changeover float, as if we were both here just yesterday.

'How is health of your ticker?' he asks.

'I'm taking these tablets. They seem to be doing the job.'

'Thank God for Doctor-ji, Mister-ji! Dentists make money, doctors earn money, isn't it?' Rajkumar smiles but he doesn't look up from the cash. His fingers are faster than a magician's.

The shop doors are already locked. At least he's learned that much since I last saw him. The baseball bat is still under the bench.

'Rajkumar, why did you tell me Siva was at the temple?'

'Little birdie is telling me nowadays you pray to Goddess Lakshmi –'

'Why did you say Siva was at the temple?'

'Siva is in Batti. Temple is in Batti. Murugan. Lakshmi. Devi. Durga. Saraswathi. Vinayagar. Anjeneyar. Many temples in Batticaloa. You knock the wrong door. Wild goose chase, isn't it? Communication breakdown.'

The computer sings. Rajkumar looks up for a moment, but his fingers are still counting. There's a fat white woman at Pump Number Four. I authorise.

'So when is Siva coming back from ... from Batti?' I ask.

'You can't really find an answer when.'

'Why not?' (I'll check the roster when he's gone, search the office. They're all in this together.)

The computer sings again: a man waits at the pump; a woman reads a map inside the car. I authorise. A pizza delivery boy stands by Pump Number Three. I authorise.

173

'Why don't you know when?'

Rajkumar stops counting and looks me in the eye.

'Emergency back home. Trouble.'

'What sort of trouble?'

'Trouble you don't know about.' His face is so serious I feel stupid. 'Trouble you cannot fathom out.'

The dwarf under his foot is ignorance.

Rajkumar feeds notes and coins into the till trays. He drops a bag of cash into the floor chute. He writes the bag number and the total on the night deposits sheet. He notes the time. *23:00.* He signs the shift control form. I remember he is an irrigation engineer. A material witness.

'Time to party,' he grins. 'You set me free.'

I go with Rajkumar through the empty shop. I lock up after him. I follow him with my eyes across the forecourt, across the tanks, across the shining spills, until he disappears into the darkness beyond the glare.

~

Giri has left me a pay packet. He's written on the envelope.

Terry welcome back

XXX from Lakshmi!!!

I suppose he thinks it's funny. But he's paying me for my time off, which is just as well. Fortune tellers and psychologists don't come cheap. I count the cash and slip it into my pocket.

I check the new roster and there's my name again across nights. On days there's Giri, Rajkumar, Naga, everyone but Siva. His office is tidy. There's a note for me, but it's not from him.

Fuel delivery due tonight.

Check tank levels.

I miss Siva's messages. I look for his scribble in amongst a pile of papers. Bills. Letters addressed to him. Notification of the next regional managers' meeting. Shift control sheets. Forms. Nothing.

I stare at the map on the wall. The floating tear-drop. *Jaffna. Trincomalee. Batticaloa.* I wonder if he's there right now, in

174

amongst the biro jabs. If he's dead or alive. If he'll ever come back. *Adam's Peak. Kandy. Colombo. Mount Lavinia.* It sounds like a story, and Kandy's in the middle of it.

And then I find a handwritten schedule of things to do. No date. Coffee stains. A change of biro halfway through. At the end of the list I see my phone number and the message: *NB Make sure Terry knows I've gone.*

The writing is a doctor's, such a scrawl that it's a wonder anyone could read the numbers. And no-one did.

§

Today I'm booked in. The usual time. I'm holding a bunch of flowers from the garage. The birds are singing. Early morning sunshine puts a gleam on the little red fox.

She opens the door. 'I half expected you to cancel.'

I nearly did. She has the knack of reading my mind. She's got the gift if anyone has.

'These are for you,' I say.

Kandy takes the flowers in her good hand and you can see she's touched.

'You didn't have to, pet.'

'I'm sorry. I don't go around smashing things like other people. I know it sounds stupid, but we've lasted longer than most marriages.'

'You coming in or what?' she says with a half smile.

I feel like saying no. I follow her inside. Her calliper is on show. It looks like a cage. Her legs are thin and puny. She's wearing a white coat, the same as a doctor's.

'Do you like it?' she asks.

I preferred the kimono.

She sits me down on the bed. She's sprayed the room with musk perfume, but it doesn't mask the smell of joints.

'The kettle's on.' She's stuffing my flowers into a jug. The sink is piled up high with dishes.

'You smoke too much,' I say.

'I know, pet, I know.' She shrugs. 'You never used to notice.'

'I used to think you were my own true love.'

Kandy fills the jug with water and grips her hand at the wrist to lift the weight to the window sill.

'And now?' she says.

'You're my own true head-doctor.'

She's quiet for a while before she speaks again. 'Your head-doctor shouldn't lose her temper.'

'Your clients shouldn't barge in on you either.'

176

'And you don't give flowers to your shrink.'

'I'm sorry, Kandy. Sorry for everything.'

She sits down beside me. She waits. 'Well, then: what's the story?'

'No story. I don't have stories. I've told you all my stories. You know me better than – you came to see me in hospital. You're my next of kin. And I don't even know your proper name.'

'There, there.' Kandy pats my head, just like a mother. 'Your garage doctor came to see you too.'

'Sivalingam Easwaran.'

'He came to hospital. He did things for you.'

'I don't know where he is. He's disappeared. I thought they kidnapped him, but he knew he was going.' Like all the fathers.

'And your savings?'

'Gone.'

'And you won't call the police?'

'No. I don't want to call the police. He's in trouble. Things we don't know about. Trouble we can't fathom.'

I feel like a dwarf. Siva is dancing on my head and I don't know the half of it.

'But I called your fortune-teller.' I say.

'Floodie?'

I nod.

'She's got the gift.'

'You really think so?'

'Well, in a way, yes, I do. Floodie helps me to ... When things get –' Kandy stops and scratches her arm. Her sleeve rides up and I spot a scab on the soft white flesh.

'We're all capable of losing our way, and even therapists have to do a bit of therapy. Every one of us. It's part of the course. Floodie's not official, I know, but she helps me see stuff from the outside.'

I suppose she means from the outside looking in. I'm thinking about the bright shiny way Miss Claire looked at me.

'How much did you tell her about me?' I ask.

'Just general stuff.'

177

'Like what?'

'Just that you two are neighbours. And you work nights. Nothing in particular.'

She must have told her more than that.

'Did you tell her that we –' I can't bring myself to say the word.

Kandy's white coat is gaping and I can see in. A black bruise on her breast. The old bruise on her temple is covered by skin-coloured make-up.

'Did you tell her that we talk?'

'You don't have to tell Floodie too much. She sees. She listens.'

'Just like you?' I'm feeling like a man in mourning, getting ready to say goodbye. The most important step is that final journey: leaving the host.

'I'm cold. I think I'm coming down with something.' Kandy clicks her calliper into the standing position and makes her way across the room.

There's steam on her windows. It's as warm as usual.

'Did you see that show on TV about sneezing?' She takes a big black jumper from her drawer and puts it on. She drags a kitchen chair over and sits herself down, right there in the middle of the bedsit.

'So do you want to tell me about your feelings?' she asks.

I lie back on her bed and gaze at the ceiling.

Kandy's acting like a therapist.

'No,' I say.

I've told her enough already.

She tries a new tack. 'It's not about what happened to you, but how you interpret what happened to you. And then how you act.'

The droplets of tar are like stars reaching forever into space. I wonder how many freckles are on Miss Claire's back, but of course I can't know. *That's the unknown,* she said, *the no.*

'It's OK to talk about your feelings, Terry.'

I can't take my eyes off the ceiling.

178

'And what about your feelings?' I say out loud. 'When are you going to stop getting knocked around?'

Kandy is quiet. She's never been porous and she's nothing if not professional. She knows not to say too much about herself.

'One day at a time,' she says.

I have no idea what she's thinking.

'I don't know how well I did in my exams,' she says. 'But I gave it a try. And you never know.'

I'm counting the brown drops. I make out the click of her lighter and the smell of fresh smoke. I hear her inhale and blow and tap the ash until she gets to the butt and lights another cigarette from it. I know without looking that she's holding it with her weak right hand, gripping hard at the wrist with her left.

We stay there without talking just like that: me lying, her sitting, until my time is up.

'Same time next week?' she says.

'Yes of course,' I reply.

I pay her and I go.

§

I open the door to my flat and turn the light on. The place smells of old newspapers. Ink. Dust. Daylight creeps in under the edges of the blinds. There's a big soft stain on the sofa. I've never noticed that before. I put my coat over it. But now I see marks everywhere: age spots in the carpet between the piles, faint stains on the ceiling. No rhyme or reason. I trip over a shiny slippery stack of special offers. Pizza. Curry. Prize draws. *Act now. Don't miss your lucky jackpot.* I kick them across the space on the floor. They fan out like cards on a croupier's table.

Kandy would throw the lot away.

My living room is an eyesore.

Siva must have seen it like this. He couldn't help himself from tidying things up a bit. He had a nerve. But maybe I should do the same.

Would Miss Claire notice? Has she seen it all in her mind's eye? No. But what would she be thinking if she was here, now, inspecting everything with her fortune-telling eyes?

I would stare at my shoes, ashamed.

She would shake her cardboard chart at me and point to the down-looking cartoon eyes and say: *What you secretly pray for, you try to hide from me.*

Miss Claire would paint my walls new, peach and lilac.

I turn on the TV. I play the sound for a moment. I press the button again and the jabbering journalist goes mute. There's a clutch of women behind him wailing over rough graves. I don't know what country. No noise.

Did they die on their feet?

There's no getting round that deep-down will to live, to eat, and to make more of your own kind. If you're a normal animal you'll have no intention of dying.

I eat. Fish fingers. Juice. Bananas. Healthy food – doctor's orders.

In the bathroom I put some ointment on my eyes and then I

180

wipe it off again. My eyes are fine. But *The Other Terry* looks back at me from the cabinet mirror and pulls a face. He shakes his head. It's as if he's given up on me.

My shirt collar is frayed. I need a haircut. I comb my hair to the side with my fingers, the way Kandy would do it with her long pink fingernails. I'm wearing a girl's lucky charm bracelet.

The Other Terry is disappointed in me. He sends me to bed until I can do better. But I make him a promise. It's a kind of prayer.

The Other Terry looks back at me and his lips tremble on tiny invisible hooks. It's nearly a smile, if I'm not mistaken.

He looks like a stranger. Foreign.

Then his face splits. His cheeks bunch into folds like curtains being pulled open. His eyes sink into a cushion of creases. His teeth are white and crooked – but they're all his own. I've never seen him smile before. From the outside looking in, he's such a strange sight I can't help but feel a tickle. His nostrils twitch. It's a kind of laughing. Quiet. Inside. He's laughing at me. Little snorts come out of my nose. I'm laughing with him.

I follow the path in the carpet.

I curl up, fitting the shape in my mattress, neat as a cocoon. Ready.

181

§

'Has anyone ever read your eyes before?' Miss Claire asks. We're sitting at her table.

I shake my head.

'So this is your first time?'

I nod.

There's a Mexican doll on a dresser behind her, with glitter on its dress and a huge sombrero. A snow-dome from Russia, or somewhere like it. A blue and white ceramic clog. She must have been all over the world.

'Have you been to Sri Lanka?' I ask.

'No,' she says. 'But I'm sure it must be nice.'

'Was Mexico ... nice?'

'I haven't been there either.'

She takes my hands in hers, just as she did last week. She seems to be studying my nails.

'Are you looking for something there?' I ask.

'Clues. Insights. Manifestations.' She's concentrating. 'But there's no point over-gilding the lily. Tonight it's the eyes we're after –' she laughs a little. 'The eyes have it! Dear me! Now look into my pupils. Pretend I am you in the mirror.'

I gaze at her. In the curve of her eyeballs I see two little pictures of myself, the sort you get in security mirrors that go round corners. I am cut in half by the green-covered table.

'This may take some time,' she says.

For a moment I watch her thin mouth move as she speaks. Her lipstick is a kind of pearly pink.

'No, no. Keep looking at – *into* my eyes!'

She doesn't seem to blink at all.

'I see illness,' she says at last. 'As a baby, perhaps as a child. I see volatile projecting.'

Everything she says sounds back-to-front.

'Of course it was you. Yes, you were ill as a child, many times. Sometimes you can look back over a life and it seems that you were always ill, but you weren't. No. Be careful what you choose to remember.'

I can't help looking away.

'You're sensitive about your eyes, aren't you?' she says.

I can feel myself blush all the way down into my collar. If I'm not mistaken, the heat of my neck turns my after-shave to vapour.

'You used to have a problem, like a persecution complex, with your family. Well, perhaps that's putting it too strongly. That's all behind you now, yes. You need to turn over a new canvas, a blank slate, and good luck to you. No point carrying a millpond round your neck. No point making excuses. Life begins at forty-something.'

Her grip on my hands has tightened. She has my eyes fixed in hers. She doesn't blink. I wonder if I'm supposed to say anything.

'After a certain point, every man is responsible for his face,' she says. 'You lost your way and then you found it. A stitch in time, if you know what I mean. Yes. Yes.'

Her hands are warm now. My little finger has pins and needles.

'You love no-one. Ah, but I'm wrong. You loved, you had loved, you were loving, you used to love. Better to have loved and lost. You love the birds. You know what I mean. You've waited, like the Lady of Shallott with her sewing. Sometimes it seems you've been waiting all your life, your halcyon days, your salad years, your misspent youth, your prime, your zenith, your nadir, your fulcrum, your crucible, just waiting for … for the crucial things to improve considerably.'

I'm not quite sure what she's saying. It runs like petrol. It pours. She's nothing if not fluent. – How does she know I love the birds?

'But I see hurt and disappointments there, side by side with expectation. They happen. You can't have sun without clouds, food without hunger, success without jealousy, cats without dogs. Think of fate. It's inexable.'

183

She sighs. There's a trace of alcohol on her breath. Sherry, I think. Sweet. I wonder if she's had dinner yet. If she's ever been to any of the souvenir places.

'But now I know, you'll be asking the simple question: what thing are you looking for? And the other simplistic question: where are you going with your life? I see the questions there, written in lines across your left iris. The left is the private side and there's a fact. The left cheek is the cheek you turn away from strangers. Abashment. Shame. Secrets. Hopes. The right is the public side, the side you show to the world, your external face. Remember that, if ever you get a pimple or a twitch.'

I think of Kandy. Which way does her smile go? I can't remember. Which hand holds the cigarette?

'And now, the answers to your private questions. The thing you are looking for is...' Miss Claire's arching eyebrows go up evenly on both sides.

'The thing you are seeking is love. You loved, you had loved, you used to love, you were loving, yes, but you will love. You yearn to love. It will happen. Yes. You can be certain of that. Yes.'

The nerves in my fingers have gone dead now, she's gripping them so tight. I don't dare move.

'As for where you are going...' She frowns. The flesh between her eyebrows gathers up like a little fountain.

'I can only tell you where you *might* be going, if you make your path with your own two feet. But it is *not* – and I quote – it is *not* a certainty. Unless of course you make it so. You know? They can make a replica of the Titanic. Same windows, same portholes, same everything. It would cost a fortune. Tickets would go for a mint. They'd sail the same journey, and it would be unsinkable. But it would all go wrong. I've got a book on the golden age of cruising –'

She sits back suddenly in her chair and sighs. My hands go with hers. I'm stretching across the green cloth. It's as if I'm falling. The table edge digs into my ribs.

'You're used to hiding things,' she says. 'You're a private

person, Terry. Eyes are the windows to your soul but to me it is perfectly apparent that you've put up nets and blinds, if you know what I mean – metaphorically speaking.' She sighs again.

I shiver. A kind of panic. It's as if she knows me.

'Do you have another question?'

I don't want to tell her specifically about my money, but it can't hurt to ask. 'Where is the thing I have lost?'

She thinks for a while. She's concentrating. A wisp of cinnamon hair has curled down onto her forehead. Her eyes are moist and full of pretty sparkles. She blinks for the first time.

'Have you looked behind the sofa? Have you looked inside the cupboard, at the back?'

S

Packets of jelly. Tins of spaghetti hoops. Soup. Two hours till I start my shift – no, less than two hours. She told me to check the back of the cupboard. Things get sticky there. Old boxes of Corn Flakes. Gravy granules. Sugar. I find everything but the vanity case. I'm hungry. I open some creamed rice and sit there in the middle of the floor, eating straight from the can. It tastes good. Sweet. I'm sweating. Of course, she might have meant a different cupboard – and she might have no idea what she means.

I go to the living room. Where do I start? Stacks of *The Truth* block the doors to my cupboards. I don't remember where everything was before Siva came and tidied my flat. He had a nerve. I haul a heap across the floor and out of the way. Another lot has to be cleared before I can open the cabinet against the wall. I hug the pile and move it a foot or two, but half the newspapers slide off the top and onto the paths in my carpet. *Woman smothered.* More gets in the way of my feet. *To hell and back.* I kick at it and pain shoots through my ankle. *Pensioner lashes out.* I've had enough.

Turn over a new canvas, Miss Claire said in her topsy-turvy way.

I hobble into the lift, bent double with the weight. It's all I can do to press the button for the basement. When the doors screech open again, I catch the smell of engines and rotting rubbish.

You'll always be rubbish. You'll never amount to anything.

I heave my hoard into the first dumper. Day after day. Week after week of *The Truth,* yellow from the light, even though I always kept the blinds down.

TV recluse death. Honour killing by family.

I feel like throwing a match in. If I was someone else I would.

Friend admits arson grudge.

I fly past Miss Claire's floor and then the invisible numbers.

The bell tings home. The door to my flat is open – I can't remember the last time I was so careless. There's no-one around. There's nothing to steal. I drag another pile of papers across the carpet and out onto the landing. I block the lift doors with it. I'm getting hot. *Dad deserved to die: daughter.*

I don't know how long it takes me to load up the lift. I squeeze into the space and head for the basement. *Youth excess fatal. Schoolgirl chooses suicide. Business chief kills wife.* I drop the endless days, weeks, seasons, years of *The Truth* into the greedy dumper. I can't help but think of *Terry's TV*, the security videos which are recycled every month. Day and night cancelled. Actions undone. Memories, nightmares, visions, wiped clean for good.

I go up and down in that grating lift. A drunk stumbles in from the ground floor. Later, two foreign boys. They don't stop arguing. An old woman, leaning on her shopping buggy, rides up with me to the fifteenth floor, and all the way down again to the basement. She doesn't know what hour of day or night it is. Neither do I.

For the first time in my life, I'm going to be late for my shift.

'Hey, Terry, man, I thought you weren't coming!' Naga isn't looking too happy. He's locked up and he's got his jacket on, ready to go home. 'I had to call in replacements, isn't it?'

'I was looking for something. I got distracted. I lost track…'

'You lost weight!'

It's 23:30 on the screen. In all my years I've never done this before. Giri must be on his way – that's the downside of being a manager. You're always on call, like a doctor. My hands are black with newspaper ink. I go to the sink and wash them. *Keep your mess to yourself, you lazy – yes, you!* I'm the only one who reads the sign. The red letters have been blotted with upward-flying splashes. Like blood.

Now Naga is doing the changeover float. The coins clatter loudly in the trays. He's probably done it once tonight already. The computer sings. There's a man at Pump Number One. I recognise him from somewhere. He looks like a boxer. A pizza delivery boy lifts the nozzle at Pump Number Four. I authorise. I authorise. I don't see their stories. I'm cured of seeing. Petrol pours and pours into their small tanks from the great tanks below the stained cement. Machine numbers are ticking over, whirring, blurring, like the racing clocks that show the years passing in some old film. When Siva opens the shop door with his jangling bunch of keys, he has the look of some famous forgotten actor. A doctor disguised as a garage manager. I broke into his flat. I'm speechless. Naga flips his baseball cap onto his head and quits the booth. He crosses the empty shop floor and meets Siva at the door. They talk. Naga disappears from the bright white glare of the forecourt. Siva bolts the shop door after him.

'Number One,' the heavyweight says at my window.

Siva swipes his ID card at the security door and taps in the code.

Cash goes into the till. Receipt and change slide into the tray. Money-germs stick to fingers.

Siva is here now, by my side. But I don't look. *Have you asked for that extra sale?*

'Oh, and *The Truth*,' the man says, still at the slot.

I pass him the newspaper. There's a battered old woman on the front. She's dead. Inevitable.

'Terry, man.' Siva slips into his office.

I can't look at his face.

'The bike,' the pizza boy points behind glass. 'I think it's Number Four.'

He pays. He goes. The forecourt is empty. The computer is silent. Siva is in his office. Just feet away. Alive. Here. He's come back. I was late. My heart is singing. And I'm wearing his shoes.

13: Hope

'I came looking for you.' My voice is puny. I can feel it shake. 'Yes, I know. I found your message,' Siva says. He looks tired. '*The more you hope, the more you gamble.* Why did you write that, Terry?'

I don't have an answer. I'm talking to a man who's come back from the grave. I broke into his flat and he knows it. I stole his pinching shoes. I found his certificate at the back of his wardrobe.

'You used to be a doctor.' It sounds like an accusation as I say it.

Siva nods. The security camera is switching from the fore-court to the dumpers to the picture of us inside his office. Me standing. Him sitting.

'I used to be sick,' I say.

'And now? How is your health now? You're looking better, Terry. Are you taking the tablets?'

I nod.

'So why were you late?' He's talking like a manager. Stern.

'It's never happened before,' I say.

'And why didn't you call up?'

He's got a nerve.

My face feels hot. 'I didn't know you'd left. Giri told me at the temple. And Rajkumar had me looking all over the shop.' I've said too much.

'Ah, he's got so many things on his plate, isn't it. You went to temple?'

I don't know if he means Giri or Rajkumar.

'I left the message for you, Terry.' Siva scratches his nose. 'I was ... I had an urgent business to attend back home.'

Ti. Ti. Ti. Ti. Ti. Ti. I can hear the computer singing in my booth. *Ti. Ti.*

'I thought you were dead.' I don't wait for his answer. I go to my booth.

'Not this time around,' he says under his breath.

There's a plump shiny man at Pump Number Six. His glasses are strapped to his head. His hair like pelt has ridges where the white fat rolls onto his neck. I authorise. I wait. I watch. Siva is sitting in his office, two paces behind me, but I can't look. I check the monitor and wait for the camera to show me the black ghost by his tear-drop map with the biro jabs. He's going through papers. If I'm not mistaken, he's pretending to work.

My customer comes to the window and pays. His tongue flicks from side to side like a fat snake. I've seen him before, but I don't remember what goes on behind his skin.

I stand at the doorway to the office.

Siva looks up.

'You don't have to be here.' My voice is loud. 'You can go home. I'm here now. I'm sorry I was late – it's never happened before.'

'Yes, I know. I have some catching up to do, isn't it.'

'But it's nearly midnight,' I say. I check the screen.

23:59

'My body is still on Batti time. You remember I told you about Batticaloa?'

'I'm sure it must be nice,' I say. It's what Miss Claire said, and she's never been there, never been anywhere. But I've read about the curfew, the army on the bridge, the bombs. Those newspaper cuttings he keeps in his drawer. I've seen it all.

'I thought you were dead.' This time I look him in the eye as I say it.

He stares at me. He doesn't say a word.

'Did you pay them off? Is that how you got out of it?' Suddenly I'm thinking his life is worth more than all my savings.

'Who, Terry?'

'I saw them on video. Two men. I saw you pay them off with my – in broad daylight. More cash than I could count.'

Siva's looking shameful now. I've touched a nerve. He hangs his head.

'Ah, you mean the agents?'

191

It's not what I expected to hear. 'Don't you mean the Tigers?'

Siva shakes his head. It means no. But he's looking guilty.

'Terry, I don't give money to the Tigers.'

The computer sings. I can't bear it. I return to my booth.

A car. I don't care who's driving. I authorise. A motorbike. I authorise.

Now Siva stands at the door to his office.

'Don't get me wrong,' he says behind me. 'I'm sympathetic. They have good reasons.'

I feel like a gaping fish with nowhere to go in my glass tank. I'm remembering the notes stuck to his mirror.

'The agents were helping me to solve a problem, isn't it.' His two eyes are making holes in my back. 'It was costly, very costly, almost insurmountable.'

A customer pays at the window. Then another. A car pulls up at a different pump. The computer sings. I authorise. I can't stand it. I still have Siva's face, four times in a row, the passport pictures he threw out. You can't see the long ear lobes. But I can, here, now. I swivel on my stool and face him.

'What kind of problem?'

'It was my first time back. It has been many years. Too many years.' He's avoiding my question. 'I saw my sister.'

'The one who wrote you the letter.'

'Ah, yes, of course. You found that letter again for me. She is my one and only sister. We didn't – we had a separation when we lost touch for a long period, perhaps it was fifteen years. She is very involved with politics and I am not. This is the root of the problem. But she revealed to me in her letter that her health is so-so – and how much time do we have left actually in this life?'

His head rocks a little from side to side as he speaks.

'Now she has high blood pressure, isn't it. Having too much coconut milk. Too much rice. Too much oil in the cooking. It is common enough. But I'm not forgetting that you know – you've also had warning from your heart.'

A customer pays at the window. Credit card. Chewing gum.

192

Receipt. Signature. Gone.

I feel tetchy. I try to hide my feet below the bottom shelf.

'You went all that way –' I start. I stop. 'You threw away –' I can hardly speak. 'Where'd you get that kind of money?'

'It's a very big debt, Terry, I know.' His eyes want forgiveness. 'Ah, Terry, man, I might be upside-down from my journey, but I can see that you are upset. What's the matter? What is bothering you?'

Siva is dancing on my head. I am the dwarf. His face is anything but calm.

The computer sings. I authorise.

He's still standing by the doorway, one pace away. The shoes on his feet are exactly the same as mine. He must have bought two pairs.

'I saw you with crooks on the video and I nearly died and then you disappear all of a sudden and no-one knows where you are and you wonder why I'm upset when you say you rushed off like that without telling me because your sister's health is *so-so*?'

His face is screwed up. He's picking at the skin around his fingernails.

My ears are full of the sound of the air-conditioning system, the rumble of fridges. I'm thinking if he wanted my life's savings I would give him the lot all over again.

He takes a deep breath and speaks. 'Because someone saw my wife in Jaffna.'

Thambi, I'm shedding tears now for your wife and children. They're dead. Silenced because of some army. As far as I'm concerned, they lived for a second. They died as soon as I heard them mentioned.

'Your wife?'

His eyes are tearful. 'I ought to have known better, Terry. It's been too long. Too many years. They saw I was a soft touch. They stirred me to chase after a scrap of hearsay in the wind.' He stops. His voice shakes. He braces himself. 'The worst troubles have been in Jaffna. Government say they're letting through medical supplies but actually it's the discretion of army officers.

Hospitals are running on empty. She is a doctor, too. Her name is Archana.'

Archana. The name on the certificate.

Archana. The word on the temple lottery ticket.

'Your wife is alive?'

'Most of the time I believe so. My children also.' Siva wipes his eyes with the back of his hand. 'But what can you believe?'

A customer raps at the window. I don't know how long he's been there.

Cash. Change. Gone.

The forecourt is empty.

'But if she's alive –' I can't work it out. 'I thought she was dead. I thought, because of the troubles –'

'You thought I was dead too. And in a way I was. Who can say what has become of her? Death is inevitable. But life is only chance.'

The lottery till-sticker is asking me, yet again: *Have you asked for that extra sale?*

'I am not difficult to find.' He's thinking out loud.

I looked for him in videos, temples, offices, streets, newspapers, flats. I didn't find him.

'My sister found me the first letter she wrote. Someone always knows someone. Like Rajkumar from the same town, or this fellow here has an uncle in that petrol station. Not forgetting the hospitals, temple, fundraising – even if you keep your head down like an ostrich. If Archana wanted to find me she could have done so many times by now. But she didn't. She just didn't.'

His face is crumpling up.

'I was compelled to cross the world again before I had this realisation, Terry. I lived in hope. Always I had hope. Up front I financed three false passports with the correct visas, and passage for three people. She didn't show up. She didn't show up! The Jaffna agent had arrangements to fill the seats and the London agents gave me one deadline. I had no choice. The rep in Colombo wanted more money, but then he disappeared. I couldn't find his contact in Jaffna, the one who called me first and passed me the

194

message from Archana. I never saw any of them.' He goes over to the sink and rips off a square of paper towel. He blows his nose. He doesn't read the sign. No-one does.

'Even when you lose, you can't stop gambling. It grips a hold of you. I laughed when I read your message,' he says.

The more you hope, the more you gamble.

He's leaning against the counter now. Standing next to the lottery till. 'Why did you write that? I thought for a moment that you could see inside my soul.'

He means it. He stares at me as if he's waiting for me to own up.

I shrug. I look away. 'I lit the lamps for Nataraja.'

'You kept him awake for very long. He needs a little sleep!'

I broke into his flat and he doesn't seem to mind. Why doesn't he mind? I wish he was porous.

'With Nataraja you can be anything,' he says after a while. 'You choose your own path, isn't it. You have to pray for many years to get boons. You need to be a strong person. You get a strong force back from him.' He smiles weakly. 'Nonetheless he also needs his forty winks!'

The computer sings. I authorise. I couldn't tell you what vehicle is out there, what kind of person, which pump. I'm caged here with Siva and he's changed. I've changed. He robbed me for all I was worth – and I can't bring myself to say it outright. It's the middle of the night. A gaggle of partygoers trips across the forecourt. At my window they're after all kinds of groceries. They pay for things separately. Water. Milk. Bread. Margarine. Crisps. Cigarettes. Biscuits. Rolling papers. Water. Nescafé. Tobacco. Cigarettes. Ice cream. Water. Matches. Chocolate. Cigarettes. Coke. Water. It takes longer this way. I have to go back and forth. I'm relieved. I'm not sure what I might say to Siva. Or what he might say to me. He doesn't move. He's stuck, like a question on a sticker. A man in overalls finishes at the furthest pump and ambles across to my slot. He complains about something. I apologise. He looks surprised. He pays and he goes. I'm left all alone again with my manager. My next of kin. He looks different.

195

'You've changed,' I say.

'You're telling me, Terry. I've changed. Like night and day.'

I'm thinking he's like a blackbird. So plain, he's beautiful.

'Did you hear your Singing Fish?'

He shakes his head. 'I went through hundred army check-points. Hundred questions. I was sick to the stomach, Terry. I went to Jaffna Hospital. Of course she wasn't there. No-one knew her. *Countless thousands of people have disappeared,* they told me. I remembered my old worries. They have this type of question, the question I was asking them – *have you seen my wife? my child? my boy? my auntie? my grandfather?* – people searching, any day, any year. The hospital was occupied by Sri Lanka Army. I went to District Hospitals. Every night I was having nightmares. Fever. Waking up sick as a man with untreated malaria. This was my past coming out of me – in my sweat! The ghosts were waking up inside and working their way out from my system. Your memory is a parasite, isn't it. Vaccine-proof.'

I shiver. *I cost her an arm and a leg, I sucked her dry, and I never amounted to anything.*

'Just think of it, Terry: I came to England because I thought that I was following her. I went back to Sri Lanka because I thought I was following her. Each time I was wrong. Chasing after delusions.'

I think of the dogs on the betting shop door, endlessly chasing. Stuck. Wrong. Both of us.

'If the children are alive, why have they not contacted me by now?'

I wonder how many times he's asked himself this question.

'Do you think they might be … not alive?' I say.

'I have confronted that possibility.'

He starts tidying the cigarette packs on the shelves behind me. He re-stocks the lines that are running low. He straightens each row behind its price. He talks to them. He's talking to me.

'But perhaps they have a new life without me. They could be voting in Australian elections. Equally they could be Canadian, or Swiss – then they are happy in snow. But it is just as likely that they live in Malaysia or India – no, I should say that they have become Malaysians or Indians, or French, or American, as I am inch by inch becoming English.'

'Why weren't they with you?' I ask.

'Terry, man, they would not be the only ones, not the first, and not the last, who dropped everything, who paid everything, and fled from their home in order to survive somewhere else.'

Siva is transferring cigarette lighters into a polystyrene holder.

'Big trouble for them if they have banned goods…' He's quoting something.

'Why weren't you with them?' I ask.

'Somewhere foreign. Somewhere alien.' He's lining up pain-killers and matchboxes now. 'Off limits,' he mutters. 'Out of reach.'

Like the coins inside a curtain.

He hasn't answered my question.

'They will have new names, any names,' Siva says. 'Possibly a new father. It is our tragedy that so many of our children grow up without knowing their parents –'

He stops suddenly and looks at me. They wrote Siva's name on the form for me, and he read it.

'Terry, you chose me as your next of kin. I thank you for this honour.'

'You saved my life.'

'But that was also my wake-up call.'

I think he's dancing on my head again. My heart is a knot. I can't speak.

The computer is singing. *Ti. Ti. Ti. Ti.*

Siva talks over it.

'My life was on hold. Waiting. Waiting for what? Actually I had given up living a long time ago. My past was my excuse.'

You can choose your background, I can't help but think.

Ti. Ti. Ti. Ti. Ti. Ti. Ti. Ti.

'Excuse?' I say out loud. 'Excuse for what?'

'Not loving. Not healing.'

197

The computer is singing.

On guard.

Ti. Ti. Ti.

An alarm.

Ti. Ti. Ti. Ti.

A warning.

I authorise. The singing stops.

My booth is full of Siva's stories. His musk. The shine of his shoes.

The petrol flows at Pump Number Six. The numbers are turning over. I've got a job to do. I count up a hefty safety deposit and drop it into the floor chute. I make a note in the register. We're low on silver. I open bags of coins into the till trays. I fill in the shift control sheet. I check the tank fuel levels. I turn off the pumps nearest the main road. I should look over the stock on the shop floor, but I don't want to leave. We have unfinished business to sort out.

My cameras peer through glass and into hidden corners like a morning sun. The forecourt is basking in glare. Beyond the light, the traffic rumbles and streams. It's the dead of night. Darker than a brown blackbird mother. Blacker than a blackbird father.

'He got away,' Siva says.

'Who? Who got away?'

'Number Six, isn't it.'

I can just about picture the back end of the car as it pulled away. A memory already. Green or black. Impossible to tell in this light. Of course I didn't catch the registration plates.

'Did you see his plates?' I ask.

Siva shakes his head.

'Or the driver?'

'My mind was somewhere else,' he says.

Me too. 'He'll be on camera. I'll –'

'Business as usual, isn't it?' Siva laughs and the sound is sudden as a bell. He doesn't care.

'Why are you in this business, anyway?'

'My cousin here opened the first door for me.'

He hasn't understood. That's not what I meant. 'No. I mean, why aren't you a doctor any more?'

'Ah, Terry, I've talked too much already.'

'And why weren't you with your family when they – when you left?' I'm pressing a pain and I know it.

'Perhaps the two things are connected, isn't it.' He's run out of merchandise to tidy. He could just leave, or tell me to mind my own business, or go back to his office and pretend to work – but he doesn't. He drags over a cashier stool and sits on it. He looks at me and smiles, but the smile reminds me of a skull: it pulls too far, too tight, and you'd be hard-pressed to say it was happy.

'I couldn't do it any more.' He wipes his nose. 'When I finished my internship, I worked as a Relief Medical Officer. The District Medical Officer was on annual leave and his area was, what you call, a trouble hot-spot. I was out and about with police conduct-ing post-mortems. The victims could not be buried until a doctor had registered the cause of death. *Mob riot* is not a medical cause of death. *Hit with a blunt weapon leading to haemorrhage* – that is. Not a job for a family man to do.'

'Your family was with you?'

'I was still a bachelor, but actually I had met Archana and fell head over heels. She took her time to make up her mind about me. We got married and came back to Batticaloa. Next year was a state of emergency. Archana graduated with flying colours. Ceylon was named Sri Lanka and our first child was born. We called her Shanthi. It means peace.'

I can see the woman with the gem in the middle of her fore-head. Wearing a sari, a suit, a graduate's outfit, holding flowers, holding a baby. The woman in the formal-feeling couple, not touching – Siva's bride.

'Shanthi looked like me. All the babies I had delivered, and here was one that looked like me!'

The first one's always like the father. It's Nature's way of keeping a man from doubting or straying. Of course it didn't work in my case. I've never found my face in any man.

The forecourt is empty. A fluorescent tube over Pump Number

One starts to flicker. The computer is silent. The cameras rove, pick us up, examine us, put us down, pretend to look at other things.

'Then we had our boy – his name is Bala. He looked more like his mother. I trained to be a general surgeon. My sister loved our children as her own. She could not have any children, and in some ways that is why she is still there. Our life was comfortable, but the message was coming in all the time there was violence throughout the country. Even if you did not see riots before your own eyes, you did see the stream of ambulances and all the patients in need of urgent surgery.'

Siva's eyes are seeing in real life the things I saw in those news cuttings.

'If a man is dead, Terry, I can only certify him, isn't it. If he needs repairs, that is definitely another matter. This is my job. This is why I am a medical man.'

'But you're not a medical man. Not any more. You work in a garage.'

'But I am. And I will be again.' He nods slowly, certainly. 'Now I will be again.'

The tube is flickering over Pump Number One. It's Siva's job to call in the electrician to fix it.

'I stopped working as a doctor in Sri Lanka. I stopped working altogether.'

The computer sings. I don't look to see who it is. I authorise.

'I went to a medical conference in Jaffna.'

I know that name from the top of his map. A city. Shreds of land.

'If you saw the causeway now you would see only minefields with barbed wire and soldiers. I was crossing the lagoon in a civilian boat. I had only my small blue suitcase with me. Man, you could *tell* it was a civilian boat! We were fired upon by the Sri Lankan Navy. I saw other people getting shot. I fell into the water. The lagoon is possibly twenty feet deep. I cannot swim, Terry, I never learned to swim, and I was full of bullets. I should have drowned, man.'

I'm looking at his face and neck and hands for scars. His eyes are dry but they're full of trouble. His life is worth all of my savings twice over.

'The Red Cross reported my luggage was found, my small dark blue suitcase. Aside from the total body count, there was no other information. Some victims were never found. With water and wild animals, Nature does the housework, isn't it.'

A customer comes to my slot. Pays. Goes.

'I was still gripping onto some rope when they captured me and took me to military hospital. Perforated lung and so on. Unconscious but all my will must have been to survive. Man, someone wrote my name on the tag like a Sinhala name – this bought me some time. And then the Army Chief was a humane person – this was my luck. Otherwise I would have been allowed to die. Whichever way you cut it, Archana knew that I must be dead. They don't want survivors.'

'Why not? Why don't they want survivors?'

'Because we will go out and tell stories to the world. I am telling my story to you.'

'I tell my stories to Kandy.'

'Kandy?'

'You met her when I ...'

'Ah yes, your counsellor friend.'

The forecourt is still empty.

'But now I was missing. Archana was under strong pressure to create my death certificate. Otherwise there was no pension for the family, you know. A doctor in Sri Lanka is a government servant, isn't it. But she wouldn't do it. She had no reason to believe that she would ever see me again in this life. But she wouldn't do it. This hope of hers made me live.'

The cameras quietly pass their views, one to the next, in relay. Seven arms. Seven eyes. Watchful. Recording everything they see. Remembering everything. Storing it up.

'When I came back home, I fell into depression. For three years I could not sleep. A piece of rope lying on the ground was always a snake to me. I managed some shifts on and off but then

201

I could not work at all. My work made me sick. At home I locked the children in their rooms. Terry, they will remember me drunk and shouting. Locking their doors. Trouble was everywhere in Sri Lanka. When my sister told me she had joined a militant cell, I hit her. It was the last straw. My wife must have wished me to be dead after all. So she made herself dead in my life – she left me. A Tamil widow with her two small children ... she was just another refugee.'

Siva gets off his cashier stool and goes over to the sink again. He turns on a tap. The sound is like a drum. Loud at this time of night. He runs cold water onto his hands. He splashes his eyes, his cheeks, the felt-tip sign. He tears off a length of paper towel to dry his face. When he comes back to me, his eyes are red. There's a drop of water on his left ear lobe. It hangs for a moment before it falls.

We're under the darting eye of the camera. *Terry's TV*. A camera never forgets. But it can only remember what it sees.

'I see that you borrowed my shoes.' Siva laughs all of a sudden.

'And you borrowed my money.' I've said it now.

He looks surprised. 'Terry, I don't know what you mean.'

'All my money. You used it to pay off the agents, the reps, the crooks.'

He looks worried now. 'Ah, Terry, I am sorry that you think that. You have not been paid? Giri I thought has looked after the salaries –'

'When you went to my flat.' I just want him to admit it. I would pay anything for his life. 'My savings.'

'Your savings?'

'I'm talking about my vanity case! My life. All my life in the case!' The words sound idiotic as I say them.

Siva looks at me in horror. His mouth drops open, but his eyes say everything.

I've been wrong. Rash and wrong. I am the squirming dwarf, hot, red. 'I talked myself into it. Everything changed. I lost everything. I lost my wits or something. I don't remember things.

202

I saw – I got things wrong. How do you know if a snake is a rope? I have to look behind the sofa. I have to look inside the cupboard, at the back. But all the papers were in the way. That's why I was late tonight. I was looking. I was hoping. You moved everything. I have to go home now. I'm sorry. I'm so sorry. It's coming out. It's nearly out. I have to finish what I started.'

Ti. Ti. Ti. Ti. Ti. Ti. Ti. Ti. Ti.

I pull off my shoes – his shoes. And I bolt.

14: Love

Have you looked behind the sofa? Have you looked? I am filled with his horror. *Ti. Ti. Ti.* Doctor Siva. Lord Siva. All Siva. Dead and alive. He's never had to stand in for me, nor has any other manager. *Ti. Ti. Ti.* The more you act, the less you see. *Have you looked?* I'm rushing, hopping, inching home without my shoes. Home is where the heart is. A hoop of fire. *Ti. Ti. Ti.* I'm out of breath. My throat burns. It's after midnight, long past midnight. The birds are singing in floodlight at the Nightingale Estate. Loud and plain and crashing, just like day.

My road. My concrete path. My tiled lobby with the blind turning. My steps. My scraping metal lift with corners damp and stinking –

Out of order, the sign says in felt-tip.

Someone has already drawn their initials over it.

I'm out of breath. My socks are muddy. I'm out of breath. I rest a while. I look up. The handrail uncurls fifteen floors.

The keys are ready in my fist, moist sweat in the teeth of them. *Ti. Ti. Ti. Ti. Ti. Ti.* I start to climb the stairs. I've got to take it easy on my heart. Winding, winding, slowly winding. Floor 1. Lucky charm. Bad luck. Life is chance. Creation. Expectation. Winding slowly, slowly winding. Second floor. Desires. Secrets. A craze for saving. Winding, winding, winding. Sloth was never a sin for tapeworms. I wait. I watch. I take a rest. Preservation. I think of my favourite videos. Winding, winding, winding slowly. The fourth floor stinks of news, decay. Dying every minute. Winding, winding, winding. Rage. Time to run away. Escape. The most important step in a parasite's life. Winding, winding, winding. Sweating. Submit to fate. The meek die faster. It's a matter of honour. Winding, winding, winding. Hot. The penny drops. Destruction. Back firing. Revenge. Life is only chance, but death is inevitable. Winding, winding, winding. I rest for a while and then I stand up. Better to die on your feet and all that. My knees are weak. I think of Kandy. Strong. A bird of freedom.

I've never known a woman like her. Winding, winding, winding. Ninth floor. I'm a leech, full to bursting. A sponge for stories. If your hand is forced, you can get round that deep-down will to live. Does suicide hurt? What happens if you have a change of heart? Winding, winding, still slowly winding. Fathers don't leave because you're ugly. All men have one name. But I have tits. And gods are she-male. Winding, winding, winding. Even-handed. No forgetting the power of abrasives. Explosives. Justice is blind and vicious. Twelfth floor, a small grain of faith can move a mountain. I pass Miss Claire's mesh door. Like silver fishnet. Veiling. Waiting. Waiting for so long. I wonder if she's in there. *Have you looked?* I take another rest. Winding, winding, winding. The more you hope, the more you gamble. The more you hope, the more you gamble. Winding, winding, winding.

I unlock my door. Three locks, one above the other.

I follow the path worn in the carpet. I trip over something. *Have you looked?* I go into my bedroom. There's the shape of me, pressed into the mattress like a heavyweight shadow. An invitation. I lie on it and close my eyes, just for a moment.

~

Ti. Ti. Ti. Ti. Ti. Ti. Have you looked?

I don't know how long I've been sleeping. It's still night. I've been dreaming. Siva was visiting me in hospital. He was wearing a bloody white coat like a butcher. He held his stethoscope to my slippers.

Have you looked?

I turn on the light. I stand in the middle of the floor, looking around me. Bed. Wardrobe. Chest of drawers. Piles of stuff I haven't cleared. I have to finish what I started. *Ti. Ti. Ti.* I stumble into the living room and turn the lights on. Sofa. Cabinet. TV. Wall-cupboards. Carpet. Empty spaces between the furniture. Shadows and stains where things used to be. *Ti. Ti. Ti.* The kitchen. Lights on. Packets in a spill all over the place. *Tea for two.* Kandy and me holding hands in a flowery heart. Empty. The bathroom. Bright. My face in the mirror. Two eyes. Shameful.

205

Have you looked?

Back in the bedroom, I open the wardrobe door against a nuisance stack of papers – I have to finish what I started.

I pick at the heap of things inside. Old shoes. Plastic bags. Clothes. Junk mail. I start a spill of shoes in a flood all around me. Foster shoes, cleaner shoes, watchman shoes, garage shoes, slippers, suckers, grippers, years and years of them. More foot-wear than a temple entrance.

Ti. Ti. Ti. And then I find him. Nataraja. Calm as you like, almost smiling. Dancing, balancing, full of grace. Keeping guard night and day with his third eye open. He hasn't missed a trick. The vanity case is underneath him, hidden at the back. I unhook the clasps to open the lid. My savings are there, pressed in tight.

Years and years.

No need to count.

It's all I have to show for my life.

Unspent.

I do not authorise.

~

In the living room I work by the flickering light of the TV. The sound is turned off. I'm wrapping bundles of money in special offers.

Buy one. Get one free!

Christmas must be like this. Or birthdays.

Satisfaction guaranteed.

I have to work fast.

Act now. Don't miss your lucky jackpot.

~

The sky is blushing mango. I press the button that says *Trades-men.*

I push the door open and make my way into the yellow gloom. My grimy feet make no sound. The stone turns to lino after the fire doors. He lives next to the storage room. Below the glass eye there's the letterbox flap. I peer through. I know he's not home. He's at the garage, standing in for me. Still a couple of hours till the end of my shift.

I press my fingers through the slot. I let go. *Act now. Don't miss your lucky jackpot.* The carpet dulls the sound of dropping. I press my fingers through again, and drop. *Clairevoyant: 98% accuracy guaranteed.* Again, I drop another lot. *Days of the Raj Pepsi special.* I let go. I drop another bundle through the slot. There's a rushing noise in my ears. I feed wad after wad after wad through Siva's letterbox, my life of nights marked out in notes and wrapped in special offers. Enough to wipe those two men off the video. *No job too big or small.* To settle his debt. Enough to pay him back for being on call. *Earn cash on all your shopping! Americano Pizza – 20% extra – free!* My next of kin. An English doctor. Inch by inch.

~

The light is lilac. The trees are twitching with birds, excited.

I slip into the slit between buildings and climb the steps. I tickle the ceramic fox. It's the end of her shift. I haven't booked. She's probably asleep. Her hair in a mess all over the pillow. Her calliper on the floor. I carefully press the letterbox in and feed my earnings through – softly, softly – no need to wake her up. Softly, softly. Years and years. *As much as you can eat.* This is the most important part of the Temple and I should offer my prayers here. My life. Her life. *Your personal invitation.* We've lasted longer than most marriages. I've never known a woman like her. Years and years. *Open now for your chance to win.* Faithful as a fiancée waiting for me after the war. I don't know if we will ever meet again. Softly, softly. *Make all the tax-free cash you want.* Inch by inch. I still don't know her name. *Buy one. Get one free!*

~

My lift, I forgot, is out of order. Someone has pissed at it, fresh and wet. I climb the stairs. My legs are aching. I stop to catch my breath and rest on every landing. I stand outside Miss Claire's mesh door gasping like an unlucky fish. I lift my feet, heavy as weights, one after the other. My body is burning.

Home is full of silver light. Streaming. Dust. Nataraja is perched on top of my TV.

Then I hear the blackbird singing. Not the *ti ti ti* of fright, but a carefree tricky pretty song that echoes up and down the public stairwell, full of disregard and teasing.

I sit for a while and listen.

I go to the sound. From the public landing, I peer down. Fifteen floors in a coil. Winding. Unwinding.

There's a hand moving along the handrail in the middle storey somewhere, getting smaller with each step. No sign of any blackbird. Nothing moves except the little hand that nearly dances as it shrinks, step by step, foot by foot, like a singer's hand on a staircase in *The Sound of Music*.

I cough.

The whistling stops for just a moment. The blackbird takes a little breath. Someone opens a door somewhere. I hear the blare of television. A clatter of plates on another floor. Whistling echoes. The rumble of the lobby door. The blackbird song is suddenly fainter.

I follow the sound.

All the way down.

~

Outside, the ground is cold underfoot.

The blackbirds are singing to me, so plain they're beautiful. They pour their hearts out from the broken walls and torn bushes. They pull at worms. They smash snails for breakfast.

A hand scatters dried fruit and cubes of bread onto the scabby lawn beneath the trees. Wood-pigeons, magpies, seagulls, sparrows, blue tits and blackbirds – there's more than enough for everyone. The Whistling Woman steps between trees and showers the birds with food. She turns to look at me. Her hair is a cloud of cinnamon curls. There's a spray of freckles on her

208

forehead. I wonder how many are on her back. Miss Claire stops in the middle of her birdsong and smiles at me, her round eyes sparkling.

I smile back.

The lipstick on her thin mouth is fresh and shiny. I wonder if it helps her whistle.

'So it's you,' I say.

Two Ravens Press is the most northerly literary publisher in the UK, operating from a six-acre working croft on a sea-loch in the north-west Highlands of Scotland. Two Ravens Press is run by two writers with a passion for language and for books that are non-formulaic and that take risks. We publish cutting-edge and innovative contemporary fiction, non-fiction and poetry.

Visit our website for comprehensive information on all of our books and authors – and for much more:

- browse all Two Ravens Press books by category or by author, and purchase them online, post & packing-free (in the UK, and for a small fee overseas)

- there is a separate page for each book, including summaries, extracts and reviews, and author interviews, biographies and photographs

- read our daily blog about life as a small literary publisher in the middle of nowhere – or the centre of the universe, depending on your perspective – with a few anecdotes about life down on the croft thrown in. Includes regular and irregular columns by guest writers – Two Ravens Press authors and others.

www.tworavenspress.com